The Tinman's Farewell

Michael Tanner

authorHOUSE®

AuthorHouse™ UK Ltd.
500 Avebury Boulevard
Central Milton Keynes, MK9 2BE
www.authorhouse.co.uk
Phone: 08001974150

First published by AuthorHouse   4/19/2010

ISBN: 978-1-4490-9384-6 (e)
ISBN: 978-1-4490-9383-9 (sc)

PROLOGUE: NOVEMBER 1884

He stared at the envelope, rubbing his palms on his breeches, probing the saliva-caked corners of his mouth with his tongue for the courage to open it.

But each time he tried the tremor worsened, for behind the silver-blue eyes fingers of cold fear crawled across his mind and numbed his senses. All afternoon he jumped each time the door squeaked open; he paced, he blew his nose, he washed his hands. He was incapable of keeping still, fidgeting more than a Spitalfields street urchin with fleas. Yet now, faced with this simple task, he seemed paralyzed.

He sat hunched and round-shouldered, grinding his fingertips into his temples until his head ached. When he finally forced himself to stop tapping the heels of his boots against the wooden bench and accept the envelope from his valet, a trickle of perspiration was gathering along his prominent top lip and he had begun to feel quite light-headed.

His slender fingers released the message and instantly ceased trembling. A smile normally alien to his hangdog features disputed possession of them and gradually won the argument. He read the four words a second time, and then a third before he allowed himself to believe them. Even then he was unable to articulate them. Elation gradually overcame nausea and he waved the telegram at his valet, fighting for breath. Eventually he managed to croak: 'I have a daughter.'

Drying his eyes on his cuff, he accepted the congratulations of those clustering around him before shying away in embarrassment. He produced a photograph of a pretty young woman from his coat pocket and pressed it to his lips. Then he filled his lungs and stood tall, as she would want him to.

On 6 November 1884, Fred Archer had stood in the weighing room at Liverpool racecourse surrounded by saddles, tack and fellow jockeys, a happy man. He was 29-years-old; been champion jockey since the age of 17; and had just landed a public gamble to win the Liverpool Autumn Cup on Thebais. Idolized by the man-in-the-street to whom the acquisition of 'tin', his slang for money, was more virtue than vice, 'The Tinman' was a celebrity for whom station-masters felt privileged to hold trains and whose presence theatre audiences felt honoured to applaud.

Yet wealth and acclaim meant nothing to England's greatest sportsman compared with the euphoria presently sweeping through him. His cheeks glowed healthily for once and he found himself conversing animatedly with colleagues he normally avoided. He was experiencing a happiness he had only ever seen in other people.

Archer would soon celebrate his second wedding anniversary. Ellen Rose Dawson was his childhood sweetheart whom he met when he came to Newmarket aged 11 to serve his apprenticeship with her uncle, the revered trainer Mat Dawson. Petite, pretty, gentle and undemanding, his wife understood how years of weight-watching had doomed him to living on his nerves: one kind look or endearment from her banished melancholy and quoshed tantrums.With Nellie beside him he faced the future with confidence. He assured friends that after two or three more seasons he would hang up his boots: train winners instead of riding them; eat instead of starve; raise a family with Nellie its heart and guiding light.

Nellie soon fell pregnant and as the birth approached Archer began to smile more often than he frowned. He told everyone that the child meant more to him than any Derby or jockeys championship and when his son was born he declared himself the luckiest man alive.

Baby William clung to life for just seven hours. Archer thought he knew pain: he had suffered the excruciating agony of having an arm practically severed at the elbow by a savage horse. But nothing prepared him for the halo of sorrow that enveloped him like a crown of burning thorns.

Now, ten months later, he had a family once more. He hurried home, the tedium of a long train journey enlivened by imaginary conversations with Nellie and his daughter. He pictured her first tottering steps and heard her tiny voice mimicking his as he read her bedtime stories from Hans Christian Anderson. He envisaged her taking turns on the rocking horse with the baby brother he and Nellie would eventually provide and how he would teach them both to ride as his father had once taught him.

Arriving at Falmouth House, the family mansion he'd commissioned on the outskirts of Newmarket, he charged up the stairs two at a time and halted outside Nellie's room. He knocked softly and entered. Nellie's ashen frailty shocked him. He wanted to hug her but confined himself to kissing her tenderly on the forehead. They were so happy they both began to weep.

Archer tiptoed across to his daughter's crib and dropped a father's kiss on the baby's nose. She was perfect. He pulled down her blanket and a clammy fist popped free, and he smelt for the second time that year the freshly soaped skin and warm bed-linen of a new-born baby. Feeling the tiny fingers tickle his lips, he kissed them and although he tried to find the words to tell Nellie how proud he was of her, he was too choked with joy. Instead he told her she must rest and get some sleep.

He pondered how he might lift her spirits and an idea came to him. She thought him so dashing in his pink hunting togs: he would amuse her by dressing up. The image of her clapping hands to her cheeks with glee sent him scurrying along the landing to his dressing room.

Archer had not reached the door before he heard screaming. He ran back to find Nellie thrashing in a tangle of bedclothes, eyes rolling wildly, her limbs jerking in a crazy semaphore of arms and legs. He struggled to comprehend what was happening: his brain demanded his body react but starved of ideas it shut down. Archer was no stranger to fear: a broken neck was only a stumble away in the heat of a horse-race. Yet he had never known fear that made him beg for divine assistance.

Archer beseeched God for help and found him otherwise engaged. Nellie's convulsions only ceased when her heart stopped beating some 12 hours later and she lay like a bundle of soiled rags in his arms. She expired without uttering a word or appearing to know him. He could not bring himself to let her go. He smothered her with kisses and buried his face in her hair, rocking in his anguish, begging her to speak to him, assuring himself she must wake up if he persevered. But he felt her grow cold. He had known desolation when his son died. Yet even that had not left him wanting to punch God on the jaw.

They dragged him from the room, mouth agape yet incapable of sound, transfixed by a grief that dare not speak. He clutched his forehead lest it contents fell out and clung to his manservant as the floor pitched beneath his feet, the steel band squeezing his ribcage reducing every breath to a silent scorching scream. He blinked repeatedly yet could not wash away the image of Nellie's face frozen in the agony of death. Finally, he wailed and collapsed unconscious.

Archer stopped every clock in Falmouth House: each morning he woke up wishing he had not. As the months passed he was persuaded to put away his mourning clothes, and day by day he willed himself into going about his business, hiding his sadness behind a facade of normality. He doted on little Nellie Rose but the loss of her mother permeated his life like the November drizzle that fell on the day he watched the cold damp earth finally take her away from him: incessant, raw, numbing.

He saw Nellie's face in every cloud; smelt her rosewater on every breeze; never went anywhere without the silver mounted keepsake of her plaited hair close to his heart. There were no longer any colours in his life. He lived in the condemned cell of his own mind. All the light went from him.

And that's when they started coming for him.

ONE

Algy Haymer trained his race-glasses (top of the range from Gregory in the Strand) on the distant figure but did not bargain for what they communicated.

He could clearly make out the jockey's knees gripping ever tighter as he folded his long legs round the horse's belly. He saw the spurred heels bite into the chestnut colt's soft flesh and watched as the animal felt three stinging swipes in quick succession from a steel-tipped whip that made him flinch as much as the horse. Even so Diavolo was flagging. And there were still some three hundred yards to run to the winning post at the top of the Sandown Park hill.

'Come...on...Fred!' Algy recited nervously as the light-limbed sensation of a failed betting coup started to make itself felt. 'We can't afford to lose another one.'

'I take it the "tin" is down then?' came a gruff voice over his left shoulder.

'What's that?'

'You going deaf in your old age?' the voice boomed markedly louder.

Algy turned and glowered. 'What do you mean, "Going deaf"?'

'No need to be so bloody touchy!' responded Montague Blackwell, fellow hack on *The Sportsman*.

'Yes. Sorry, Monty.'

'Merely suggested Archer's carrying some big bets, that's all!' replied Blackwell through plumes of earthy smoke from a Punch ninfas.

'You could say that! Fred's carrying a lot of money. Some of it mine!'

Algy struggled to hold his glasses steady but the blood seemed to be draining out of his fingertips. He tightened the focus on the jumble of silks and squinted through the lenses.

He drew some encouragement from the sight of Archer's legs and arms working in a brutal unison of thrusting and flailing, his extra-long whip snaking around Diavolo's rump, its steel tip tearing through the animal's flesh. He knew Archer loved horses. Yet he also knew his love for winning races ran deeper. Algy winced at the sight of Archer's spurs puncturing Diavolo's skin. But no more than that. His conscience was clear. It had to be done if the bets were to be landed.

Archer shut everything out of his mind bar the image of Diavolo passing the post in first place and hit the horse six times across its hind quarters in quick-fire succession. Algy watched its low-headed reaction to the power being generated by the strongest lever in race-riding and knew that Archer had set his mind on winning this race.

In the 20 months since Nellie's death, he had seen Archer channel his remaining spirit into the only thing he knew: ride even more winners, establishing a new record of 246 in 1885 that included four of the five Classics. It was the eighth time he had ridden a double-century of winners; no other jockey had managed it once.

Archer told Algy how he hoped Nellie was watching, proud of him. But Algy reckoned she would also have been frightened for him. He now approached race-riding with a ferocity that was short-sighted and frightening in equal measure, causing friends like Algy to fear for his health - physical and mental. They saw a man eight inches taller and half a stone heavier than the average jockey reduced to walking with a round-shouldered stoop as if his spine could not cope; a stick-thin man in need of a square meal; the blue lines etching his hollow cheeks so livid they could have been described with greasepaint.

Algy knew for a fact that throughout the nine-month Flat-racing season Archer paid three visits to the Turkish bath every day and consumed copious drafts of a noxious purgative prepared by his doctor for the specific purpose of stopping him filling out his 5 feet 9 inch frame. Algy once tried a thimbleful of 'Archer's Mixture' and barely reached the lavatory in time. His friend swallowed it by the sherry glass.

It struck Algy that Archer often acted as if life was not worth living. He told Algy how he saw her everywhere he looked; in the playful face of their daughter at bath-time or peering through the crowd of backslappers after a race: by the end of each day his head was reeling and the headaches were relentless. He believed he was slowly going insane. Too many things had a habit of going wrong. Just like this race.

Algy could hear Blackwell chuckle. 'I do believe you're not going to collect. The Tinman's beat. Charlie's got him. Doesn't always pay to be one of the lucky few on the receiving end of Archer's tips, eh?'

'Smart arse!' was the best riposte Algy could find as the emptiness of defeat began sweeping through him.

Archer was feeling the same. He had detected the one sound no jockey liked to hear: the 'hiss-hiss-hiss' of breath whistling through the bared teeth of a jockey working hard to galvanize his mount. What was Charlie Wood playing at?

Horse-races came no humbler than the Ditton Selling Plate for two-year-olds, contested by a motley collection of first-season youngsters considered so unpromising that the winner would be offered for sale. There were eleven runners but only two possible winners. One was Lal Brough, the favourite ridden by Charlie Wood, and the other was Diavolo. Archer had told Algy that Diavolo was a stone-cold certainty.

'Charlie!' the champion growled, as he drove Diavolo up to Lal Brough's quarters. 'Take a pull!'

Wood continued exhorting the leader. Archer caught sight of the winning post, panic shot down his right arm and fired it back and forth, each vicious stroke of the whip lashing Diavolo closer to the point of exhaustion. Yet only when he heard the wheeze of surrender and felt Diavolo stagger did Archer drop his hands.

Wood's victory on the favourite came as no surprise to most people at Sandown but Archer was not one of them. He had not just hoped to win this insignificant contest, or even merely expected to win it. He believed he was *meant* to win it.

In fact, he had put £5,000 on it - more than enough to buy ten Diavolos - because he was badly in need of a big win. The new season of 1886 had not gone well. Despite riding fees, prize money and presents from grateful owners and gamblers pushing his annual income well beyond that earned by the Prime Minister, he was crippled with debt, besieged by creditors ranging from the builders and outfitters of Falmouth House to his bookmaker. What alarmed him most was the nagging thought that he had lost his once infallible racing judgement: his betting book for the current season, no more than three months old, was already showing a five-figure loss equal to the construction costs of a small warship. Diavolo's defeat would begin financing another.

Algy's loss was a trifling £500, irritating but bearable. He soon caught up with the exhausted Diavolo and made eye contact with its jockey. Archer's eyes were blank. Algy shrugged. Diavolo's owner received an equally swift touch of the cap from Archer before the jockey headed for the sanctuary of the weighing room.

By now his dark features were more saturnine than ever. He suppressed the urge to put a fist or boot through the nearest door and confined himself to slinging his saddle in the direction of his long-serving valet, William Bartholomew. The object he wanted to hit was not yet present. 'Solomon, that twister Charlie Wood's done for me.'

The valet continued about his business. The wisdom of the biblical king that had won Bartholomew his weighing room alias ensured he knew better than to pass comment.

Archer glared round the room, a fuse looking for a match. Conversations ceased abruptly and heads buried themselves deeper in copies of today's *Sportsman*. His silver-blue eyes were his most elequent form of expression and right this minute they spoke unequivocally. He was incandescent. His redundant black cap sailed across the room.

'Take no notice of the tin-scraping miser, Solomon,' ventured a lone voice from the far corner of the room. 'Give him a sandwich!'

Archer had come to expect aggravation from George Barrett, whom he had replaced on the season's unbeaten star Ormonde to win the Derby. He resisted the temptation to put Barrett in his place: he did not want the distraction.

'Tell us about your posh dinner with old Six Mile Bottom the other week?' Barrett said, taking a bite from a hot mutton pie.

Archer's arms began shaking by his sides. 'Have some manners!' he snapped. 'You're talking of a great lady!'

He was accustomed to hearing riff-raff like Barrett use the oddly named Newmarket landmark when referring to the well-upholstered

Duchess of Montrose: but only behind her back and certainly not in front of him, her favourite jockey.

'The flunkey placed a lovely plate of roast beef in front of our Frederick and what does he do?' continued Barrett. 'Why, he only scarpers, without so much as a "By-your-leave, Your Grace"…'

Barrett sauntered over to Archer and waved the steaming pie beneath his nose. '…and, would you believe it, he only goes and throws up outside in the corridor!'

He chortled and looked around, encouraging others to join in the fun. None did.

Archer felt himself becoming nauseous when the weighing room door clicked open to reveal the perspiring figure of Charlie Wood.

Wood's face would not have looked misplaced on a wanted poster, always full of bug-eyed and hook-nosed villainy whether he was coming back having partnered a winner, ridden a loser or pulled a dead cert. He sidled over to Archer and sat down beside him. Barrett began giggling. He guessed what must have happened in the last race and edged closer to eavesdrop.

'Look, Fred,' Wood said straight-faced, using finger and thumb to flick the sweat from his beaked-nose onto the floor, 'I know I said I'd bury him in the pack but he was too fresh. The bugger was going too well for me to take a pull. I had to let him go, believe me. The stewards would have to be pissed not to have spotted it otherwise.'

Wood grinned at the Barretts and deposited his saddle on the long table that ran down the centre of the room.

'We'll get our losses back soon enough, Fred. You can be sure of that.'

Archer bared his teeth and his eyes appeared to dissolve into deep blue pools of anger. He had listened in silence, dissecting every phrase for signs of the truth and didn't believe a word. Wood had put him away. Wood had decided to take the price about Lal Brough and had reneged on their arrangement.

He got up and went through the door that led to the lavatory. He could not get the smell of mutton out of his nostrils and it was making him feel muzzy. Suddenly his legs gave way and he just made it to the bowl before he began retching violently. His stomach knotted and he moaned:

he knew there was nothing in his stomach to bring up because he had already purged himself with the 'mixture' to rid himself of the biscuit that had passed for breakfast.

The contractions eased and he tottered to the nearest washbasin. He studied the reflection staring back at him from the mirror above with rising disgust for he saw a pitiful man being eaten away by self-pity. His face crumpled with dry gasping tears and he pressed his forehead against the glass rather than look at himself any longer. He commanded himself to take a series of long, deep breaths and after splashing his face with cold water eventually he felt able to re-enter the weighing room.

He called Solomon over and dropped his voice to a barely audible whisper. 'Go and find Brusher. Ask him - no tell him - to come round to the back door of the weighing room. I need to see him. Tell him it's urgent.

Archer made his way to the rear of the weighing room. He began to shiver. It seemed cold enough for an overcoat yet he felt sweat dribbling off his nose. His thoughts began racing. He would need to recoup his losses tomorrow aboard Minting in the Eclipse Stakes if he was to have any chance of squaring matters with Mo Fenner. Defeat for Minting was out of the question.

TWO

The Honourable Algernon Reece Melvill Haymer, younger son of the Ninth Marquis of Belton, strode purposefully past the row of saddling boxes that stood near the gates of Sandown Park while checking gold hunter for the second time in the last few minutes. If he hurried he might just make Esher station in time to catch the 3.20 train to Waterloo that would get him back to London in around 30 minutes and enable him to relay Archer's apologies to Mo Fenner.

Haymer was approaching his 28th birthday. Standing just over six feet with the solidity of someone who had never shirked hard labour whenever it had presented itself, he had corn-coloured hair and attentive eyes blue enough to make the sky jealous and ladies swoon. On the rare occasions he chose to unlock it, he was also blessed with a smile that might give a sunburst a run for its money. So, he had good reason to be vain about his appearance: yet it meant no more to him than an extra pair of hands; superfluous and an irrelevance.

Any scar tissue was on the inside. He had never quite come to terms with his privileged background for he regarded anything that came for free as dangerous. Everything worth having had to be earned, whether it be praise, wealth or happiness. He constantly sought proof of his worth, from his friends and his family - especially from his father who had the unerring capacity to antagonize him with his first comment and humiliate him with his second.

Only those closest to him called him Algy. The majority knew him as 'Brusher', the soubriquet bestowed on him at Uppingham thanks to a rebelliousness that precipitated numerous brushes with authority. His housemaster took grave exception, for example, to his initiation of nit races on the basis that it undermined Uppingham's reputation for cleanliness and diligent grooming. A bored and unrepetent Algy, by contrast, merely regarded them as the best available betting medium in the regrettable absence of thoroughbred racehorses.

Team sports he shunned in favour of solitary runs cross country, punctuated by bouts of shadow boxing and, in time, assignations with the under-porter's wife in Wardley Wood that led to the loss of his virginity at the age of fourteen. He became a breaker of bodies as well as hearts for being handy with one's fists proved an asset to a good-looking youth such as he if the advances of dormitory predators were to be repulsed. Further kudos was won courtesy of his ability to mimic virtually every master in the common room and the nerve to bellow his own less than respectful lyrics to the school song at Sunday chapel.

Contrition was an alien concept to him. At Oxford his contention that knocking the bowler hats off the 'bulldogs' with his cane constituted a sport rather than a crime failed to impress these University policemen and saw him rusticated from Corpus Christi College. Shinning up the college's ornate sundial pillar surmounted by a stone pelican to tie a scarf round the inscrutable bird's neck before lighting a fire beneath the two beehives in the fellows' garden, where bees had been kept ever since the civil war, only served to make his temporary exclusion permanent. Had his father, a Corpus man himself and a generous college benefactor, intervened on his behalf he may have avoided being sent down, but Lord Belton was one of those individuals who said what he liked, liked what he said and forgave wrong-doing in nobody but himself. He chose to remain silent.

Donning a pair of horns could not have made Algy any more of a maverick. Some people, it struck him, aspired to be mainstream and some did not. He did not. He chose to stand apart, to watch and to listen, draw his own conclusions and trust his own judgements. Some thus considered him odd. To those of that persuasion, however, he paid no mind: were he interrogated by the face in his shaving mirror he would gladly have confessed to glorying in his misfit status – even courting it - and taking pleasure in responding to unjustified criticism with a quick tongue and, if riled sufficiently, even quicker fists. On leaving Uppingham he even drew deep satisfaction from his headmaster's warning that were his self-destructive streak left unfettered it would see him dangling at the end of a rope.

This transparent contempt for authority reduced an Army career to the level of a high-wire act that would have pleased Blondin himself: curled lips soon accused him of marching to his own drum. In any case, he was far too intelligent to play the subletern for long, lacking dullness - which also ruled out out the church. He would debate with both God and authority but genuflect to neither. As for the City, it smacked of too much duplicity and mendacity; besides, he concluded, an office or bank would be asking a falcon to share a cage with a bunch of canaries.

No, Algy's brand of irreverence, unlimited charm, quick wits and streak of waywardness made the racecourse his ideal habitat; a way with words and a sharp brain meant racing journalism might have been invented for him. However, the talents that endeared him to the ladies of the fast set were, understandably, lost on the members of his own sex inside the Press Room. They only saw those that undermined their own. Consequently, Algy Haymer had few male friends.

Chief among this select circle was Archer. They had met when the jockey won the Leicestershire Oaks on Lord Belton's filly Petunia and Archer frequently stayed at the family's ancestral home, Haverholme Priory, whenever he was up hunting with the Belvoir or Blankney during the winter. His closeness to Archer led to accusations of toadying because it had its compensations: Archer's tips invariably paid off. Algy reciprocated in whatever guise he could. Since Archer could barely read or write, it was Algy who dealt with most of his correspondence.

One of his other tasks was placing Archer's commissions with London bookmakers. For years he had been a regular visitor to No 2 Hill Street, Berkeley Square, the residence of society bookmaker Henry Brockford, but Archer's recent ill fortune had seen him run up big losses and forced him into placing bets with less reputable men who preyed on compulsive gamblers down on their luck. Placating a notorious moneylender-cum-bookmaker like Mo Fenner would stretch Algy's limited powers of diplomacy but he owed it to his friend to try.

So it was imperative he caught the early train. He acknowledged the groom standing guard outside one of the saddling boxes but politely spurned his invitation to inspect the colt of his father's due to run in a later race. He marched on, oblivious to the fact that every step of his progress had been closely monitored.

'Oh, my!' called out a husky female voice cultivated in the Shires and honed to Parisian perfection at a finishing school on the Boulevard Haussemann. 'If it isn't the Honourable Algernon Haymer.'

If his favourite Cafe Royal dessert had been blessed with a voice Algy knew it would have sounded like this one: smooth, rich, enticing. It was a female voice he knew intimately, very intimately in fact, but the last one he wanted to hear at this precise moment. It belonged to a woman who knew she enjoyed too much freedom, too much money and too much sex - but, she thought, not enough love.

Algy turned to feast on the winsome, willow-waisted and satin-clad figure of Lady Constanza Swynford.

'Ah, Connie! Can't stop!'

'My, don't we look smart today,' she declared in the modulated tones associated with the female members of her class, her vowels as polished as the family fish knives. 'Well, at least by your standards.'

'You are, as ever, most kind!'

'The cut of that shirt is rather fashionable, isn't it? Rather daring for an old stick-in-the-mud like you! Where did you find it?'

Algy recognized a throwaway line when he heard one but played along all the same. 'From a new shop two chaps opened last year just round the corner from my rooms, names of Reginald Turnbull and Ernest Asser.'

'You must show me next time I visit Jermyn Street,' she said, struggling to maintain the pretence.

Algy shifted from foot to foot and gave that curled lip of indifference which she detested. 'Request noted, Dotty!' he said.

Connie felt herself colour and wanted to slap him.

'I've told you before not to call me by that silly name!' she snapped as her freckles rapidly did their utmost to endorse the childhood nickname she abhorred.

'I never realized you were so sensitive about your freckles!' Algy lied.

'Then why do you continue to refer to them?'

'No reason,' he shrugged. 'Possibly because the red hair and freckles make you what you are. They identify you. Brand you. They make you stand out from the crowd, an individual.'

The hard lines fled Connie's face and the freckles softened. 'Is an invitation too much to ask?'

Algy was already on the move; then he tensed. He was not in the mood for another row with Connie but he could only tolerate so much. 'An invitation like that of last week perhaps?'

Connie's hands flew to her cheeks. 'Oh, God, it completely slipped my mind!' she babbled, searching for a plausible explanation. 'How could I have been so stupid!'

'If you say so.'

'Willingly forfeit an evening with you?'

'So it would appear.'

'No, it wasn't like that!'

She struggled to complete the explanation. 'I had to go...'

'You had to go where?' he said, eyebrows rising.

'I had to...' she mumbled, her face colouring. '...oh, never mind.'

She turned her head this way and that to avoid his gaze since she could not bring herself to tell him. She knew her whereabouts on the evening in question would have excused her but the child in her refused to divulge them. She felt she had already lost enough face.

'I must fly!' he said. 'Train to catch!'

As he moved so did she. She had staged this meeting and had thought out her tactics.

'Not staying to see your father's colt in the Victoria Cup?' she said.

The question achieved its objective. Algy stopped, his sandy skin darkening with temper.

'I've done it again, haven't I?' she wailed. 'You're still not speaking, are you? But I was so sure I'd seen you chatting in the luncheon room!'

Connie felt a heaviness gathering in her chest. She was frightened he would leave her. She scrutinized his face. She did not care whether he was upset or not, so long as he stayed with her a little longer.

'It must have been someone else you saw,' he said. 'I've not seen him for months.'

Lord Belton might have been any small boy's hero and he had been to his younger son. He was an accomplished and fearless rider to hounds and a university pugilist of some repute. He had forged an heir in his own image, however, and saw no reason to devote the same attention to his other son; the younger boy's achievements were belittled and his imperfections ridiculed. At a time in a young man's life when it is more important how he looks than who he is, for example, the onset of adolescent acne saw his father dub him 'plague-boy.' Whenever Haverholme entertained thereafter young Algy took to skulking in the orangery with a book of poems or else lost himself in the top yard where he might sport with the scullery maids or jaw with the stable-men and farm hands.

'You and your father still at loggerheads after all these years? That's so sad,' continued Connie, trying to ease the tension.

Algy's head dropped as all Connie had done was exacerbate it. He had reached the conclusion long ago that his father was impossible to please; that his father viewed him as some kind of threat whom he would resort to any measures to quosh. These teenage wounds festered and fed the need to challenge every authority figure he encountered. The evening he threw a glass of Nuits-Saint-Georges in Lord Belton's face at dinner after listening to his mother being abused for dismissing a pregnant housemaid marked both his coming of age and his departure from Haverholme. And it made him just as angry reliving it.

'Isn't it obvious?' Algy replied sourly.

'But you're so alike.'

'Rubbish!' he thundered. 'The only thing he passed on to me was a love of cats!'

'No trace of cynicism? The piercing stare?' Connie ventured, cocking her head to one side. 'That caustic wit?'

'Are you trying to annoy me because you're doing a bloody fine job!'

'How could you think that!' she said, praying she had not pushed things too far.

Connie had observed some of Lord Belton's inadequacies emerging in Algy for some time: the repressed emotions and the vices. Especially the vices for she saw his life being coloured from the same intoxicating palette of women, gambling and liquor as his father's. Less vividly, perhaps, but no less evidently. And Algy recognized it too, an epiphany filling him with a corrosive self-loathing that reinforced his fierce sense of grievance.

'I can't talk to the man without the conversation disintegrating into an argument, so I stay away from him,' continued Algy, head bowed. 'I swear that man is determined to expire with not one drop of venom left unused!'

'What of your mother?'

Algy's eyebrows hastened toward his hairline. 'My mother? My poor downtrodden mother? She opted for martyrdom when she chose to marry my father.'

'I know she's rather...'

'She could no more bring herself to confront him than she could bring herself to cuddle me when I was a small boy howling with toothache!'

'Perhaps, if I were with you...'

'Are you kidding?' Algy exploded. 'You're one of the problems!'

'Well then, we could all sit down and discuss the situation like adults.'

Algy looked into Connie's eyes and saw their dewy honesty. But he was not in the frame of mind to revisit an old argument.

'Look, Connie, it's been nice chatting but I really must dash!'

'But Algy,' she cooed, gliding closer to him, 'it's been so long since I've seen you.'

She ran a hand through his mop of unruly blond hair that was a source of constant frustration to both Trumpers and comb alike owing to its habit of imitating a haystack in the wake of a thunderstorm.

'Must you rush off?'

He made an exaggerated show of reaching into the waistcoat pocket of his four-buttoned, olive-green tweed suit in search of his watch. Tailored by Halls of Oxford, the suit was ten years old but still fitted him like a glove.

He need not have bothered with the charade of checking his timepiece. Connie hunted him down and placed her mouth over his ear.

'I want every inch of you,' she whispered. 'From that blond-thatch right down to the tips of those shiny Grenson boots you're wearing.'

She gripped his wrists and led him into a saddling box, sliding the bolt behind them with her foot. With each step Algy began to tingle. Did he have the time? He would make time.

'Don't move a muscle,' he said, palms up in mock surrender. 'Just let me look at you a moment. I want to savour everything about you... your freckles, your breasts...the smell of you.'

That's more like my Algy, she thought.

He surveyed the carpet of straw beneath her feet and felt every nerve-end in his body spark into life. There was something irresistibly sensuous to him about the aromatic cocktail of Connie and straw ever since the day he escorted the Earl of Kesteven's teenage daughter on a day's hunting with the Belvoir and one thing had led to another in a barn outside Burton Coggles.

'First things first!' Connie said playfully.

'Why? What's wrong?'

'Why, nothing at all. That is, unless you count the performance of Archer's horse in the last which you advised me to back.'

'Aaah! That was a blow, right enough...' he said, reaching for her waist.

'You wouldn't have put us all away would you?' she replied, retreating.

'I'm afraid I don't know what you mean.'

'Don't be obtuse! You know very well what I mean. You spread the word that Archer's told you to back Diavolo on his behalf...everyone invests a monkey or two...a public gamble develops. But it's all just a front, isn't it? Admit it! The horse didn't carry one penny of your money, did it?'

'Connie, you're imagining things!'

'This wasn't meant to be the animal's day, was it? It wasn't "off", was it?

'Connie, I can assure you the horse was definitely trying! Both Fred and I backed it.'

'And so did Seger and I!'

Algy threw back his head and laughed heartily. 'Seger backed it!'

'Yes!'

'On your say-so?'

'Yes!'

'That's cheered me up enormously! Why on earth do you consort with such a...'

Connie waved away his question. 'What happened to Diavolo is the question! You and Archer have laid the beast out, haven't you? When it is "busy", we mugs will have given up on it because we got our fingers burned, leaving you two to get a bigger price.'

'Connie, you couldn't be further from the truth.'

'Foolproof and absolutely priceless you mean, unless you happen to be one of those whose money unwittingly helped you set up the coup!'

He laughed. 'Nice theory, Connie. Yes, we both know it can work like that. But, on my honour, Archer expected Diavolo to win.'

Her nose wrinkled. 'When have you had any honour?'

Smiling impishly, she pulled him into a corner, slowly peeled-off her silk scarf and tossed it provocatively to the ground.

'I demand *sat-is-fac-tion*,' she purred.

'Connie! No!' he protested, suddenly remembering what he should be attending to. 'I just haven't got time for this.'

'Are you asking me to believe that Algy Haymer is a cat who loves fish but is afraid of getting his paws wet? When have you ever not had time for this!'

He knew she was right. She had the kind of body that drove cavemen to chisel on bare rock and mere mention of past encounters set the familiar ache prickling through his loins.

Connie had never looked more tempting. The fiery green of her feral eyes shone through the dimness and her plump bottom lip invited sucking as if it were a dribbling peach. Her skin glowed like amber, bringing out the freckles that dotted her cheekbones; sensuality oozed from every one of them. Only the small blemish high on her left temple near the hair-line left her beauty just shy of perfection: at the age of six she had jumped from an apple tree to see if she could fly and discovered she could not.

'I want to lick every inch of you,' Algy panted, accentuating every syllable with a lasciviousness that left her in no doubt he meant it.

Connie took hold of his hands and drew him toward her, leaning back against the cool wall of the box, her generous mouth welcoming him like a shark greets a seal pup. She nipped his lips and his tongue, one hand playing with the tight curls behind his ear while the other slipped down to his groin. He responded by shoving her back against the wall and kissing her hard on the mouth; she made to twist her head away but he merely pursued with his own. She pushed him off.

Algy knew his Connie. She wanted him. But not yet. The certain knowledge she was driving him crazy only made her lissom body pulsate with a greater desire to be fondled. She wanted to be naked, rolling with him in the straw, smelling his manliness. But she was in no hurry. She would make him wait until he could not distinguish pain from ecstasy. He would thank her for it in the end.

Algy's right hand went to the luscious mound of flesh topped by a hard nipple that was her left breast. She cursed the satin from coming between mouth and flesh and made do with imagining him gorging on her as he lifted her skirt and petticoats with a flourish. She finally surrendered. And he leered.

'Don't look at me like that!' she admonished. 'I'm not one of your Covent Garden tuppenny knee-tremblers!'

Algy knew she was fantasizing herself just so - and he was happy to play along. He had enjoyed himself too often up against a wall in Slingsby Place after a night at the Opera House not to.

Connie pulled his mouth onto hers, drawing a drop of hot blood from his lower lip, and lifted her left leg as high as she could, enabling them to couple with the urgency of honeymooners yet the intimacy of old stagers.

'It's been too long!' she declared with the throaty whimper of a woman who felt she was closer than ever to snaring the one man she loved, the one man she wanted to be with until the day she died. 'Please don't stop!'

'What a whore you'd make!' he gasped, ever grateful to Connie's Parisian education that had incorporated extra-curricular tuition from a mademoiselle who plied her unique skills in the back alleys of Montmartre.

Connie felt him shudder and washed his face with kisses knowing she had fulfilled his fantasies. She clung onto him, kissing his hair his cheeks, his lips, refusing to yield. She tried to stall her tears but failed. She never ever wanted to let him go because she was afraid she would never get him back again. Only when he begged did her fingernails relax their grip on his buttocks.

'Connie, you are shameless,' he said, breaking free. 'Beyond redemption!'

She tossed her head and dabbed her cheeks with the back of her hand before doing likewise, for she did not want him to see this encounter had meant more to her than to him.

'Actually, if you must know, I was just going to say the same about you!'

'You're an incorrigible minx and you know it!'

'Well, we know what that makes you, don't we?'

Algy was too perceptive an individual not to appreciate his minor role in the little tableau they had just enacted for Connie's pleasure. He had merely played the role of itinerant tom cat. But a very willing one all the same, for on his list of weaknesses Connie Swynford came very near the top. He smiled to himself and made directly for the door, picking bits of straw from his jacket as he went.

'Must you rush off?' she pleaded. 'Can't we go on to the Cafe Royal for supper? Or what about Simpson's...a little of that pot-braised chicken you love so much...and that plum and apple cobbler you find so irresistible! Please say you will!'

'No, I'm already late.'

'I do hate it when you leave me so quickly.'

His hand paused on the bolt as he felt his conscience calling.

'Are you here again tomorrow?' he asked at length.

'Of course, I wouldn't miss the Eclipse!'

'I'll see you tomorrow then, and perhaps we can go back to Jermyn Street for supper...'

'And a long talk? About us? Our future?'

'I didn't think we had one!' he said petulantly. 'I heard you were half-way down the aisle with George Seger.'

'Don't be silly!' she chided. 'Say we'll talk.'

Algy kicked up a clump of straw and slowly nodded, though he remained unsure what common ground they would unearth.

'Oh, Algy, I do love you,' she said, unleashing a smile that would have melted all the snow in Switzerland.

He smiled at her and pushed the door ajar. He stole one final glance as she stood there preening herself and realized why he felt the need to try.

Algy saw a woman who defied categorization. The kind of free spirit no amount of aristocratic breeding, expensive education or fine clothes could ever hope to conceal or constrain. That's what he loved about her. That's why he liked having her around. Even if she did court trouble. Even if she was forbidden fruit. Where Connie was concerned he could not help himself.

Was he in love with her? Did he think they had a future together? He didn't know. But two things he did know. One: it gave him headaches thinking about it. Two: she was the kind of woman for whom a bishop would kick a hole in a stained glass window.

THREE

Algy ran onto the up platform at Esher Station just as the last carriage of the 3.20 train to Waterloo was vacating it.

Consequently, it was gone six by the time he crossed Waterloo Bridge and headed up St Martin's Lane. As he reached Seven Dials he quickened his step and instinctively pulled up the collar of his jacket. He tried to pretend this was due to a blustery wind with drizzle in its teeth,but he could not fool himself: the trickle of liquid in the small of his back was more cold sweat than raindrop.

This was one area of central London in which property developers and speculators were disinterested: ten acres of prime location its upright citizens wished to avoid. No one of sound mind wandered hereabouts unless they had an exceptionally good reason because to proceed onwards up St Giles High Street was to enter the infamous district, a city within a city, known as the 'Holy Land.'

Algy chased off the pack of street urchins and yapping dogs his arrival immediately attracted and trudged on between rows of houses so decrepit that they seemed to be falling down even as he looked at them. The colour of bleached soot, their doors hung from their hinges on worm-eaten posts, their window-panes mostly replaced with straw or brown paper. Running off the High Street to his left and right he could see any number of the twisting alleys, so narrow a man might scrape the walls as he walked, that linked a disorienting warren of claustrophobic yards and gave The Holy Land much of its evil celebrity as an underworld stronghold; a sanctuary for welshers and footpads, be they fugitives from the gaming houses of Leicester Square, the high-class brothels of Bloomsbury or the drinking dens and dosshouses of Soho. Its elaborate network of unways and bolt-holes provided escape routes up and over roofs or down and up interconnected cellars that were revealed to outsiders on pain of death.

Even the Metropolitan Police thought twice before sending men into this hostile environment.

At the heart of this criminal citadel stood 'Rats Castle', a fortress of iniquity that in local parlance amounted to somewhere between a slap-bang and a suck-crib: in other words a cheap beer shop that served slop passing as food. It also served as a front for Mo Fenner's money-lending and bookmaking operations. This was Algy's destination.

He had been told the signposts: left at Rostov's tannery and left again at the corner where pigs trotters are boiled. An attack of retching denoted he had found the second landmark for the rancid odour was redolent of Uppingham's refectory every Thursday when pork more fat than meat was the staple fare. Ever since then he had taken the trouble to pare every scintilla of fat from his breakfast rashers with the painstaking touch of a consultant surgeon.

He put a handkerchief to his mouth and nose, vaulted the stagnant gutter running down the centre of the passage, and pressed on, determined not to display any signs of a vulnerability that was bound to invite trouble instead of assistance.

The clock of St Giles's church was striking seven as he crept down the precipitous flight of steps leading to the dark fetid cellar that was the entrance to Rats Castle. The iron-barred door guarding the entrance had a Judas-slit in the middle, which he tapped. The slit opened, Algy showed his face, and he was allowed in.

The place was window-less and seemingly airless, the fumes of several raw gas-jets that provided light and heat only adding to the pollution. The indifference that greeted his arrival struck him as positively hostile. He felt like the new boy in the dormitory all over again: fresh meat wondering where the first challenge, the first attack, would come from.

Algy looked around. Apart from one corner-booth equipped with an oak table and leather chair, the furniture comprised a handful of trestle tables, constructed by laying bare boards on top of vegetable crates. He paused to read the sheets of paper nailed to the wall that listed today's runners at Sandown and shook his head at the cramped odds Fenner had offered his desperate punters: 10 to1 shots were shortened to 5s; even-money favourites were at odds-on. Alongside were the rates charged on loans: Existing customers 20%; Trustworthy Types 60%; Total Strangers

500%. Presiding over the lists hung a painted sign that warned: 'Debts not cleared are punished by payment in kind'.

Algy remained mystified as to how Archer had got tangled up with a man like Fenner despite appreciating his friend had something Fenner prized: inside formation. If it paid off and Fenner made money off other bookies, Archer got a present. Algy guessed that on Archer's say-so, Fenner had laid Charlie Wood's horse to lose this afternoon and backed Archer's to win. And that Fenner must have incurred heavy losses.

Fenner's customers presently comprised three men and a woman. Two of the men sat at one end of a table rolling dice and sucking on roll-ups more paper than tobacco, while at the other a tart and her posh beau sipped from a bottle of the notoriously potent gin called Old Tom and slurped from saucers full of what seemed to be shell fish drowning in an unnaturally green slime.

Algy made for the relative comfort of the booth.

'Not there!' shouted the pot-man. 'That's for Mister Fenner's private use only!'

Algy's first inclination was to sit down anyway but he reasoned there was no point asking for trouble. He chose another table, called to the pot-man for a glass of beer, and nervously reached into his waistcoat pocket for his gold hunter. It was a 21st birthday gift from his mother (from his father he received nothing) customized by Asprey with the family crest and motto 'Forever Loyal'. He was in the process of extricating it when he remembered where he was and that it was no place for displays of ostentation.

'Has anyone seen Mr Fenner this evening?' he asked the room.

There was no reaction other than a gob of spit being projected toward the spittoon near his feet. It missed its presumed target and spattered Algy's boots. He decided to take no offence but began to gather himself for the worst by identifying the nearest exit.

A ferret-faced little man brought over his beer, though its appearance hardly suggested the description was warranted.

Algy inspected the grimy rim of the glass and took out his handkerchief to rub it clean with the thoroughness of an optomertrist. He took a cautious sip and grimaced. His taste buds demanded he deposit the watery apology for beer in the spittoon. But there was no point looking for trouble, it was likely to find him soon enough. He described a circle on the greasy wooden surface in front of him with a leather-patched elbow and put down the glass.

'Mister Mo Fenner? Anybody seen him?'

His second enquiry elicited no more response than the first. The beau whispered something in his judy's ear and she giggled out loud.

Then he detected movement to his left. The two dice-players towered above him. Algy ordered himself to remain calm and, above all, to show no fear.

He stood up and eyed them one at a time. Both were shabbily dressed and as if they had just completed a shift at the tannery, the last soggy inch of a roll-up stuck to bottom lips. It was clear they had not come to extend pleasantries or engage in Socratic debate.

'It's you is it?' said the first ginger crop-head.

'And who might that be?'

'Fred Archer's errand boy!'

He flicked the ash off his roll-up into Algy's glass.

'Mister Fenner said you'd be on yer way!'

Algy watched the ash swirl to the bottom of the glass.

'And you might be?' he said, picking up the glass and scrutinizing its contents. 'I'm afraid you have the advantage of me.'

'Watch yer flamin' mouth!' added the second tearaway, tossing his own dog-end into Algy's glass. 'We don't like toffs round here!'

The pair stood there like two hounds barely controlled by their chains, challenging Algy to make the next move.

'I can't say the beer had much flavour,' Algy said with a thin smile. 'You may just have improved it!'

He grinned and raised the glass to his mouth. The yellow-toothed expressions froze on their faces. Bullies, he had calculated during his schooldays, tend to fear madmen. Just how mad could he be?

Algy smashed the glass down on the edge of the table, spewing ale and shards of glass everywhere, wrapped an arm around the nearest yob's neck and thrust the shattered stump of the glass under his chin. Blood spurted down onto Algy's fingers.

'Now, listen!,' he growled to the other nasty piece of work, his eyes flickering like blue flames. 'If you don't bugger off out of here, I'll be jamming this into your mate's neck and you, my foul-smelling friend, will be swimming in his blood.'

The yob backed away, arms outstretched in surrender. Algy relaxed his grip and flung his captive onto the floor. 'Now, you can bugger off after him!'

He placed the broken glass on the table and asked the pot-man if there was a back way out. He was directed through a small side door and emerged into a narrow passage. He glanced left and right and then cursed. It was a blind alley.

He doubled back; and was cracked round the head. Confronting him he could just make out the two louts: one slapping his palm with a cosh; the other brandishing a knife.

Algy steadied himself and used his wrist to parry a second blow from the cosh while kicking the chiv clattering across the granite setts but, he could not prevent his arms from being pinioned. He stamped his right boot into the instep of the tough restraining him and drove his right elbow back into his gut. A putrid blast of beer-and-baccy breath testified to the blow's effectiveness and Algy threw him round into the path of his mate's swinging cosh. The yob hardly had time to feel the torrent of thick warm blood gushing from his slashed cheekbone before he crashed to the ground like a barrel dropping off the back of a dray.

The remaining ne'er-do-well dropped the neddy and made a run for it. Algy chased after him, grabbed him by the jacket and slammed him against the wall. One look into Algy's cold blue eyes made him cry for mercy. They told him Algy's thoughts had gone beyond retaliation. He wanted retribution. He was consumed by a brutal and ferocious desire to maim.

Algy dug a forefinger into the lout's eye as if he were needling a winkle and followed it up with a kidney punch that he confidently expected would make him piss blood for a week. He watched the man drop to his knees, caught hold of his right wrist and twisted his arm up his back before jerking it up and out. The sickening crunch of sinew was followed by a pop and erstwhile hard-man writhed on the ground feeling as if someone had bisected his chest with a cleaver.

Algy suddenly saw his father screaming up at him. His face twisted and darkened. A rage ripped through him over which he had no control nor wanted to have as he punched and kicked in a blind fury. He felt nothing and he saw nothing outside of the vague outline of tattered clothes. He stopped only to draw breath and only then did he feel his skinned knuckles stinging with his blood and that of his victim or notice how his once pristine boots were scuffed and smeared with skin and hair.

The man fell silent. Algy stood over him, shivering with a pleasure so tangible he could clamp his teeth on it. He shook his head and looked around, wondering who could have half-killed the human lying at his feet.

Slowly it dawned on him and he felt ashamed. He winced as he staunched the blood leaking from the cut on his cheek, straightened his jacket and then hobbled away.

******

Algy limped out of the Holy Land, half expecting to be waylaid around every corner. Reaching St Martin's Lane, he paused to shake the numbness out of his leg and recoiled at the sight of a tooth falling from his trouser turn-up onto the pavement. He stamped the blood-encrusted molar into dust: he had made a total hash of his mission and he would have to think of a solution very quickly if he was not to fail his friend or possibly even place him in physical danger.

Anger began to fuel his progress. He crossed New Row and as he neared Charing Cross he thought he spied a familiar figure up ahead entering the large building that stood on the corner of May's Court. Although they were separated by twenty yards of bobbing heads, he could have sworn it was Connie. He called out but the woman disappeared inside without acknowledgement.

Turning the heavy iron key in the lock and pressing her back against the doors, Connie bit her knuckles and braced herself for the sound of Algy trying to gain entry. She prayed to God he would pass by. She heard his footsteps approach the door with the threatening tread of a bailliff and held her breath as the handle clanked under his touch. When it refused to budge, she heard him pad away and she slid down to the floor with the bilious taste of relief in her mouth, snagging her dress on the door furniture in the process.

The fire in Connie's green eyes was doused by tears as it struck her just how much she was the prisoner of her own egoism. She thought she had got her priorities right at last. She knew she had more than her fair share of good fortune, yet every advantage - the exorbitant allowance, the sumptuous clothes, the lavish parties, the endless holidays - was ultimately overwhelmed by the sheer emptiness of her existence. She desperately yearned to change, to inject some meaning into her life. And she had resolved that this was to be the year she did.

Yet even now, as she ransacked her brain to identify why she had thrown away this perfect chance to show Algy another side of herself, she could not find a rational explanation. Every time she got close, her brain was befuddled by a chorus of voices all talking to her at once: Algy and Seger; the mother she missed and the father who nagged; her banker and her bookmaker. She began to feel dizzy, her thoughts spinning round in her head like the moving pictures on the zoetrope she used to whirl faster and faster in the nursery: the world flashing past with herself a dazed observer, going nowhere fast. She began to snivel.

But the last thing Connie wished was to make an exhibition of herself in this particular place. She pummelled her knees angrily and made herself to get up, only to tread on the hem of her dress and transform a small hole into a huge tear.

Her shriek attracted a swarm of young bare-footed ragamuffins, their faces as grey as their calico dresses, all eager to know why 'Miss Connie' was wearing a tattered skirt. Connie gazed from one set of saucer eyes to another and took hold of the nearest hands, suggesting they all go and finish the summer dresses they had started making last week. She told herself not to cry as she trudged down the corridor, each step demanding greater and greater resolve as she sought an excuse to leave.

A few hundred yards away Algy was crossing Piccadilly Circus having erased all thoughts of Connie from his mind. He had examined the name carved into the arched stone lintel above the heavy studded double-doors and realized he must have been mistaken. The words spelt out: Doors of Hope For Orphaned Girls.

If the woman he had seen entering the orphanage was Connie, he assured himself, she must be a finer actress than Lily Langtry and Sarah Bernhardt rolled into one.

FOUR

Around the same time as Algy was entering the Holy Land, back at Sandown Park Minting's trainer Mat Dawson was leading his vet toward the racecourse stables to check that his prized colt had arrived safely from Newmarket.

'Mannington, mon,' the veteran handler said in his distinctive Scottish burr, 'ye're aboot to gaze upon one of the finest-looking horses you'll ever see! Almost 17 hands, and bone the like of which ye'll nae find every day!'

The vet smiled benignly, then nodded in capitulation. 'I know your opinion well enough! You've been telling me for a year that Minting is the finest looking three-year-old colt in the country.'

'And the best!'

'But he couldn't beat Ormonde in the Guineas!'

Dawson pink cheeks reddened brightly above his white whiskers. 'Away mon!'

'You may criticise a man's wife but not his horses!' said Mannington, not wishing to offend. 'You've trained the winners of 22 Classics, Mat, so I'll bow to your opinion.'

'Minting will redeem himself in the Eclipse!' Dawson declared. 'There's no Ormonde in the field tomorrow! Aye, Minting'll show them a clean pair of heels tomorrow. I'll stake my reputation on it!'

'Counting the prize money already, Mat?' teased Mannington.

'Don't be so silly, mon!'

'Just keeping you on your toes!'

'It's too strong a field to be counting chickens.'

Mannington suddenly felt quite stupid. Old Mat had not become the most lauded trainer in the land by taking victories for granted. 'Quite so.'

A first prize of £10,000, more than double the amount Ormonde collected for winning the Derby, had attracted a fine selection of horses for this innovative clash between the current three-year-old Classic generation and their elders. Ranged against Minting would be the 1884 Derby winner St Gatien and the dual Classic-winning filly Miss Jummy, plus the promising Gay Hermit running for the Duchess of Montrose and Bendigo, a big black six-year-old who loved a scrap as much as his namesake, the renowned bare-knuckle boxer.

'But I've a trump card up my sleeve, Mannington!' Dawson said slyly after they had walked on a little farther.

'And what might that be?'

Dawson stroked his luxuriant white whiskers like an elderly pussycat anticipating his next meal and a post-prandial a snooze in the sun.

'Yon tin-scraping Archer is itching to ride him.'

'Aaah! Lord Alington is willing to forego his claim and let him off Candlemas?'

'Aye, in order to ride for his old master - and the uncle of his dear departed wife - I do believe His Lordship will give his consent. Mark my words, Archer will ride Minting for me.'

'The Tinman's presence in the pigskin would make all the difference.'

'Aye,' said Dawson with a broad smile as they finally reached Minting's box, 'that's right enough.'

Within the coolness of the box, the strapping bay colt stood obediently in a corner while his stable lad busied himself at his feet. But instead of forking up the straw into a fluffy yellow bed or twisting a handful into a switch ready to buff the colt's coat to a mirrored sheen, he was busy securing a piece of cloth around Minting's off-fore pastern. Once he had fastened it, he pulled a small hammer out of his coat pocket and struck the target with one sharp, carefully-aimed blow.

Fingers of fire shot up the bay colt's leg and he fly-jumped in pain just at the moment

Dawson drew back the bolt on the stable door.

'Good God, mon!' Dawson exclaimed. 'What in heaven's name do ye think ye're doing?'

The groom dropped the hammer, pushed Dawson out of the way and fled, leaving poor Minting standing forlornly on three legs.

'How bad is it?'

'The skin's not broken but he's made a damn good job of it,' replied Mannington, squatting on his haunches to inspect the leg at close quarters. 'The leg's filling already.'

'Badly?'

'Enough to rule him out of any exercise for the next 24 hours at least. That's the end of the Eclipse, I'm afraid.'

'Curse the mon!'

The three words were an inadequate summation of Dawson's feelings but he was a God-fearing man who would no sooner resort to profanity than feed his horses inferior oats.

'Young Archer will be grievously disappointed,' Dawson added, beard scraping his chest.

Mannington was too preoccupied with Minting to fully appreciate the depth of Dawson's concern for his protege.

'He obviously intended just to lame him,' he said getting up from his haunches, 'and was taking great pains to cover his tracks.'

'If I ever get my hands on the mon!' mumbled the trainer, his face now as white as his whiskers. 'Whatever could have possessed him? He's been with my me for years. He was one of my best lads - that's why he was entrusted with Minting.'

'Someone must have put the fear of God into him.'

'Bookmakers, I'll be bound!'

'Obviously one who didn't want Minting lining-up tomorrow afternoon,' said Mannington. 'This definitely smacks of money talking.'

The vet eyed Dawson ruefully.

'Have you backed him, Mat? Is it your money they're after?'

Dawson returned the look with one of indignation.

'He was nae carrying any of my money! The prize money was good enough for me.'

'Whoever ordered this must have been running scared of someone's wager!'

'Ye're probably right,' said Dawson, 'but whoever's backed him, their money's in the bookmakers' pockets now!'

Dawson was correct. Even as Minting was being crippled, Fenner's agents were offering stumer odds of 10 to 1 about the 7 to 4 market leader in a ploy to coax last-ditch commissions from mug punters.

Their boss was not a man to stand idly by when anyone double-crossed him. Particularly if they were the sort who considered themselves a cut above everyone else and untouchable; the sort who looked down on a man like himself who had, quite literally, fought for his position in life. He had spent his formative years pandering to the whims of people like this, putting his life at risk for their entertainment and amusement. No longer. Their boss had no intention of allowing Minting to save Archer's skin by winning the Eclipse Stakes. He had Mister High-and-Mighty Fred Archer in the jaws of a vice he was planning to tighten. Mister Archer owed him. Weak excuses and paper promises would not suffice. Mister Archer would have to find some other way to appease Mo Fenner.

******

The man suspended by his feet from the meat-hook was as naked as the day he was born. surrounded by swaying sides of beef, his arms pointed limply toward his clothes heaped on the stone floor of the cold-store, for they had lost all the strength to protect his modesty. The only sound he made amounted to not much more than the occasional gurgle thanks to the apple jammed firmly into his mouth.

The smaller of the two men standing guard over him paced back and forth. He was protected from the numbing cold by a thick overcoat and a woollen scarf wrapped tightly around his head from chin to crown that would have made his eyebrow-less white face look like the man in the moon's had it not been for the crimson sore underlining his blackened and half-closed right eye.

Every now and again he poked the human carcass dangling in front of him with a sharpened stick to make sure it was still alive and to amuse himself.

'You blew the gaff!' he snarled as the body showed some semblance of life by twisting on the rope and providing him with a further opportunity to prolong both its suffering and his enjoyment. 'The boss don't like people who bugger up!'

His eyes narrowed while he decided which part of the man's anatomy to target for optimum pain. Suddenly he jumped back.

'You dirty stinkin' bastard!' he yelled as a spout of steaming urine splashed his coat.

He nodded in the direction of his companion who ceased thumping his hands together and stamping his feet long enough to pick up a bucket of ice-cold water and hurl the contents over their prisoner.

The force of the water caused the body to execute a half-turn whilst making a noise that reverberated around the arctic cavern like someone treading on a igantic frozen puddle. The body quivered, barely imperceptibly, for it could not withstand much more.

'Cocky, can't we go nah?' whined the second man, who had one of those lop-sided faces that looked as if its owner had just received pieces of good and bad news simultaneously. 'I'm freezin' me balls off!'

'Nah! Not yet. Give 'im some more.'

He did as he was ordered. He flinched as the water sprayed back at him off the body but he could tell from the whites of Cocky's eyes that the role of torturer was too satisfying to relinquish.

The victim's lips were now a deep sapphire. Icicles hung from his fingers, his nose and his genitalia; ice crystals starting to form all over his body made it resemble a frosty windowpane. Had he been able to speak they would have heard him begging for death and welcoming it.

'E's a goner, Cocky. Let's go! It's bleedin' brass monkeys in 'ere!'

'Eli, you don't know shit from sugar!'

'I got a judy to sort out!'

'You know your trouble?'

'What?'

'Your brain's in yer dick!'

'That's choice, coming from you wiv an' 'andle like Cocky!'

They guffawed and turned away, their job done. They left him hanging there, as lifeless as the carcasses providing his only company.

When the first of Smithfield's meat-porters opened the cold-store at four o'clock the following morning to extract some sides of beef, he discovered Minting's former stable-lad frozen solid among them. A man to whom cadavers meant nothing was promptly reduced to shielding his eyes and throwing-up against the nearest wall, sickened that any civilized human being could stoop to such butchery.

FIVE

The rain beat a relentless tattoo on Algy's malacca-handled umbrella and ran down the back of his Burberry waterproof as he hurried through the gates of Sandown Park a little after one o'clock on the afternoon of the Eclipse Stakes. He was desperate to speak with Archer.

No opportunity had presented itself the previous evening in the aftermath of his altercation with Fenner's roughnecks. After leaving the Holy Land he had dined at his club, the Turf in Carlton House Terrace. He was not exactly the clubable type, suspecting that any club soliciting his membership was not the sort of establishment he wished to be part of, but he made an exception in this case because Turf Club gossip guaranteed a supply of juicy tit-bits for his thrice-weekly column in *The Sportsman* that appeared under the pen-name 'Spyglass.'

Algy could hear the circumstances surrounding Minting's surprise defection from the Eclipse being loudly debated in the adjacent dining room as he twiddled his thumbs in the lobby waiting for Satterthwaite, the Club's doddery septugenarian major-domo, to fetch a letter hand-delivered some 30 minutes earlier and marked for his 'Urgent and Personal Attention.'

He began fingering open the envelope half-heartedly while pondering the likely involvement of Fenner in Minting's injury until he felt the touch of something soft and painfully familiar. The blood drained from his lips, leaving them resembling two taut white lines as he drew out the small rectangular card onto which was pinned a tiny white feather. Algy knew there was no point inspecting the card for the name of its sender. He ran his tongue around his mouth and, glancing left and right, thrust the coward's badge into his trouser pocket.

Though finding he had suddenly lost his appetite, Algy forced himself to eat a light supper of poached salmon and creamed potatoes, confining

36

himself to a single glass of Tremblay-Bouchard, before politely rejecting Blackwell's invitation to make-up a four at bridge in favour of retiring to his Jermyn Street rooms where he made directly for the walnut veneered bureau occupying the alcove beside the hearth. He slid the catch which released the hidden drawer and, after pausing a moment, took the white feather from his pocket and placed it with all the others. Then he sought the comfort of a long hot soak wherein aching mind and body might be soothed while he considered his next move.

The former proved more achievable than the latter but, after much subsequent pacing and thinking aloud, the recent exertions with Connie and Fenner's henchmen finally caught up with him and he fell asleep in an armchair.

A more restful night's sleep would have put Algy in a better mood to negotiate a Sandown Park heaving with a record crowd of 30,000 - among them the Prince of Wales - for this first running of the Eclipse; it took five frustrating minutes of elbowing and prodding with his rolled-up umbrella to force a path through the hordes milling around in front of the entrance reserved for Press. Once inside the course he had not gone more than a few yards before he felt someone tugging at his sleeve. A ferret-faced figure hiding beneath a grey billycock hat, who looked vaguely familiar, was holding out a small brown-paper parcel.

'Mister Haymer, sir, could you see that Mister Archer gets this, please?'

'What is it?'

'I don't know, sir, but I believe he's expecting it.'

'Really? Hand it over then.'

The man handed over the parcel and Algy lifted it to his ear and shook it. 'I hear no ticking! Seems harmless. I'll see he gets it.'

He gave the man 'a guinea for his trouble' and tucked the parcel under one arm before resuming his meander through the social climbers who had started to pack the lawns bordering the paddock in the hope of seeing and being seen now that the rain had eased. Among them he caught sight of Connie talking with Lord George Seger and his perpetual court jester and snitch, the Honourable Douglas Deek.

Algy promptly lowered his head and sought a detour. He never relished being within fifty yards of Seger and Deek: he detested the pair of them.

Algy had first come across Deek at Oxford. Initially, he decided Deek's was a personality too pallid to inspire anything so positive as dislike; soon he reached the conclusion that Deek was as wooden as a railway sleeper and about half as useful. Deek was thin of hair, corpulent, without a chin but with the tiny hands and long eyelashes of a girl, and had been dubbed 'Tea-Pot' by his Corpus contemporaries owing to his squat body and extra-long 'spout'; he was also so overburdened with self-importance that Algy had seen him take drinks from college scouts as if they had done him personal injury not service. He had no occupation - if one excluded scandal-mongering - and wore the permanently doughy expression of an obese child who had just seen the last slice of chocolate cake stolen from under its nose. Indeed, it was the kind of face Algy felt instinctively compelled to punch but had never considered it worth bruising his knuckles.

Seger unsettled him in a different way, and had done from the day of their first encounter at Uppingham where his odd slanting eyes displayed the disturbing habit of straying toward a boy's crotch. He had been regarded as a 'mummy's boy.' And an oversized one at that. Most of his six feet was taken up by legs and neck like a length of lead piping atop which sat an undersized head permanently cast in gloom. Seger looked as if the devil's black dog had walked over him, scoring his cheeks, blue-black even after a close shave, with sharp lines and licking the waxed moustache until it curved like an inky scimitar. Algy likened being in his presence to being trapped in Haverholme's crypt and joked that he felt like reaching for a crucifix every time he encountered him.

Yet beneath Seger's heavily pomaded hair, he sensed a cold brain that revelled in its own cleverness, one that had already capitalized on a web of aristocratic connections to get him elected to the Jockey Club. All Seger lacked was a suitable lady on his arm to lend him total respectability.

Algy was too slow. Connie had spied her lover burrowing through the crowd like a lost leveret and hailed him.

'Good to see you again so soon!' she said, flashing a row of white teeth in a smile that dazzled like the sun coming over the mountains.

'Likewise, I'm sure,' he lied in view of the company she was keeping.

Seger tipped the brim of his hat with his cane. 'The hero of Isandlwana, no less.'

'Don't you mean the survivor of Isandlwana!' haw-hawed Deek.

Algy felt as if he had been skewered through the guts and rendered incapable of speech: his throat felt tinder-dry and his mouth struggled to manufacture one speck of saliva.

'A lot cosier,' he finally managed to croak, 'hiding behind Chelmsford's skirts 12 miles away, enjoying a picnic lunch, than facing Zulu assegai!'

'One did not choose the responsibility of being honoured with a place on His Lordship's staff...'

'No, your spineless chums-in-high-places saw to that!'

A flash of colour at last began to illuminate Seger's dull cheeks and he raised his cane until its ivory pommel menaced Algy's jutting chin. Both men seemed to grow an inch, sensing this was one of the rare occasions when their antipathy to one another might actually spill over.

'That's enough of the past!' said Connie, stepping between them and forcing a smile. 'What about the present? Don't you think I look splendid?'

'You look lovely,' Algy eventually managed to grunt without releasing her two companions from a glare now verging on the maniacal.

'Do you really think so?' the peace-maker continued.

He blinked and took a proper look at her. Connie's appearance acted like a sobering wet cloth for she looked ravishing. She shimmered in a figure-hugging, lacey yellow frock that complemented the fire of her titian hair and green eyes. The allure of a red-headed woman, all bar the milk-white red-heads whom he found to be as cold as they appeared, was simplicity itself. They smelt of sex.

And as for the colour of her dress: it suddenly dawned on him that it was not canary yellow or lemon. It was straw. Connie knew what she was doing: she was trying to titillate him with coded signals. The dress itself defied convention: it had no bustle. Connie's figure needed no artifice to advertize its splendour. High-waisted and buttoned tight to her slender neck, it triumphantly showed off her trim waist and the swell of a bosom he had salivated over five years ago when he first saw her in hunting gear out with the Belvoir. Judging by the present stirring in his loins, it had not lost the ability to arouse him. If he could have had his way he would have peeled the dress off her but he had to make do with undressing her with his eyes.

'No hat, Connie, on such a miserably wet afternoon?'

'Why should I spoil the view!' she replied.

Algy smiled inwardly for he appreciated that going bare-headed on such a social occasion as Eclipse day was just one expression of Connie's nonconformity which enabled her to draw attention to yet another: a penchant for cropping her golden locks boyishly short rather than submit to the *chignon* favoured by ladies of convention.

'Pity, that dress must have cost you a small fortune!' Algy added. 'Or should I say, it must have cost your father a portion of his large one!'

'I'll have you know I manage my own financial affairs quite satisfactorily without the help of my father! He doesn't own me and in any case what I do with my money is of no concern to you or anyone else!'

'Someone sounds as if they're on a losing streak!'

'You sound just like my father!'

'Is that a compliment?'

'Now, you two!' Seger interrupted. 'You're behaving worse than a couple of tight-kneed spinsters squabbling over the bride's bouquet!'

Algy aimed flaring nostrils in Seger's direction. 'Is that a hint of lavender I can smell?' he sneered.

'I don't like your tone, Haymer!' Seger replied. 'What are you suggesting?'

Algy giggled at Seger's girlish response and restricted himself to saying that an xplanation was surely unnecessary.

'There's no need to be so snide!' admonished Connie.

Algy grabbed her wrist and pulled her to one side. 'Why in heaven's name are you mixing with a pair of ageing poodlefakers like these two?'

'Older men are so much more resourceful, financially and emotionally!' she said, seizing her opportunity to give a smirk of her own.

'Really?' said Algy, hearing his voice rise.

'And they're only a few years your senior! Besides, they entertain me and make me laugh.'

'I'd have thought a chin-less wonder like Seger possessed all the qualities of a poker – excepting, of course, the occasional warmth.'

'I don't care what you say, he makes me feel I have something to contribute.'

'Nothing to do with all those estates in Gloucestershire, then?'

'No,' she snapped. 'Not one jot!'

'Keep your voice down!'

'George, and Deek, listen to me. They're interested in what I have to say.'

'And I suppose I don't?' Algy hissed, tightening his grip on her wrist.

'And so charming!'

'About as charming as a dead baby, the pair of them!'

'I'll not be treated like one of your old Grensons that you can slip into just when it pleases you!' she snorted, pleased with her riposte.

'You don't think,' Algy continued regardless, 'this pantomime is more a case of you knowing full well the very thought of those morons fawning on you is guaranteed to annoy me?

Connie rolled her eyes and tugged herself free of his attentions. 'Actually, Seger has asked me to marry him!'

Algy emitted a noise somewhere between a snort and a cough. 'You've turned him down, of course?'

Connie's mouth widened with undisguised glee until its corners curled in triumph, causing all Algy's cockiness to desert him; he felt a coldness invade his stomach.

'You've not said "Yes"?'

'I may have,' she said, nose wrinkling.

'You can't love him,' Algy harrumphed.

'How could you possibly know!'

'He certainly can't love you...'

'And why ever not?'

'Because men like him are incapable of loving anyone but themselves!'

Algy's thoughts suddenly turned to hot air and blew away; instead of completing his diatribe he mumbled something about needing a drink.

Yet he made no effort to go and find one. He and Connie stood eye-ing each other like two divorce lawyers waiting for the other to make the first offer of settlement. The difference was one yearned to be swept off her feet by an enraged lover while the other was mummified at his being cuckolded.

'I see,' Algy said with a heavy sigh. 'Then there's no more to be said.'

He turned and executed a mock bow toward the brooding figure of Seger who had been trying in vain to follow the gist of their tete-a-tete. 'I really must apologize. I was completely unaware of the circumstances...'

'Well, don't be such an absolute cad!' interjected Connie, playfully tapping Algy on the wrist with the handle of her parasol. 'There's really no call for you to be so grumpy!'

Her companions duly laughed on cue but she paid them no attention. She had eyes only for her elusive paramour whom she had reduced to cringing with pain.

'It's nothing, Connie,' Algy protested. 'Caught it in a carriage door, that's all.'

'More like caught it sliding down a drainpipe when the husband returned unexpectedly!' guffawed Deek, looking around to check that he had been heard.

Connie handed her parasol to Seger and undid Algy's cuff-link, pulling back the sleeve to inspect his wrist.

'This may need strapping!' she said. 'And, yes, you've a bruise coming up beneath your eye!'

'It's nothing, I can assure you.'

As he fumbled to re-attach his cuff-link, Connie snuggled as close to him as propriety permitted and homed-in on his good ear.

'I do hope you weren't caught by an angry husband,' she whispered, her hot breath warming his neck, 'because if you slept like a baby last night I want to have been the cause not some trollop in Mayfair.'

The fragrance dabbed behind her own ear made him want to take the plump pink lobe into his mouth.

'No, it didn't give me a sleepless night since you ask,' he said. 'I'm perfectly fine and I'm afraid I've better things to do than bandy words with you. I must speak with Archer.'

Connie's face lit up. 'Oh, do introduce me to The Tinman! Please! I've so wanted to meet him!'

'Didn't I see you talking with him only the other week at...'

'No!' cut in Seger, lancing Deek with a cold stare. 'That must have been Celia Wilding. Connie has yet to make Archer's acquaintance.'

Deek displayed the verging-on-tears expression of a child who knows not why it has been reprimanded as Connie scolded him for being so stupid as to mistake her for someone as plain as Celia Wilding.

'You did promise!' she simpered, turning her attention back to Algy. 'Those lovely big sad eyes of his remind me of an adorable spaniel puppy! Oh so glum and begging for a good cuddle!'

'I'm sorry, Connie,' said Algy, 'but that's an impossibility at present. Fred has a lot on his mind. The last thing he needs is you on his trail.'

'My, aren't we the protective one!' jeered Seger, a sardonic smile contorting lips as thin as Deek's were thick.

He rolled his next words around his mouth to extract maximum impact and satisfaction from them. 'What's Archer to you other than a convenient meal ticket now and again. It's not as if he's family or anything.'

Algy's knuckles whitened and he jabbed a finger to within an inch of Seger's chest. 'That's enough frippery from you! Watch what you say or I'll knock you from here to kingdom come!'

Seger's insinuation was nothing new and nor was Algy's reaction. He first endured these scrap-inducing taunts at Uppingham and had been coming to terms with them ever since. Archer's quaintly aristocratic mien and Lord Belton's reputation as a womanizer fuelled rumour that there was more to the Belton connection than the principals were prepared to admit.

Algy grew to hope the gossip might be true. He had always been too frightened to air the subject with either of his parents: his self-effacing mother, he knew, would look away to hide her fears and he would feel ashamed of himself for hurting her; his father would most likely reach for his horse whip. And he knew what that would spark. He recognized his dilemma: it was easily enough diagnosed yet no less difficult to treat. He wanted to believe he and Archer were brothers so much that he could not bring himself to seek confirmation in case his hopes were dashed.

'Calm yourself!' said Connie, stepping between them.

'He's nothing but a poodle-faker!' said Algy.

Needled or not, Algy remembered where he was and allowed his fists to drop. He watched Connie pout as only a woman who has engineered a spat between two warring suitors can.

'Now, where were we?' she continued officiously. 'Ah, yes! My little request. How could you deny me this one teeny favour?'

'I can't exploit Archer's friendship for…'

'You think I'll just badger him for tips?'

'Well…'

'In that case, it falls to you to give us a winner?' she said quickly. 'And I *mean* a winner this time!'

'Connie, you should know better than to chase your losses,' he replied with a mixture of impatience and disapproval

'Oh, I didn't lose *that* much yesterday!'

'Can't say there's anything I'd recommend.' He did not believe her for a second and was damned if he was going to be party to further financial embarrassment.

'Don't be such a spoilsport, Haymer!' brayed Seger.

Algy sucked his teeth: Seger was beginning to have the same effect on him as a hungry mosquito. 'Sorry, Connie, I really must crack on. I've wasted enough time already!'

'Haymer, there's no reason to be so damnably rude…'

'George, do shut up!' demanded Connie as Algy walked off.

She raised herself on tiptoe and craned her neck in an effort to make herself heard. 'Shall we meet later? If it's any help I can offer you a ride back to town! I have daddy's brougham!'

'Sorry! I'm busy this evening!' Algy shouted back.

'But you promised!'

Connie's face crumpled as Algy passed out of earshot. She did not know whether to run after him or scream. Instead, she counted to five under her breath and then asked her two lap-dogs if that was roast chicken she could smell coming from the luncheon room.

What Connie found impossible to ignore over luncheon was the sure knowledge that her teenage infatuation showed no sign of abating.

SIX

Algy bounded up the steps of the weighing room two at a time. The very idea of Connie and Seger having a relationship, let alone a marriage, raised a head-shaking smile but the thought of more important issues saw it vanish just as quickly.

He found Archer engaged in quiet conversation with Lord Alington, for whom he would after all partner Candlemas in the Eclipse. One glance at the jockey's downturned mouth suggested his friend knew Minting's injury had been malicious in origin and that Algy's bid to pacify Mo Fenner had failed abysmally. Algy wished he could conjure up some means of avoiding the conversation in prospect.

'Good afternoon Lord Alington, good afternoon FA,' he said. 'When you've finished your chat, perhaps I might have a word with you, FA? I think we need to talk.'

'I think we do.'

'Somewhere a bit more private.'

Archer turned to Lord Alington. 'Excuse me M'Lord. Do you think Haymer and myself might use the stewards room for a moment, please?'

Alington raised no objection and Archer led the way. The smell of polished wood and leather tainted by the smoke of countless cigars hung heavily in the panelled room, affording Algy painful reminders of his father's study. The calm was disturbed only by the sonorous ticking of the large clock mounted on the wall behind the broad judicial table that separated stewards from miscreants.

'I'm sorry, Fred,' Algy said, and sat the parcel down on the gleaming table-top. 'It's entirely my fault. I got there too late. Fenner had already set the dogs on you.'

Archer stared at the portrait of himself on the 1880 Derby winner Bend Or that hung over the fireplace. 'You tried your best. And the problem was of my own making.'

'Good of you to say so but I might have tried harder if only...'

Archer stood with his back to Algy, splay-footed, whip tucked under his right arm, head cocked to one side.

'Fred, are you listening?'

'He was a good horse that day, Algy.'

'Pardon? Who was?'

'Bend Or,' Archer replied, gesturing toward the painting with his whip, 'the day he beat Robert the Devil.'

'Ah, yes, the day you rode with your arm in a iron brace! You must have been mad but By God you made us some money with that ride.'

Archer sat himself down in the chair in the centre of the table reserved for the senior presiding steward and began fiddling absent-mindedly with the string securing the parcel. He wished he was riding Bend Or this afternoon in the Eclipse instead of a no-hoper. Then he could have got himself out of this mess.

'I thought as much when I heard what happened to Minting,' he said, finally addressing Algy's point. 'How could anyone do that to a dumb animal?'

'Fenner has no scruples, Fred. You must know that as well as I do.'

'I suppose so,' Archer replied while studying every square inch of the yellow-stained ceiling as if he were in the Sistine Chapel.

'I find it incredible that you bother to have any dealings with him.'

It was now the jockey's turn to look flabbergasted. 'Don't be silly, Brusher!'

'You can't be that hard-up?'

'No?'

Algy was irritated by the need to explain further and did so only after walking the extremities of the room and pausing to look out of each window.

'Let's think about this. You receive a five-guinea fee for riding a winner and your retainers must come to at least £3,500.'

'Yes, I imagine so.'

'Good God man, that comes to £8,000 or more. Every year for the past decade!'

'Possibly so.'

'And then there are the special fees on top of all that! Lord Stamford offered you £1,000 just to ride Geheimniss in the Leger!'

'But I couldn't.'

'That's immaterial! There have been plenty more like it. And then there are presents from grateful owners!'

'A lot don't bother! They think I've had a good bet already so they don't bother to give me anything!'

Algy inhaled deeply and rubbed the back of his neck. 'Fred, a few years back it was common knowledge that you were worth £¼ million! That kind of money doesn't just blow away in a west wind!'

Although he had anticipated this topic might come up, Archer was no better prepared to cope with it. He began rubbing his palms on his knees and, the proximity of a decent fire notwithstanding, he felt a chilling inability to order his thoughts.

'I'm not doing so well this season,' he answered with the alacrity of a glacier.

'That's just an excuse and you know it. Just a smokescreen, that's all!'

'There's my weight. I struggled to do 8 st 8 lb at Ascot, you know. Wood is getting away from me in the table. He's seven ahead of me now. I just don't think I'm riding so well.'

'Nonsense! You won the Derby! And Ormonde's sure to win the Leger - and heaven knows what else! The money will start rolling in again.'

'But will I ride him? Barrett rode him at Ascot for his last win, don't forget.'

'Only because you were claimed for Melton by Lord Hastings!'

Algy realized he was fast losing his temper: he wanted to help his friend so much it was making his chest ache but he hated anyone defending the indefensible.

'Fred, listen to me, don't sell the brush before you've caught the fox. The Duke and Old John aren't going to drop you for George bloody Barrett.'

Archer heard Algy but he was not listening. 'In any case I've had a lot of expenses lately,' he continued, 'what with finishing-off the building work at Falmouth House. And decorating and furnishing doesn't come cheap you know.'

'Even so, Fred…'

'I'll be in Carey Street before you know it!'

The absence of irony in Archer's voice shocked Algy and his indignation vanished.

'You mean,' he said, chosing his words with care, 'you're so strapped for cash you actually fear bankruptcy and you're having to borrow money and rely on your betting to stay solvent?'

Archer ate a yawn, chewing on it two or three times. He began to think about which story he would read his daughter tonight.

'So, you've been to Cork Street and dropped-in on Sam Lewis?'

Still no answer. Algy knew Archer could be as deaf as a white cat when he wanted to be.

'I suppose you could do worse than old Sam. He drives a hard bargain but he's a man of his word and pretty honest.'

'That's what I've heard,' mumbled Archer at last, having tired of daydreaming about Goldilocks and the Three Bears.

'You mean you've not used Sam's services?'

'No, I haven't,' he said after another lengthy silence.

'Let's get this straight, shall we?' continued Algy, his earnest expression stating he had suddenly appreciated the gravity of the situation.

'You're borrowing money and you're gambling heavily?'

'Things haven't been going as well as I'd like.'

'And Brockford has cut you adrift completely?'

'Yes.'

'And what about Pulleine?'

'Him too. After I had a bad Ascot.'

'But, Fred, you won five blasted races at the meeting!'

'I know. But I got beat on Woodland and Whitefriar. They were my banker bets.'

Algy shook his head. 'So, things are so bad that only Fenner will take your bets and you've put yourself totally in his hands?'

'That's about the size of it.'

'Fenner, of all men! I can't believe you'd ever share the same room as a thug like Fenner let alone have dealings with him! How on God's earth did you even get to meet him?'

Algy watched Archer shrug his shoulders and knew that was the only response he was going to get. 'How much, exactly, do you owe him?'

The two men looked at each other. Both had churning stomachs: one because he did not want to give the answer and the other because he was expecting to dislike that answer.

'£30,000.'

Algy thumped his forehead. '£30,000! Fred, you're not getting involved too deeply in his nasty little schemes are you?'

Archer tilted the chair back until he could bring his feet up to rest on the rim of the table and began rocking it back and forth as if he were riding an imaginary finish. He was in a world of his own.

Algy could not help marvelling at the champion's exquisite balance and had to force himself to concentrate on the point at issue.

'Fred, this is deadly serious! Fenner is an animal.'

'Maybe, maybe not. He's never been charged with anything.'

'And we all know why! People are petrified of him! He rules by fear! People are frightened to death of crossing him!'

Algy rested his knuckles on the burnished table top and followed Archer's eyes with his own until they grudginly paid attention. 'Look, why don't you come and stay with me over the weekend until it all blows over?'

'Thanks, Algy, but I can't.'

'I've got plenty of room in Jermyn Street. You can have my bed and my man Edgecombe... you've met my manservant?'

'Yes, at Haverholme.'

'Then you know he's the soul of discretion and can be trusted implicitly... he can make up the cot for me.'

'I shouldn't put you out,' said Archer, by now waving an imaginary whip at his chair.

'I'll be fine on the cot,' insisted Algy. 'There's no racing until Goodwood starts on Tuesday - and I wager you're staying with the Rapers at Selhurst.'

'That's right.'

'Well, so am I. We can travel down together.'

'But I really should return to Newmarket tonight,' answered Archer, who had ceased riding the chair and let it bang to the floor.

'Why?'

'I read Nellie Rose her bedtime story whenever I can.'

'Of course,' said Algy sympathetically, although in truth the attraction of small children was a complete mystery to him. Nothing more than messy crying machines in his view, best avoided until they were old enough to fend and think for themselves.

'She's all that matters to me now,' Archer said, blinking. 'If anything happened to her, I don't know what I'd do.'

Algy acknowledged Archer's concern but pressed on regardless. 'Your sister, Mrs Coleman, is at Falmouth House isn't she? And Captain Bowling?'

'Yes, they are and right glad of their company I am.'

'Well then, little Nellie will be well looked after. You could put your own life in Bowling's hands. There's no finer man alive.'

'That man's so generous he'll most likely die in the poor-house.'

'There, you see, she'll be perfectly safe.'

Archer began licking his two front teeth, tossing Algy's assurances over in his mind. Perhaps he was mollycoddling Nellie Rose. He had been at home most evenings this past week. Perhaps a few nights away would buck him up a bit. She probably won't notice, he convinced himself.

'We'd better send the Captain a telegram,' he said. 'It's a lot to ask of him.'

'Of course. I'll attend to that, don't worry.'

'Well, all right then.'

'Capital!' said Algy, patting him on the back. 'We can sit, relax and talk.'

'I suppose a few days away won't do me any harm.'

Algy's face split into a broad grin reflecting the buoyant mood that had come over him since Archer had begun to weaken. He had waited years for such an opportunity as this and his mind already raced with plans.

'I've one idea for taking your mind off things.'

'What's that?'

'I happen to know of a certain entertainment taking place tonight that might appeal to your sporting instincts and provide the opportunity for a small flutter - no big stakes, you understand.'

Archer suddenly became interested. 'And what's that?'

'Ratting!'

'You're joking! I thought that was illegal?'

'No, certainly not. The police don't interfere. The only crushers you'll find there will be among the punters if truth be told!'

'Better than dog-fighting, I suppose,' said Archer quietly. 'I couldn't stand for that.'

'I agree. But rodents excite rather less pity!'

'Where is it? Far away from Rats Castle, I hope.'

'Far enough. A pub in Clerkenwell, The Cock and Hen in Compton Street. We'll clean-up first and have a bite of supper in my rooms...'

At the mention of food Archer turned away. Talking about food meant thinking about food and painful experience told him that only led to headaches and nausea.

'Whatever takes your fancy,' said Algy apologetically. 'Perhaps a sliver of chicken...a nice glass of champagne?'

'No!' Archer said in a raised voice. 'I couldn't. I've got to watch my weight. Perhaps a sardine...'

'You can't go through the day without eating something!'

'You know very well I take a drop of castor oil, a dry biscuit and a small glass of champagne before racing every day.'

'That's not food! That wouldn't keep a bug alive!'

'I don't feel the hunger any more. The less you eat, the more your stomach shrivels...'

'...and the less you need to fill it. Yes, I've heard it all before from you jockeys!'

'It's true!'

'Then your stomach must be the size of a grapefruit by now!'

Archer saw the funny side and laughed.

'How about those new Heinz beans then?' Algy continued enthusiastically. 'Lots of energy without any weight gain.'

'I had some of those in America the other winter. They made me...'

Algy began to snigger. 'Break wind rather a lot?'

'That's right. Something awful.'

'Well, what's it matter among friends!' laughed Algy. He could see that Archer remained unconvinced. Famished though he knew he would be, the prospect of having Archer to himself superceded any thoughts of the inevitable hunger pangs: he suggested they forget supper and stuck to the ratting.

Archer rubbed his nose. 'But, I'm sure to be recognized. I couldn't bear a scene.'

Algy needed a second to think of a solution. 'I've an overcoat that's two sizes too big for you. That and a trilby pulled down over your eyes should do the trick. You'll be completely incognito. They'll all be too drunk to notice you in any case!'

Archer had removed one of his boots and begun furiously rubbing away between his toes. 'This blasted itch is enough to drive me mad! Solomon's not keeping these boots clean enough!'

'Try peeing in them!'

'Are you kidding!'

'No, I'm absolutely serious. It's what the old sergeant advised in South Africa. Washing your boots out with urine kills the fungal infections a treat!'

Archer harrumphed and stamped his foot back inside the boot.

'What's in this?' he said, turning his full attention to the package.

Algy was too preoccupied with planning the evening's entertainment to hear Archer's question first time of asking.

'I've no idea,' he replied second time round. 'It's not mine, it's for you. Some strange little fellow passed it to me on the way in. He said you were expecting it.'

Archer pulled a face. 'Can't think what for, but I'd best open it then.'

He began untying the string and permitted himself the glimmer of a smile.

'Perhaps it's some money! Charlie's organized a whip-round!' he said, amused by his wittiness. 'What do you think?'

Algy's thoughts were so far away that he neither answered nor noticed Archer lifting the lid of the cardboard box he had found inside the brown paper. He was dragged back to reality by Archer's face contorting in horror as he dropped the box onto the table, spilling its stinking contents in a bloody heap that would have been more at home on a butcher's block.

Archer began retching violently and was on the verge of swooning. Algy got him into a chair and poured a glass of water from the jug provided for the stewards.

'Is it offal of some kind?' he said, peering at what appeared to be two lumps of putrid meat. 'Jesus, Fred! It's a pair of horse's testicles.'

Algy held his nose and swept the offal back into the box with his free hand. Then he noticed a piece of paper pinned inside the lid.

'Fred, did you see this?'

'What?' Archer replied, sipping water which he hoped would stop him retching again.

'There's a note.'

'What's it say?'

Algy cleared his throat. 'It says "Do as you're told or next time it will be yours for the chop."'

His friend's situation was more perilous than he had imagined. Algy tore up the note and wondered what he had got himself into.

SEVEN

Some hours later Algy and Archer alighted from a hansom cab at the corner of Clerkenwell Road and St John Street as dusk was falling and the sound of a church bell striking nine could be heard in the distance.

They turned into Compton Street and the clamour coming from the Cock and Hen pinpointed its location. The noise fired Algy's enthusiasm for the evening ahead but not so his companion.

'Is this really a good idea?' Archer said, his stride shortening.

'Don't be an old woman,' Algy hissed out of the corner of his mouth as they crossed the street. 'Just pull down that hat and pin those shoulders back and even Bowling wouldn't recognize you.'

While Algy approached one of the men flanking the door, Archer hid his face and read the curling hand-bill nailed to the wall: 'Ratting for the Million. A Sporting Gentleman who is a Staunch Supporter of the Destruction of the Vermin will give a Gold Repeater Watch to be Killed For by Dogs under 13 ¾ pounds Weight.'

'Two square-rigged mashers on the randy, eh?' said the sentry with a smirk. 'That'll cost you an alderman.'

Algy dropped a coin into his outstretched hand and they were waved into the premises. Archer asked whether they had strayed into another country since the populace obviously spoke a language other than the Queen's English.

'Fred, this is another country,' Algy assured him. 'A little of the local lingo goes a long way!'

'So, what did he say?'

'We were a couple of swells out for an evening's entertainment and the entry fee was a half-crown.'

Archer laughed so much his eyes watered and he almost dislodged his hat. 'Well I never!'

Algy steadied the hat and returned the laugh. Fred is starting to relax, he thought. Seeing him laugh from the eyes is a good sign. Algy flung an arm around Archer's shoulders and pushed through a pair of swing doors whose spring matched that in his step. He could hardly wait for their real fun to begin.

The room they entered was low-roofed and bereft of the adornment generally considered essential to make a tavern welcoming. The jars of gin and brandy littering the counter were blistered by the heat coming from innumerable gas flames and what few gilt fittings there were had been blackened beyond recognition by the thick smoke that stung the eyes and drastically impaired visibility.

The front of the long bar was crowded with men from every social stratum, all smoking, drinking and talking about dogs. Coachmen still in their livery; soldiers in uniform; tradesmen who had merely slipped a frock coat over their shop clothes - even two slaughter-men still wearing their bloody aprons; plus the expected gaggle of the unwashed and un-shaven. There was not a woman to be seen. More importantly, everyone was so preoccupied with the evening in prospect that no one bothered to scrutinize the stooping trilby-hatted figure in their midst.

Most had brought along their 'fancy'. Various black, brown or white terriers lay curled in their masters' laps while several small bulldogs rested in the crooks of arms, their flat pink noses rubbing against Algy's sleeve as he passed. Sleeping in an old chair lay an enormous white bulldog with a head as round and smooth as a clenched boxing glove. As Archer squeezed past his lair, the dog rose menacingly on legs as bowed as a sailor's and growled.

'Come on! He'll not harm you!' said Algy.

'I thought he was going for me!' Archer replied, clutching Algy's elbow in a way that suggested he was unconvinced while the tavern gave the slobbering canine bruiser the kind of spontaneous and heartfelt applause reserved for a genuine gladiator. 'Look at the size of those jaws!'

'I shouldn't worry.' said Algy. 'I doubt if there are any teeth in them any more!'

Algy distracted Archer by directing his attention to the wall above the fireplace on which, hanging from a nail, was the silver collar that awaited tonight's victorious dog and a large glass case containing a stuffed terrier: 'Tiny the Wonder Dog,' Archer read on the brass plate, 'only 5 ½ pounds in weight, represented here with one of the 200 rats he killed in one contest and wearing a lady's bracelet as a collar!'

Archer phewed. 'I've seen animals achieve marvellous feats, but that takes some beating! Will we see the like of that tonight?'

'I shouldn't think so. Tiny was to ratting what you are to race-riding! We may see a Barrett or two perhaps!'

'They'd pass for a couple of rats!'

Algy observed the silvery twinkle in his friend's eyes and knew they were going to enjoy themselves. Archer thought so too.

The dogs being readied to fight were standing on different tables, open to inspection. One or two yawned as if to invite examination of their teeth while others took to stretching out their limbs as if to satisfy the onlookers of their soundness. Almost every animal carried visible, and pronounced, scars of past battles.

Suddenly a broad-shouldered man with a set of magnificent mutton-chop whiskers dangling down below his jaw clambered onto the top of the bar and called for silence.

'Who's that?' asked Archer.

'Cropston Batty, the proprietor and self-styled 'Rat and Mole Destroyer to Her Majesty.'

Batty was suitably attired in an ankle-length scarlet surcoat on which the letters 'VR' were emblazoned in purple velvet. Once he had obtained silence, he roared theatrically 'Light up the pit!'

The very sound of Batty's voice set the dogs to howling, those tethered to tables scampering to the end of their leashes and thrashing their tails like landed eels as though they actually understood what he had said. The said pit was a small circle some six feet in diameter demarcated by a wooden rim that reached elbow height on the average man. Over it hung three gas lamps that lit up the white-painted floor.

'Who wishes to rat first?' Batty called above the din, his eyes scanning the dog-tables for an answer. 'Mister Rathbone, I see, and his white bitch Snowball!'

Rathbone brought up his terrier and Batty placed her in a canvas stretcher that was slung over a beam above the bar and attached to weights. 'Snowball weighs in at ten pounds!'

'No overweight?' chuckled Archer. 'Must've supped some of my "Mixture"!'

Batty's announcement was greeted with raucous cheering. 'What do you say, Mister Rathbone? Fifty? In, shall we say, two minutes?'

Snowball's owner nodded.

'Then gentleman, you may wager as you wish!'

Batty jumped into the pit and asked for the rats to be delivered. His request caused a stampede for the front-row and a comfortable spot resting elbows on the wooden planking. Algy and Archer were content to mount a table - which, to the champion jockey's disgust, he found far more onerous than mounting a thoroughbred racehorse.

A large flat basket, similar to those Algy had seen fetching chickens to Smithfield market, was brought to the pit. Beneath its iron top could be seen small mounds of densely-packed rats. Batty poked a stick inside the basket and stirred the mounds into activity. Then the pit-master began pulling the biggest ones out by the tail and dropping them into the pit.

'Gentlemen!' he announced. 'Freshly caught this very day by Mister Jimmy Shaw, of Windmill Street, professional rat-catcher!'

'What's that awful smell?' gasped Archer, reaching for his handkerchief as the rank breath emanating from tens of clammering dogs was overwhelmed by an even viler stench.

'Obviously urban sewer rats!' explained Algy. 'Easier and cheaper to find! But lethal! It's all the extra germs they carry! The dogs may get infected mouths. You'll see the owner rinse the dog's mouth out with peppermint and water afterwards.'

Archer clutched his handkerchief ever tighter to his nose and mouth and sank into his overcoat wishing he was back in Falmouth House reading Nellie bedtime stories.

Algy, by contrast, was overflowing with bonhomie, shaking a hand here, thumping a back there, even though he had no clue to whom they belonged. There were few sporting pleasures he could pursue alongside Archer apart from the odd day hunting: his teenage dream of competing under Rules as a Gentleman Rider and sharing a track with him had died when he began to sprout in his late teens. He had waited years for the chance to play the role of brotherly companion and *eminence grise* and he was determined to enjoy every minute of it, stench or no stench.

'Country-caught barn rats can cost a shilling apiece!' he added helpfully. 'And this fellow probably takes delivery of, oh, between three and seven hundred a week!'

Suddenly one of the rats scrambled out of the pit. To cries of 'Watch yourself! Rat's away!' the crowd parted and Algy spotted the fugitive making directly for their perch.

'Hold onto your happenny, Fred! The blighter's coming our way!'

Archer turned white at the thought of the desease-ridden rodent sinking its teeth into any part of his anatomy and stood on tiptoe as if the extra few inches would make all the difference.

The rat jumped half-way up the table-leg to be met by the pendulum of Algy's right boot which sent him straight back where he had come from. The rodent was dead before it thudded into the centre of the pit. Batty held up the corpse by the tail and Algy took a bow as the company roared its approval of his deadly marksmanship.

Archer struggled to combat the jelly in his legs because the entire episode had frightened him more than he was prepared to admit. He was accustomed to noisy crowds. But friendly ones. There was something menacing about this one. His eyes flitted round the room and imagined every man there to be one of Fenner's bruisers intent on breaking his legs. He began to bite his nails.

Batty continued selecting and counting rats into the pit until stopping at fifty. All the while odds were being given and taken in every corner of the room.

'What do you think, Fred? A bit more life than Ascot or Newmarket, eh? Real people here!'

'At this particular moment I wish I was at Ascot or Newmarket! At least I'd not have wear this disguise and risk being savaged by rodents!'

'I think we can risk a finny,' said Algy, too interested in his own pleasures to detect Archer's increasing anxiety. 'What do you say?'

'I'm just watching,' grunted Archer. 'I don't know the form!'

Algy belly-laughed, leaving himself breathless and squeezing tears from his eyes.

'I'm glad you're enjoying yourself so much,' said Archer, 'because this place is beginning to frighten the life out of me!'

Algy's shoulders ceased rocking once he detected the panic shaking itself through Archer's body and he suddenly felt ashamed.

'I'm sorry, Fred. I didn't realize,' he said.

'I'll be all right in a minute. I'm just behaving like an old woman. All the excitement brings out the emotion in me. I just can't help it.'

'I'm the complete opposite,' Algy said softly. 'I bottled up so much emotion as a child that that I scarcely recognize it in other people. My father drilled into me that it was a sign of weakness to show people what you're really thinking.'

Archer's eyebrows came together. He could not admit he was thinking only of Nellie and not some excuse for entertainment called ratting. 'I suppose some things are probably better left unsaid.'

'I learnt that the hard way!' laughed Algy. 'I was five at the time! My father sent me from my own birthday party for giggling after he burnt himself trying to light the candles on the cake. I couldn't understand why he was so angry. It was so funny, seeing him hopping with rage. But he wasn't laughing.'

Algy chewed his lips at the recollection. 'You only laughed when he laughed. I soon learnt to keep my thoughts to myself.'

Archer saw the doleful expression on his friend's face and recognized a kindred spirit but before he might utter a consoling word Algy's attention had returned to ratting.

'A finny says Snowball necks three dozen o' more!' he cried, waving his five-pound note in the air.

'I'll take some of that!'

Algy spat on his hand ready to shake on the bet. It was left suspended in mid air.

'Don't I know you?' said the rat-fancier.

'Surely not,' Algy lied once he found himself staring at the brow-less pasty face of a ginger-haired man with a nasty black eye and a weeping cut on his cheek.

The man's mouth tightened. 'I'm damned if I don't! You're the bleedin' toff who broke my mate's shoulder!'

'Fred!' said Algy instantly. 'Run for it!'

Algy pushed Archer ahead but in his haste knocked off his trilby.

'Bugger me if it ain't Fred bleedin' Archer!' yelled the yob at the top of his voice.

Algy quickly shepherded Archer toward the door as a swelling chorus of 'It's The Tinman! Archer's here!' engulfed the room and drowned the outburst of excited barking.

Every man in the room appeared intent on getting close enough to the revered Tinman to shake his hand or slap him on the back. Tables over-turned and stools went flying. Within seconds a stray boot kicked out one of the planks bounding the pit and tens of terrified rats frantically ought escape and safety. Mobbing the Tinman was one thing but the prospect of themselves being mobbed by 50 crazed rats sent men running in as many different directions as the rats.

The mayhem afforded Algy and Archer just enough time to make it out into the street. Men were now tumbling out of the pub and brought back to their senses by the cold night air. Among the first was Algy's adversary from Rat's Castle who spied the fugitives catching their breath and gave chase: the light from a gas lamp caught the blade in his right hand.

'I'll buy some time!' shouted Algy. 'Find a hansom and I'll meet you back at Jermyn Street. Number 27b! Quickly man!'

He followed Archer for a few yards before ducking into the first avail-able alley. As their pursuer passed, he threw a lassoing arm around his neck and yanked him back into the darkness. Just as swiftly, he made a grab for the knife-hand.

'Still quick with that chiv of yours, eh?' he snarled. 'I'd hoped you'd learnt your lesson the other day!'

The man struggled but Algy had surprise, technique and sobriety on his side. He pressed his back firmly against the alley wall to gain the extra purchase to tighten the headlock and felt the strength of two arms channel into one: he twisted the knife-hand inward toward the man's groin.

'Friend, what's your name?'

'B-bollocks!'

Algy pressed the knife down onto the man's genitals and proceeded to jab them. 'I don't think I heard you properly!'

'C-Cocky Arnull,' the man mumbled, all bravado gone.

'Well, C-Cocky, how appropriate a name is that? Do you know how much blood a man loses along with his cock and his balls?'

Cocky was in no state to answer. He felt as disoriented as if he he had wandered into a Whitechapel fog because Algy's headlock was fast cutting off his air supply.

'No? Then I'll tell you,' said Algy. 'Not as much as a poor defenceless horse, but enough.'

He squeezed and manipulated Arnull's hand until it slashed through the tatty fabric of his own trousers and he felt the steel against his skin.

'They say there's enough to fill a small bucket. Never seen it myself but I'm prepared to believe it. How about you?'

Algy wedged the blade under the scrotum and prepared to slice. 'Shall we find out?'

Arnull felt he was about to lose control of his bladder and hoped he lost consciousness before finding out.

Algy was not going to allow him that luxury. He relaxed the headlock just sufficiently for Arnull to get some oxygen into his brain and croak a reply. 'Pl-please, no!'

'All right, then,' Algy said. 'Now, you tell everyone - and I mean everyone - to leave Fred Archer alone. You and your kind are not worth the hairs in the crack of Archer's arse! Stay away from him!'

He lifted Arnull's member with the knife-blade and felt him wriggle like a sausage in a hot frying pan. Though he did not like admitting it, Algy was deriving considerable satisfaction from Arnull's suffering. He knew he ought not be so inhumane and that his priest would take a dim view of his excuses but the man surely had it coming.

'Don't you dare piss on me!' he whispered. 'We don't want my hand to slip, do we? Now, Cocky, just nod your head if you understand.'

Arnull did his best to nod and control his bladder at the same time.

'That's settled then,' Algy said with a smile.

He released his hold but held his breath as Arnull folded like a clapped-out accordian, wheezing to his knees in an incontinent heap. Then Algy tossed the chiv over the wall and coolly strolled off to hail a cab as if he had merely concluded a leisurely stroll along the Embankment.

******

Algy reached Jermyn Street without further mishap and let himself into a typical set of rooms for the discerning City gent, which amounted to an extension of his Club.

He walked into a hallway laid with a geometric pattern of coloured tiles and presided over by a simple Gillows hat-stand, which led into a dimly-lit drawing room paying homage to the revival in Gothic furniture. He skirted the gate-legged table just big enough to dine *a deux* and collapsed into one of several leather armchairs sitting on a large, slightly worn, white, brown and black Alloucha carpet from the Tunisian city of Kairouan.

Algy rested his head on the back of the chair and let his tired eyes flick along the wood-panelled walls lined with book shelves and sporting art. Two impressive prints faced each other on opposing walls, one recalling the celebrated bare-knuckle bout of 1845 when Bendigo humbled the giant Ben Caunt and the other depicting the finish of the 1880 Derby when Archer on Bend Or just touched-off Robert the Devil. Both prints were dear to him for each had been signed and dedicated to him by the victors.

This was as much as most visitors saw. Only a highly select few, all female apart from Archer, got to see Algy's simple brass bed or deposit their jewellery on his rosewood dressing table and admire his collection of jade and erotic Japanese drawings.

Algy knew he was home as soon as he felt the familiar battered upholsterery of his well-loved Charles Bevan reclining leather armchair which constituted the solitary piece of swag he had purloined from Haverholme - that is, if one excluded Edgecombe. He plucked a copy of 'Silk & Scarlet' from the bookcase that lay within easy reach of his right hand and felt himself relax as soon as it touched his skin. He loved the look and feel of books: the way the smooth elegance of red Morocco leather complemented the creamy roughness of top-quality parchment paper; even the musty smell each page gave off as he turned it gave him sensual pleasure. He did not so much read them as fondle them.

'Ah, Edgecombe, still up then? I rather thought you'd be in bed,' he said somewhat disingenuously since the manservant was stood in front of him still attired in his Belton livery of green-striped waistcoat and bow tie. 'Did Mister Archer return safely?'

'Yes, sir. An hour or so ago,' Edgecombe replied, cocking a bald head that bore a strong resemblance to a kindly flamingo to one side in a show of affectionate deference. 'He retired immediately - to your bedroom.'

'Excellent, that's as we arranged it,' said a relieved Algy.

'Shall I make up the cot for you, sir?'

'No, you cut along,' Edgecombe's master heard himself saying with that superior air he wished he might eradicate. 'And we'll probably sleep late tomorrow as Mister Archer is not riding.'

'In that case, sir, with your permission, I'll return home to Mrs Edgecombe in Kennington rather than use my quarters.'

Lionel Edgecombe had been one of the Belton family's most trusted retainers since boyhood and had never left the estate apart from the annual staff holiday on the Norfork coast until being passed on to Master Algy by Lady Belton once her younger son made it clear he was leaving home for good. He was the general factotum *nonpareil* and it was said Algy saw more of him than Mrs Edgecombe. In truth, he was more of a father to Algy than a manservant and treated him like the son he had lost.

'That's fine. Just let yourself in in the morning and you can pack the portmanteau for Goodwood then.'

'Very well, sir.'

'And there's no need for you to travel down with me. I've arranged for one of Sir Felix's men to look after me. You have a well-earned rest with Mrs E.'

'As you wish, sir.'

'There's just one thing,' remembered Algy, tapping his forehead. 'Mister Archer and I will be taking the train down to Selhurst on Monday, so you had better arrange for Mister Archer's gear to be sent on from Newmarket, including his best bib and tucker. There's a rather grand dinner on the Wednesday.'

'Very well, sir,' replied Edgecombe. 'May I prepare a cup of Epp's for you, or perhaps pour you a night-cap before I depart?'

'No, that's all right. No cocoa tonight. I'll help myself to a calva, perhaps.'

'By the way, sir, a telegram arrived for you. It's on the tray.'

'Thank you, Edgy. And good night.'

'Good night, Master Algy.'

Algy collected the telegram from his grandmother's silver tray and slit it open with her pearl-handled paper knife.

It read: 'Off to Goodwood. Stop. Made arrangements to stay with the Rapers. Stop. Look forward to seeing you there. Stop. Connie.'

Algy screwed the telegram up into a tight ball and threw it onto what was left of the fire. He snatched the poker and continued pushing the ball of paper into the glowing embers until it crackled into flame.

'Bugger!' he said, pouring himself a stiff measure of Boulard Pays d'Auge. 'That's all I bloody well need!'

EIGHT

Always it began the same: with a noise, a rumble like an approaching train.

Then he saw himself come into focus, scarlet tunic torn open at the collar, face caked with sweat and blood, his blond hair bleached white by a South African sun presently shrouded by thick clouds of cordite smoke so acrid that it stung his eyes and choked his sleep even seven years later. Black waves of Zulu impi were breaching the red-uniformed walls of the British camp on the flanks of Isandlwana mountain, 20,000 assegais drumming on cow-hide shields in time to stomach-turning shrieks of 'uSuthu!' as the warriors swarmed onward, stabbing and hacking every soldier in their path. His body tossed and imprisoned itself in the damp bed-sheets as his mind relived the carnage and wailing of a battle lost.

He dreaded the images that always followed. He knew he would catch sight of his teenage batman flinging his arms around the neck of a bug-eyed Basuto pony and bringing it to a standstill before urging his officer to save himself, his puppy-fat face quivering with the terrified acceptance of his own fate. Somehow Jimmy always managed to leg him into the pitching saddle and somehow he always saw himself stretch out an arm to haul his boyhood friend up behind him only to watch him lose his footing on the blood-greased scrub.

Then his sleep would be wrecked by that other sound: a gutteral sucking noise redolent of Haverholme's weary plough-horses dragging heavy hooves out of deep Lincolnshire clay at the end of a wet autumn day. It ushered in events and emotions that made him want to shut his eyes and keep them shut forever. Jimmy's back would bend like a drawn longbow and those last words freeze on his lips as the iklwa's heavy 18-inch blade was driven into the small of his back and withdrawn to the onomatopoeic sound that earnt its Zulu name, first skewering him and then sucking the life out of him.

Now the Zulu was picking up Jimmy's discarded rifle: a darkly athletic figure, every ebony muscle tensed, white teeth bared in a noble chiselled face framed by his leopard-skin headband and ear-flaps, bloody fingers fumbling for the trigger. He felt himself grabbing hold of the Martini-Henry's barrel, and screamed at the memory of how white-hot it was from action and how he had suppressed the pain, knowing he might otherwise be just moments from death. He swore to God for the strength to wrestle the Martini-Henry from the Zulu's grasp and smashed a booted heel into the warrior's face, causing the rifle to discharge with a deafening retort against his left cheek, scorching his ear lobe and singeing his blond curls charcoal. His frenzied grey pony reared and zigzagged away between the thorn bushes and boulders toward the Buffalo river and the sanctuary of its far bank.

Algy suddenly came to, head rolling from side to side, mumbling through gritted teeth – and screamed at the spectre he saw standing at the foot of his cot.

'Jimmy…I'm…sorry…' he stammered.

But it was no phantom he saw, only his night-shirted house-guest.

'Are you all right?' Archer enquired haltingly. 'You've been hollering something awful.'

Algy sat up on the cot, left hand clutching his jaw, his eyes stinging with tears and his throat as parched as it had been on that distant afternoon in Zululand.

'Sorry, I'll be fine,' he lied. 'Bad dream. You go back to bed.'

Algy scraped the matted hair from his forehead and padded to the bathroom, where he washed away the nightmare with splashes of cold water. He stared into the mirror but all he saw were the shrunken features of Jimmy Edgecombe, his truest boyhood friend and the only child of Lionel and Olive Edgecombe; eye sockets picked clean, lips peeled back to reveal yellow teeth locked in a grotesque smile, his remaining skin taut and blackened in death by relentless South African sun. Once more his eyes leaked tears that began to roll uncontrollably down his cheeks.

There was not a day when the mental scars from Sunday, 22 January 1879 failed to hurt. On the unforgiving slopes of Isandlwana, some 850 of

Queen Victoria's rifle-carrying redcoats were slaughtered by Zulu assegai and knobkerrie in the space of two hours. Only five of her officers escaped. Lieutenant Algy Haymer of the 14th Hussars was one of them.

All too often he wished he was not.

******

Algy and Archer travelled down to Chichester on the London, Brighton and South Coast Railway from London Bridge on the Monday morning.

If anything could banish the recurring nightmare that was Isandlwana from his thoughts, however temporarily, it was the prospect of 'Glorious Goodwood.' Algy felt like a small boy with his finger in the cake mix. He loved this meeting above all others in the racing calendar for it amounted to nothing less than a carefree racing holiday at the Sussex seaside, possessing neither the rowdiness of the Derby nor the stuffiness of Royal Ascot; and having Archer by his side enthused him all the more. What his companion loved about 'Glorious Goodwood', on the other hand, was the chance to cherry-pick mounts from a clutch of quality thoroughbreds and replenish his dwindling finances.

If he could wangle the invitation, Algy invariably stayed as a guest of his godfather, Sir Felix Raper Bart., at Selhurst Grange, on the south side of Upwaltham Down overlooking Chichester and just a lazy carriage ride from the course.

'You've not ridden for Bumbo, have you FA?' said Algy as they settled into their first class compartment.

'No. Doesn't have enough horses to interest me. I heard he was a drunk. A mind sieved through brandy, somebody told me.'

'Wait till you meet him,' replied Algy, ignoring Archer's last comment. 'Bumbo's rough round the edges but loyal to the core. And a tremendous card!'

'He'd have to be with a name like that!'

'No one knows how he got the name either!' laughed Algy. 'Do you know what he keeps as a pet?'

Archer remained silent for it was a matter of supreme indifference to him.

'No dogs or cats for Bumbo! He only rescues some bedraggled brown bear from a travelling circus! The animal goes everywhere with him! He once rode the blasted beast, christened Doris, into Selhurst's great hall wearing full hunting regalia, just to see the looks on the faces of his dinner guests!'

Practical jokes notwithstanding, Raper had a lofty reputation as a generous host who provided a 'groaning board' and a splendid cellar to go with it. Such *largesse* would be no skinnier this year, especially as Algy knew he was keen to drum up some publicity for his expanding racing operation in his godson's newspaper column. Unfortunately, Raper had several other godchildren beside the Hon Algy Haymer. And one of them happened to be Lady Constanza Swynford.

Archer soon tired of paying lip service to his travelling companion's anecdotes about Raper and sought solace in the gallops reports in *The Sportsman*. Somewhat miffed, Algy wiled away the rest of the journey with his head buried in a collection of poems by Lord Alfred Tennyson. Literature, both poetry and prose, was the only subject that remotely fired his imagination at Uppingham: on special occasions he was even moved to compose verse of his own.

One of Selhurst's drags was waiting for them at Chichester Station and it was not long before their conveyance swung through Selhurst's main gate and past the south lodge. The driver instinctively flicked his whip on meeting the rising ground up the lime-flanked avenue to the house, which stood at the confluence of two small wooded valleys. The drive through the rolling Sussex Downs on a warm and bright July morning had made Algy feel glad to be alive again, a sentiment he fervently hoped was shared by his companion. But Archer gave no intimation one way or the other. His thoughts were concentrated on finding winners.

Raper was still out exercising his string when they reached the Grange. They heard him before they saw him: his voice like the incoming tide sifting pebbles. The imposing figure who eventually burst into the morning room and wrapped his godson in a bear hug that Doris might have envied sported shoulders as sturdy as a ship of the line and forearms that had withstood the slash of sabres. With that one hug Algy was transported back to his godfather's tales of spiking Russian guns at Balaklava and crawling through dried-up river beds until his knees ran red to escape the Fuzzy-wuzzies of the Sudan.

'So good to see you, Bumbo!' said Algy warmly. 'I don't think you know Fred Archer?'

Raper moved to envelop the jockey in a further hug until Algy intervened.

'Steady, Bumbo!' he cried. 'I think you'd crush poor Fred to death! A handshake will do!'

Archer thought so to. There was something rather disconcerting about his host. His face seemed eerily reminiscent of his ageing pet bear's, skin falling in comfortable folds around his mouth and eyes, which were slightly bloodshot. Raper's complexion exuded the healthy ruddiness of a man who spent most of his day outdoors but his appearance did not. He was clad in his habitual uniform of the thinnest linen shirt and trousers; no tie, no socks and on his feet he wore a flimsy pair of sandals. Even in the depths of winter he seldom donned anything warmer unless out hunting with the Southdown.

'Will you take a drink gentleman?' he asked, lining up three glasses on the sideboard.

Algy demurred, citing the earliness of the hour, and Archer shook his head.

'Please yourself,' replied Raper with a wave of the glass. 'Actually, if you must know, I only drink to steady my nerves.'

'Is that a fact!' said Archer.

Algy's brow furrowed as he watched his godfather pour an inch of water into a whisky tumbler before filling it to the brim with a yellowish-green liquid that promptly turned the contents cloudy.

Algy and Archer chose to revive themselves with a jug of freshly-made lemonade in preference to coffee as their host swallowed the absinthe with one tilt of the glass.

'Once I was so steady,' he said, welcoming the aniseed-flavoured, brain-tickling hit of the thujone delivered by the liqueur, 'I didn't move for two days!'

Archer felt sorry for him and refused to laugh but Algy did so heartily. Despite being aware of the dangerous addiction his godfather's self-deprecation was attempting to mask, he was not going to embarrass him in front of Archer by lecturing him yet again about curbing his drinking habits.

Before leaving to discuss the morning's work with his head lad, Raper motioned to a side table - Sheraton wagered Algy - on which lay a bundle of telegrams addressed to Archer that Bowling had forwarded from Newmarket. The sun came out on Archer's face for he knew they must contain various offers of mounts for the week.

Algy watched Archer rip open his telegrams with the enthusiasm of a child opening birthday cards; or was it the dexterity of a bank clerk counting notes, which in a manner of speaking they were. Algy could not decide. Archer divided them into three piles that Algy knew represented 'definitely', 'perhaps if there's nothing better' and 'absolutely not' until he had one left. He read it. Scratched his forehead. Folded it and then unfolded it. Read it again. Moved it from hand to hand. This request seemed to be covered in itching powder.

Distracted by the sight of Archer's antics, Algy put down the paper he had begun to read and offered his advice. Archer passed him the telegram: it was from the Duchess of Montrose. She wanted Archer to ride her good three-year-old colt St Mirin on Wednesday in the Sussex Stakes. The message finished: 'Dinner invitation to Selhurst Thursday. Hopefully a celebration?'

Archer felt the heat burn his cheeks as Algy read the telegram and wished he might loosen his starched collar. If he gave the Duchess half an inch she'd eagerly assume the same role in his life as Connie Swynford did in his friend's. The very thought alarmed him more than Batty's rats.

Archer had much to be wary about. Caroline, Duchess of Montrose - known on every racecourse in England as 'Carrie Red' - was an exception to Algy's rule, for she was one red-head easy to resist. For a start, her hair colour owed more to a bottle than mother nature; and she was now 68 years of age, twice married and twice widowed. Nevertheless, she was still as formidible in the flesh as ever: keen of brain and waspish of tongue, war-painted and heftily bosomed, she stood tall with no trace of a dowager's hump. Disqualified from owning horses in her own name by virtue of her sex, she raced under the *nom de course* 'Mr Manton' which suited admirably her masculine racecourse apparel that was invariably topped by her trademark homburg hat.

But mocking the Duchess was undertaken at one's peril. She knew both the studbook and formbook intimately and had orchestrated countless betting *coups* to the benefit of numerous trainers and jockeys. However, her trainers and jockeys rarely stayed in favour for long.

One who did was Fred Archer. An invitation to ride her best three-year-old colt should, by rights, have gone straight into the 'definitely' pile.

'Oh, I see the problem,' said Algy cagily.

'Then what shall I do?'

'He's a decent horse...'

'She's been pestering me all season to ride St Mirin. She offered me a retainer of £6,000, you know!'

'That much, was it?'

'I'd agreed to ride Saraband in the Guineas and I wasn't going to break my word.'

'I know.'

'And I was hardly going to get off Ormonde to ride St Mirin in the Derby!'

'No, of course not,' said Algy, returning to *The Sporting Times*. 'But you did win on him at Ascot.'

Archer was now on his feet, pacing the carpet and snatching at his collar.

'I know what her real game is. She wants me to ride him in the Leger and is trying to tie me down. That's impossible when I can ride Ormonde.'

'Obviously. Plain as day.'

'I can't ride St Mirin this Wednesday and that's that! Lord Alington says Candlemas is going to run in the Sussex - and he has fourth claim on me.'

'That's problem solved then?'

'But I know she'll keep nagging away at me,' continued Archer, his pale face beginning to display vivid pink blotches. 'She never takes "no" for an answer! She'll try and get round me, I know it! It'll be invitations to dinner again or the theatre.'

'Lucky you!' laughed Algy.

'It's no laughing matter! It's embarrassing.'

Archer looked round and lent forward conspiratorially, beckoning Algy to do likewise. 'She says she's in love with me,' he whispered.

Algy, like everyone else attuned to racing gossip, was perfectly aware the Duchess had been on the prowl for Archer's services - in more ways than one. It was an old story. His fingers flicked over to the next page of his paper.

'She's old enough to be your mother!'

'That's as may be but she follows me everywhere. She appears on the gallops, outside the weighing room - everywhere!'

'It's just an infatuation,' Algy said unconvincingly. 'One of those powerful-and-ageing-woman-admiring-the-talents-of-a-younger-man situations. It'll blow over.'

'No, you don't understand!' cried Archer, screwing up his face. 'She says she...wants to marry me!'

Algy fought to hold his breath, fearful that if he did not he would dissolve into fits of laughter. He managed only ten seconds before breaking down.

'You don't say! Sorry, Fred, I know I shouldn't laugh but...'

Algy set himself for an emotional outburst from Archer but the slender frame started to shake and after a couple of false starts he began to laugh.

'In any case, marrying her wouldn't make me a duke, would it!'

'I'm afraid not!' replied Algy, wiping the tears from his eyes.

Their schoolboy giggles eventually petered out into an empty silence with each man waiting for the other to speak. Emboldened by the sound of Archer laughing as if he meant it for the first time in months, Algy wondered whether he might fill the void by raising the subject matter he had long rehearsed.

'Fred,' he ventured hesitantly, 'you must have heard the tittle-tattle about my father and your...'

Archer was not listening. 'She is a menace though!' he said before Algy could complete the sentence.

'So I've heard!' said Algy, forcing a smile and rueing his timing. 'But a very rich one all the same.'

'I'll say. She makes me look a pauper!'

'Could be a menace worth suffering,' Algy continued, 'so long as you insist on a joint bank account but separate bedrooms!'

'I'll pretend I didn't hear that last remark!'

'Let's see what happens on Thursday, shall we? You never know, you may change your mind!'

'You keep her away from me, you hear!' said Archer, once more wandering around the room as if some corner of it hid peace of mind. 'I'm still mourning Nellie and always shall be, as long as I live.'

'Sorry, Fred, I apologize unreservedly,' said a shamefaced Algy.

Already deflated from his previous gaffe, Algy was suddenly overcome by that familiar heavy-bellied feeling he routinely endured when chastised by his father.

'That was most insensitive of me,' he blurted. 'Of course I'll do my utmost to keep her out of your way.'

Algy determined to do his damnedest but the possibility crept into his mind that he would most likely already have his hands full attending to the machinations of an entirely different female guest.

******

Archer's humour lifted immeasurably on Goodwood's opening day. He not only outscored Charlie Wood two-one in winners but also managed to avoid anything other than passing pleasantries with the Duchess of Montrose. There was even the hint of a smile when he entered the winner's enclosure after the March Stakes.

Every step of his long walk back to the weighing room after that second success was watched from the edge of the crowd by a man of singularly unique appearance. He was of average height but his upper body was conspicuously, and substantially, more developed than the lower. Whereas his legs - albeit bowed - seemed perfectly normal for a man of his height, his barrel chest and bulging forearms suggested someone who had grafted for his living in a profession where strength was essential not optional: his biceps and pectorals were so bulky and well-defined that his expensive jacket appeared one size too small. This physique made his age difficult to discern. Generous observers may have put it nearer 50 than 60; but beneath the regulation panama hat was a thick stubble of shocking white hair that devalued his bushy black eyebrows and hinted strongly toward the latter.

From his bull neck upward significant clues existed as to that earlier profession. First of all, there was no neck to speak of: his exceedingly large head seemed to be attached directly to his deltoids so that the collar of his shirt was wedged so far under his chin as to be invisible. Secondly, spread across his flat and heavily-veined bulldog face was an equally large fleshy nose undoubtedly broken on more than one occasion - to the detriment of punctuating his speech with thick adenoidal snorts.

The final clues to his former occupation were the cauliflower ear and the badly-sewn wound at the corner of his left eye from which a rheumy secretion required his constant attention. Frequent dabs from a neatly folded white handkerchief (smelling strongly of lilies-of-the-valley) were essential if he was to avoid looking like a man squinting down the barrel of an invisible rifle.

There were plenty of ways a man might incur such an unfortunate affliction. This particular man, for instance, had served time in a debtor's prison where vicious fights were a brutal fact of daily life. Generally, he had acquitted himself well, so well that his potential was spotted by a prison visitor who cleared his debt, obtained his release and directed him toward a new career.

This, in fact, was a man who had spent no fewer than 21 years earning his living as a prizefighter in pursuit of 'The Noble Art' or 'The Fancy.' Here was a man who had gone 49 rounds with Bendigo before retiring with a dislocated shoulder and had also shared a ring with two other prizefighting legends, Tom Sayers and Jem Mace, for an aggregate of three hours and six minutes, fighting a draw with each man. The latter decision came when he had Mace over the ropes and was in the throes of strangling him; a riot broke out and he was charged with inciting a breach of the peace, which cost him a month in jail. This was a man so hard that his bottle-man joked even his spittle had muscles.

The deformed knuckles the size of walnuts and the fingers swollen like sausages, other prices he paid in the course of accumulating his fortune, were masked by a pair of white silk gloves that, even in high summer, were obligatory to ward-off painful arthritis. Whether he had lost any teeth along the way, however, was difficult to ascertain because he never opened his mouth wide enough for anyone to find out. He seldom offered a smile and a hearty laugh was as foreign to him as a plate of frogs legs.

Once this pocket leviathan who bore an uncanny resemblance to Cropston Batty's bulldog had seen enough, a path was cleared for him by his minions and Mo Fenner waddled away.

There was something he wanted to bring to a speedy resolution.

NINE

Archer was sipping from a glass of lemon-infused water in the weighing room after the March Stakes when Lord Alington relayed a message from Mat Dawson asking to see him in the racecourse stables: he wanted a second opinion on the condition of Melton, Archer's intended mount in Wednesday's Chesterfield Cup, who had not eaten-up since arriving from Newmarket.

Archer slipped a jacket over his silks and left through the back door, which enabled him to dodge the crowds. He reached the stable yard and asked for Melton's box number. The horse was in the far left-hand corner, the quietest spot in the yard, a typical mark, he noted, of Dawson's concern for his horse's welfare. The door of box was slightly ajar and, hearing voices, he went straight inside.

'Welcome, Mister Archer. We've been expectin' you,' announced a disembodied voice from the shadows.

Archer cupped a hand over his eyes and peered through the semi darkness: what he identified was as welcoming as an open coffin and glazed his face with perspiration. He turned and dashed for the door but found two men barring his exit.

'Eli, step outside and see we're not disturbed,' said Mo Fenner. 'An' Cocky, you give Mister Archer a seat. 'E looks worn out.'

'It's you, Mister Fenner,' Archer spluttered. 'I'll stand if you don't mind.'

'I won't 'ear of it. Look at you. Shakin' like a jelly. That's not nat'ral.'

'I'm all right.'

'No, I can't believe that!' Fenner snorted. 'You don't eat. Yer always dashing around the place. I bet you never get any sleep at nights either.

Can't sleep for thinkin' 'bout that poor dead wife of yours, what was 'er name?'

'Nellie.'

'That's it, Nellie. Tragic way to die. Must 'ave been awful watchin' 'er go like that? An' the boy as well. Fair rots the soul, eh?'

Archer felt the strength draining from his legs; he watched them quake and was afraid he was going to fall over. He stuck out an arm.

'I think I would like to sit down now,' he said, chin wobbling.

'I thought you might,' replied Fenner.

Arnull unfolded a canvas stool and placed it opposite the one occupied by his boss.

'Now, you an' me 'ave got some talkin' to do,' Fenner continued, flexing his gloved hands on the handle of the cane propped between his legs.

Archer sat down and clasped his arms around his knees like a toddler at a Sunday-school story-telling.

'That Diavolo business the other day cost me a lot o' money. You gave me duff information. Led to an embarrassin' situation. So, what are we goin' to do 'bout it?'

Archer searched furiously for an answer. Could he blame Wood? No: the Turf's self-preservationsit supreme would have acted by now and his own stuttering version of events was unlikely to sound more plausible than that of the weighing room's master manufacturer of tall tales. He looked about him for inspiration. All he saw were the walls closing in on him.

'Shall we tell 'im, Cocky?' sniffed Fenner, dabbing a handkerchief to his left eye with one hand and drumming the fingers of the other on his cane.

Fenner took his time. He had never made a habit of going for a quick kill when he had punched an opponent to a bloodied mess during his time in the ring and he was not about to start now. He had travelled all the way down to Sussex to see Archer reduced to a quivering nonentity grateful for any quarter and he wanted to eke out the warm glow he was currently enjoying, a thrill he had not experienced since his last visit to Calloway's knocking shop in Denmark Street.

'Mister Archer, please watch carefully,' he said after a good minute had passed. 'See that mutt Cocky's holdin'? Nice little feller ain't 'e?'

Archer twisted round on the stool and looked up to see Arnull holding a bottle to the mouth of a small mongrel. Arnull grinned and thrust the bottle between the dog's jaws and tipped it up. The dog whined once, shook from toe to tail as if it had just climbed from a stream and flopped back lifeless, a dribble of white froth bubbling from its mouth.

Archer retched and gripped the edges of the stool, suddenly obsessed with the need to urinate.

'Let Mister Archer take a closer look, Cocky!'

Arnull tossed the dead dog into Archer's lap and watched gleefully as Archer catapulted off the stool.

'Now sit yerself down, Mister Archer,' said Fenner softly. 'We all know yer an animal lover - even though you're partial to spurrin' an' whippin' an 'orse. But 'e was only some poor stray. Most likely better off dead, if you ask me.'

Archer's pained expression suggested he disagreed and he concentrated on burying his feet in the straw.

'But it's amazin' 'ow quick arsenic works, ain't it? Bit like that mixture o' yours in a manner of speakin'. A little does a lot!'

Fenner took a moment to chortle at his own joke and to dab his eye.

'What do yer think a bigger bottle would do to old Melton over 'ere?' he added, pointing his cane toward the horse tethered to the iron ring in the corner.

'You wouldn't do that to a horse like Melton, a Derby winner!' Archer cried out, 'He's worth a fortune at stud.'

Archer lowered his eyes but at a signal from Fenner, Arnull took a tight hold of his head.

'One word from me an' Cocky will dose that 'orse an', if 'e 'as to, 'e'll force open your eyes with matches so yer can see what you've caused. That animal will feel like someone's stuck one red-'ot poker down its throat an' another one up its arse!'

'No! No!' screamed Archer.

'And you'll be feelin' every second of it with 'im, eh?'

Fenner started to fidget. He had had enough of this dingy stable, its musty straw and its smelly horse. It was starting to irritate his sinuses.

'Unless, a'course, you agree to a proposition,' he said, sneezing into his handkerchief. 'Now, what do you say?'

******

Throughout the following day's journey to and from the track Archer sat silently.

'Archer, did I tell you about the day I pretended to be a highwayman and held up a carriage full of hunting chums while mounted on Doris?' asked Raper, trying manfully to lift his spiritson the return trip to Selhurst Grange. 'No?'

The tale, complete with all the requisite noises and actions, had Algy in stitches by the time they passed Red Copps but had no impact on Archer. The jockey stared at the trees but saw not leaves on the branches, only the rotting corpses of dead dogs and poisoned racehorses.

'Then there was the day I disguised myself as a beggar and begged at my own kitchen door,' Raper continued. 'The servants began beating me with brooms! Would have maimed me, too, had it not been for the sudden intervention of dear old Doris! She recognized her master at once! Amazing animal! Don't you think, Archer?'

Not a cell of Archer's face so much as twitched. It was as if he had already donned his death mask.

Raper rolled his eyes at Algy and fluffed out his mutton-chop whiskers. He sat back and began whistling. He had tried his best.

Something was troubling Archer deeply, that much was plain to Algy. He watched him flex his jaw continuously and pull at his collar as if it were choking the very life out of him. But what was it? Algy did not know. It was certainly not missing a winning ride in the Sussex Stakes because St Mirin could only finish second.

It came as no surprise to Algy when Archer absented himself from dinner, citing a slight headache. Later on, he took a cigar and a glass of Krug upstairs to his room but was denied admittance. Algy slowly began to think the unthinkable: Archer was sinking into a deep depression from which no one might rescue him.

Archer's humour was no better on the Thursday. He passed the post first in the week's richest race, only to be disqualified for barging into the second. The knowledge that the promoted animal, Timothy, was usually his ride and sported the all-scarlet colours of this evening's special dinner guest - Carrie Red herself - compounded his aggravation. Although customarily abhorring profanity, he swore at Solomon and refused to speak with anyone, spending the time between races in the lavatory. Anyone listening outside the stall would have heard him crying; not angrily as he had after being accused of 'stopping' Lord Falmouth's Galliard in the 1883 Derby but softly, like a child on his first day at boarding school.

Archer had no rides in the last three races and Algy persuaded Raper that it might be a good idea if they got Archer out of the track and back to Selhurst without delay.

They waited for the distraction of the next race and then half-carried Archer into the carriage, assuring anyone who spotted them that the champion was suffering from a slight chill. They covered him with a blanket and watched him fall into a fitful sleep, mumbling and throwing his arms across his face as if suffering the worst nightmare. By the time the carriage reached Selhurst, it seemed to Algy that Archer must be verging on some sort of mental breakdown.

'Fred, are you all right? Answer me man!' he said, shaking his arms. 'Come on now! You're starting to frighten me!'

Archer's eyes opened wide and he sat up soldier-straight. 'What's that you say?'

'You've been a bit delirious, old man,' said Algy, tucking the blanket beneath Archer's legs.

'Nothing serious,' added Raper. 'Probably a bad dream.'

He registered the worried expressions on their two faces and tried to forget the recent horrors.

'I think I must be a bit dehydrated, that's all,' said Archer matter-of-factly. 'It's been a hot afternoon. Once I've had a good drink of water I'll be as right as ninepence.'

'Yes,' said Raper, 'you'll want to be on top form for tonight's dinner, what with the Duchess coming!'

Algy grimaced at the prospect. A formal dinner, he surmised, was the last thing Archer needed in his current state of mind but he would be unable to hide in his room tonight. He saw Archer safely to his room and told him to call on him if need be, whatever the reason.

******

The second dressing gong was sounding as Algy was completing his ablutions by brushing his teeth with Odonto dentifrice, taming his hair with a drop of MacCassar Oil, splashing his face with Mouchoir de Monsieur and by checking that his fingernails were suitably manicured. One of the earliest lessons Edgecombe had drummed into him was that 'you can always tell a gentleman, Master Algy, by the condition of his hair, fingernails and shoes!' Even without Edgecombe he had no need to concern himself with the state of the remaining member of his manservant's holy trinity ('The secret with shoes, Master Algy, is to work a little claret into the leather.') since one of Raper's senior footmen had been assigned to him for the week and his John Lobb Oxfords gleamed beside his dressing table.

'Fred, is that you?' he called when there was a knock at his door while he was tying the second. 'The door's open! Come in!'

He heard the door open and then click shut. 'Just dressing! Be with you in a tick.'

Pulling on his best waistcoat of silver shot silk as he walked, he went through into the bedroom.

'Fred, so glad you decided to dine with us this evening,' he said, shooting his cuffs. 'I'll take care of the lady in question.'

'And wot laay-dee might that be, guv'ner?' said a cut-glass voice doing its trademark – albeit poor - impersonation of a tart's. 'Ave you booked more than one of us? My, ain't you a gree-dee boy.'

'Why, Connie!' said Algy, genuinely startled. 'When did you arrive?'

'An hour ago,' she replied, reverting to an accent more befitting the Shires. 'Just in time to get myself ready for you!'

'And, my, have you succeeded!,' he replied, eyeing her up and down. 'I think we can say without fear of contradiction there'll not be another dress like that on show this evening!'

Connie's saucy grin acknowledged that was the intention. She stood before him a vision in scarlet from tip to toe, encased in an off-the-shoulder velvet sheath that clung to her bosom and showed off every line and curve before plunging straight to the floor; the *ensemble* was completed by a matching velvet choker from which a gold locket descended between her breasts.

Algy decided the gown was either a wonderful work of engineering on the part of her dressmaker or else a wonderful testament to her firm flesh because it appeared to him that the only things causing it to defy gravity were Connie's nipples which stood out like protruding nails. He smiled appreciatively for experience told him there would be nothing underneath that gown bar the shoes on her feet. She, in turn, knew he would be aware of her nakedness beneath the dress and knew it would drive him wild all evening thinking about how one layer of velvet was caressing another.

'Truly a scarlet woman for all to see!' declared Algy, noting the only thing missing were scarlet lips: he disliked lipstick. Connie's lips were red enough without artificial aid and right now they seemed dripping with raspberries and cream he could almost taste.

'And haven't you scrubbed-up well this evening!' she replied in kind. 'Very suave! For this lady, I suppose? And who might she be?'

'You know very well. Otherwise you wouldn't be trying to upstage her by wearing scarlet!'

Algy tweaked his bow tie. 'The Duchess will either love you or hate you for it - there'll be no in between!'

'I'm positive she'll feel honoured at the trouble I've taken,' Connie replied shimmying towards him.

'Perhaps!' he said, backing away.

'It's just a little frock I had run-up as an afterthought!'

Algy tapped the end of his nose at her fib. 'I will admit, though, you do look good enough to eat!'

Connie eyed the four-poster bed in the far corner. 'Well,' she pouted, 'what's keeping you?'

The pair stood there mentally undressing each other when the sound of a dinner gong drifting up the staircase suddenly reduced them to helpless laughter.

'I think we can safely say that's what they call being "saved by the bell"!' said Algy, leading her toward the bedroom door. 'Let's go and join the rest, shall we?'

'Wait!'

Connie stood him to attention ready for inspection as old Nanny Maltby did before permitting him to leave Haverholme's nursery and set about plastering down some unruly strands of hair that were beginning to re-assert themselves.

'Hold still!' she said as Algy grew irritated. 'That hair looks as though you dried it with a windmill - and you've a mark on your cheek. You must have nicked yourself shaving.'

Algy sighed and took a crisply laundered handkerchief from his pocket. 'Where?'

'Here, let me! Can't have your Greek-god looks spoiled, can we?'

Connie unfolded the handkerchief and used her tongue to moisten one corner as if she was licking the finest gelato from the Zattere. She slunk over to him and attended the offending spot while shamelessly wiggling her chest against his so that her nipples hardened and he might gaze at them down the front of her dress. Algy gorged himself on the pair of upstanding pink sentries and inhaled the fragrance that wafted from between them, something redolent of narcissus and jasmine with the faintest hint of orange blossom, definitely French and probably from the House of Fragonard in Grasse.

'There, all done! Now you're fit to be seen with me! You may escort me to dinner!'

Algy retrieved his handkerchief and refolded it. There was no sign of blood on any of the four corners. He smiled inwardly at yet another ploy straight from the Connie Swynford manual of feminine wiles.

His sensed a devilish evening ahead.

TEN

Algy stood back at the top of the stairs and allowed Connie to descend first so that her entrance might command the kind of attention she had planned. All conversation ceased as she sashayed down the staircase as if she were Lily Langtry, every eye drawn to her including, Algy noted grimly, those of Seger whom he spied cosying-up to the Duchess. He sighed with resignation because he knew a cigarette paper could not divide Seger and the Duchess when they were in the same room or on the same racecourse; but, he thought to himself, Seger's presence might conceivably keep her away from Fred.

Algy watched the Duchess greet Connie warmly with a kiss on each cheek and invited Seger to follow suit. Archer was beckoned from the large group feting him to do likewise. His white tie and tails made him appear more gaunt than ever, and he wished they might hurry-up and go in to dinner so that he might escape all this attention. His hope that the company might act as a distraction by occupying his mind was proving ill-founded.

The Duchess sought Archer's arm - while Connie dodged Seger's and latched onto Algy's - and led the procession into dinner like a galleon escorting her prize into port, heaving upper deck festooned with jewels instead of guns. She bestowed a gracious smile on the young couple, albeit baffled by Algy's childish giggling: too much rouge, Connie had whispered, made her look like Old Mother Hubbard vainly trying to repel Old Father Time.

The magnificently vaulted great hall they entered was the finest room in the house, dating from the Restoration when Sir Francis Raper built the Grange with money he received from Charles II for services rendered during the Civil War. Generations of Rapers who had given gallant service to the crown were represented by impressive canvases around the walls, notably one painted by Sir Godfrey Kneller of Sir Flixton, who fought alongside Marlborough at Blenheim, that peered - or was it leered, Algy couldn't quite make up his mind - over Connie's left shoulder.

Although it would be unfair to say Selhurst's part in the social fabric of west Sussex was not what it was, tonight's dinner was the closest it had come for a good few years to a proper banquet. Dominating the table was a magnificent centre-piece in the form of a heron passant (the Raper family crest) carved from a huge block of ice that drew admiring gasps from the diners. The faint whiff of rosemary-infused lamb wafting from the kitchens suggested Raper's chef had learnt much during his time as underchef to the renowned Alexis Soyer at London's Reform Club; a glance at the menu confirmed that he and his master had designed a banquet to amuse both the Duchess's palate and funny bone. It commenced with Consomme 'Caroline' followed by Lobster 'Timothy', Pigeon a la 'Duchesse', a Crown of Selhurst Lamb a la 'Montrose' and concluded with poached pears 'Mr Manton' for dessert.

Archer sat morosely at the end of the table, flanked by Algy and Connie. While they ate heartily and gossiped, he nibbled at one slice of York ham, half a peeled pear and a shaving of stilton, and sipped nothing but water throughout rather than risk a sip of the Pauillac or Corton that his neighbours quaffed enthusiastically. Every so often Algy or Connie tried to entice him into conversing but he flatly refused to make any concession to small-talk.

'Archer,' the Duchess said eventually in a voice that would dry leaves, 'I must raise my glass to you in return for presenting me with such a hand-some prize this afternoon!'

As the Duchess got to her feet everyone looked toward Archer but he remained impassive.

'To Archer,' she said raising her glass, 'and we ought not forget Goater who rode Timothy so admirably - and who sends Archer his thanks for his share of the prize money!'

Her joke at Archer's expense got its laugh but not from the man himself who was looking at her, but also straight through her.

'You do not seem amused?' she said imperiously.

Archer's eyes deglazed. 'I'm sorry, Your Grace, I...I had other things on my mind.'

'Very well!' she said. 'We must see if we can't get your attention some other way!'

After toasting his good health, the Duchess settled back in her chair. Judging by her hatchet-faced expression she was intent on some serious conversation with Archer. Algy prayed she had not been riled.

'Now, Archer,' she said shrilly, 'what shall you be riding in the St Leger?'

Archer coughed, shunted his plate around, and eventually answered as if his every word was taxable. 'I think the whole company knows the answer to that question, Your Grace.'

'I take it you mean that infernal nuisance, Ormonde!' she roared.

'Well, Your Grace, if he runs and my retainers allow me to accept the mount, I'd be foolish not to choose him. He's a bloomin marvel!'

The Duchess summoned her fiercest expression. 'So,' she boomed, glaring disapprovingly down her nose at Archer, 'you dismiss the chances of my St Mirin out of hand!'

'He couldn't beat Ormonde in the Guineas or the Derby, Your Grace, and I don't believe he can beat Ormonde over a longer distance of ground in the Leger.'

The Duchess stuck out her chest and shuffled in her seat like an egg-bound hen.

'It'll make not a scrap of difference to his chances who rides St Mirin,' Archer continued, playing with the cheese knife that lay across his plate. 'He cannot beat Ormonde in the Leger.'

'Shame on you!' boomed Seger.

The Duchess was a fearless defender of her horses. But she was no fool. She knew Archer was correct. She waved Seger down.

'Then what sort of race would you suggest was in Her Grace's colt's best interest?' he inquired with a hint of apology in his voice.

'He would be better kept to a shorter trip, M'Lord,' Archer replied before turning toward the Duchess. ' The Cambridgeshire, at the back end, would be ideal, Your Grace.'

'But as a three-year-old,' she reasoned aloud, 'he'd surely be allotted a low weight that might inconvenience you.'

'I'll manage, Your Grace. The "mixture" will do its job.'

Nervous laughter rippled round the table as the tension was relieved.

'I'm certainly relieved that I have no need of it!' exclaimed the Duchess, thereby prompting a second outburst of mirth.

'And there's more scope for a decent wager in a handicap like the Cambridgeshire,' volunteered Seger at the top of his voice.

The Duchess's broad smile stated the last point was well made. 'And a race, Archer, I believe you've never won?'

'That is correct, Your Grace,' Archer replied before adding, 'nor you.'

'*Touche*! Then perhaps we can win the Cambridgeshire in tandem!' she cried, throwing up her hands.

Seger triggered universal approval of the proposal by banging on the table and demanding all present raise their glasses to that effect.

'Now, Brusher,' said the Duchess, quelling the enthusiasm and becoming maiden aunt in tone, 'when are you and Lady Constanza going to tie the knot?'

Connie covered her face with her hands but her attempt at coyness proved feeble and short-lived. Her freckles brightened with the alacrity of a gas lamp being turned up at dusk and she flashed a toothsome smile informing Algy he could not look to her for any help in diffusing the situation. He felt his cheeks burning the colour of her gown. Had he glanced toward Seger he would have seen the same fires being stoked.

'Everyone saw what a divine couple you make,' the Duchess continued. 'I'm sure I wasn't the only one who discerned a proprietorial twinkle in your eye when the pair of you made your grand entrance together! Why, you already act like a married couple!'

Algy spluttered to find the right words, indeed any words, as cries of 'Yes!' and 'When's it to be?' went up all round the table.

'I think I - I mean we - can say that an announcement will be made shortly!' interjected Connie helpfully.

'Trust the lady to be the decisive member of the partnership!' said the Duchess, striding around the table to kiss the future bride on both cheeks before planting two more on her intended groom.'

Algy grinned like a gargoyle. He had been made to look an utter fool and he felt like one. He was fuming. He glowered at Connie and she knew what he was thinking: he wanted to strangle her.

Connie was the least of Algy's immediate worries, however. Archer was visibly flagging and looked in danger of fainting at the table. Algy begged the company's pardon and said he was sure no-one would object if the exhausted champion took to his bed in preparation for tomorrow. Archer lent on the table, rose unsteadily to his feet, thanked Algy for his kind thought and was clapped from the room.

The Duchess seized the moment to suggest it was time the ladies withdrew and left the gentlemen to their port and cigars. Algy rose along with them: there was something in Archer's expression that had put his teeth on edge.

'In the circumstances, I'll not feel happy unless I look in on Archer. He's clearly not been himself tonight,' he said. 'So, Sir Felix, gentleman, please excuse me.'

Connie immediately halted in the doorway. 'I agree,' she said perkily. 'I'll come to!'

Seger watched her pass, his flushed cheeks fast assuming their usual darkness, before taking his seat and using his cigar-cutter with the vigour of someone who was imagining its blade slicing through the vital organs of his bitterest enemy.

ELEVEN

Algy marched straight past Connie and into the vestibule without speaking. His mind was occupied with more important things than her girlish schemes. Archer, he was informed by Raper's butler Hopkins, had not gone upstairs but was seen leaving the house in the direction of the Italian garden. Algy swore and ran outside. He felt the muscles of his chest and shoulders tense with a surge of affection he had come to recognize as fraternal in origin and intensity.

Connie raised a hem in a vain effort to overhaul him but her dress had been designed with seduction in mind not running and Algy ignored her pleas to slow down. Finally, screwing up her face in a manner that suggested a tantrum was imminent, she abandoned all decorum, took her skirts in both hands, kicked-off her shoes and broke into an unladylike trot down the gravel path that led to the Italian garden.

'Algy, what the devil's got into you!' she said once she got near enough to grab his arm and bring him to a standstill. 'You're acting like a total arse! What's wrong?'

Algy was not all right, that much was true. The left side of his face felt as if sand had been poured in his ear, a side-effect of the perforated ear-drum sustained while defending himself in his Uppingham dormitory.

'I must find Archer!' he railed. 'He's not a well man! I'm afraid for him, if you must know!'

'I'm more important than Fred bloody Archer!' she screamed. 'If I thought for one minute that Archer was the cause of you blowing so maddeningly hot and cold whenever the subject of our future arises, I could understand! But it isn't and you damn well know it!'

Algy rubbed the mastoid bone behind his ear which now hummed like it was being excavated with a broken nail. He had never told Connie about this chronic neuralgia, even though it was incurable and might be triggered by stimuli more innocent than nervous tension: wind; water; the onset of a cold. The only relief lay with the strongest painkillers until the attack, which might last from hours to months, passed of its own accord. Right now, his tablets were upstairs in his room.

'Connie, I haven't got time to go through all this again!' he said, pressing his left ear and wincing.

'All what?' she protested. 'What is it that I've done?'

'You have the nerve to ask after a performance like that! You've made us a laughing stock!'

Algy tore his arm from her grasp and stood staring at her in disbelief.

'Do you *really* need to ask? Even after all these years?'

'But, Algy, we could make it work! Think about it for a moment!'

Algy did. The white part of his brain saw only the beautiful woman standing before him amid the scented blooms of an English country garden, her exquisite face scintillating in the July moonlight: that part wanted to sweep her up into his arms. The black side of his brain warned of a siren whose way led only to disaster. Somewhere lost in the confusion was a lone voice fearing what it was about to say.

'Connie, we've no future! You must forget this obsession!'

'Don't be so silly!' she shouted back. 'Of course we have a future! Yes, it's an obsession! Being in love is the sweetest kind of obsession! You're meant to feel insecure! You're supposed to revel in the danger!'

'No, it's you who is being silly! It's just not feasible!'

'Why? Tell me why?' she implored, her mouth starting to crumple as her anger turned to desperation.

Algy knew he was going to hurt her badly but he felt cornered. 'Your father loathes me! You know it and he knows I know it. He's never forgiven me for Burton Coggles and he never will.'

'But he will if I ask him,' she blinked, stepping into his arms, trusting the swell of her bosom and the salt of her tears would achieve what words could not.

'I'll ask that of no man, especially a man who has gone out of his way to blacken my name at every opportunity. Even my own father has turned his back on me because of the muck your father spread around...and then there was the South African business.'

'You're still not reconciled then?'

'There's more chance of Gladstone marrying Disraeli!'

'I'm so sorry. I had hoped...'

Algy had worked himself up into the kind of smouldering bate where he was one word away from lashing out.

'Child-snatcher! Baby-lover!' he yelled. 'That's what your father said about me! That rubbish got me sent down from Oxford!'

Connie hated to see him in such turmoil. His rage frightened her and she began to weep uncontrollably.

'I know it's all my fault.' she grizzled. 'I know I shouldn't have told anyone but...I...was...just...so...happy.'

Algy wiped her eyes with his handkerchief. 'Dotty, you were *only* fifteen! It *was* wrong. I took advantage of you. I should have known better. But...'

He held her tight and enveloped her mouth with his.

'...you were so divinely gorgeous...'

'Like a rich plum, you used to say, that had to be picked.'

'Yes, so I did.'

She blinked to stem the tears. 'Am I still?'

'What do you think?'

He kissed her on the mouth and then kissed away her tears.

Connie reached for the gold locket snuggling between her breasts and opened it. She took out a tiny square of paper and carefully unwrapped it so that it did not tear. It was too dark to see the writing upon it but that did not matter. She knew every word by heart. She clasped the paper to her bosom and began to recite in a tremulous voice.

'A love that lingers long...when silent does no wrong...the fruits of love undone...no harvest to be won. The price of love is high...that, no-one can deny...aching in its yearning...continually burning. To talk is not to touch...to dream, scarce up to much...tis true, no joy awaits...the love that lingers long.'

Algy focused on the dust covering his shoe-caps: there was nothing much he could say faced with his own words.

'Fancy you keeping that!' he blathered. 'Not the best verse ever written.'

'To me they are words beyond compare!' she said, returning them to the locket. 'Did you mean them?'

He hesitated. He did not know what to say. What he felt he wanted to say sounded trite and mawkish, and insincerity was a gift he had never mastered.

'Algy! Did you mean them?' she said, clutching the piece of paper to her bosom.

'Yes. But they're only words.'

'I carry them round with me every day. They've been next to my heart every single day of the four years since you sent them to me on my 21st birthday. They will always with me until we are finally together!'

'Love in a cottage, you mean? Because that's what it would amount to! And I can't see you living in a style you're unaccustomed to!'

'I could live in a hovel if you shared it with me.'

Algy gripped her by the elbows and looked into her eyes. 'Baking bread and planting potatoes! Flour in your hair and mud under your fingernails? Somehow I can't see you settling for that!'

'I promise I would try!'

'Do you really think you love me that much?' he sighed. 'What is there to love about me?'

'Oh, Algy...'

'My looks? My egocentricity? My grouchiness? My outstanding military record?'

'You're sensitive, kind, loyal...you can't bear injustice...'

'Connie, really,' he interrupted sarcastically, 'you'll have me in tears in a minute!'

'Algy, don't run yourself down so!

'I live in cramped rooms. I scratch a living as a hack. I must amount to splendid marriage material compared to a George Seger!'

'Now stop it!' she scolded. 'You're making me angry. Neither of us is perfect...'

The list of Connie's imperfections seemed so long to Algy that he decided against interrupting her.

'... and we both know it. But somehow we fit together.'

Algy looked up at the stars. His heart was telling him one thing, his head another. And the vice torturing his jawbone was now screwed so tight the pain was boring through his temples like a maggot.

'Dotty, please listen to me! You must be realistic. It's about more than just you and me!'

'No, it isn't!'

Algy stood in front of her, arms akimbo, his blue eyes shining like chips of glacier ice in the moonlight, and began to address her as a fraught professor would an obdurate student.

'Neither of our families wish to see us together.' he intoned gravely. 'Especially yours. Your mother thinks I'm a cad and never looks me in the eye. Your father, on the other hand, makes a point of looking me in the eye in the hope that looks really might kill! How could I ever stand at the altar alongside him and accept his daughter's hand? His only daughter! The heiress to a most of south Lincolnshire, for God's sake!'

Connie buried her head in his chest.

'I'm sorry, Connie, but it's true! He'd rather vote Liberal than see me benefit from his wealth. And how could I rest easy providing him with the grandchildren he craves so much, eh? I'd rather vote Tory!'

Algy swept his hands through his hair, picked up a piece of gravel and hurled it high into the air.

TWELVE

The sudden screech of a hunting vixen cut the stillness and brought Algy back to reality.

'It's getting late,' he said brusquely. 'I sincerely hope Archer is not out here still. He'll catch his death. Come on, Connie, we must find him.'

They scrunched along the gravel path, round a huge bank of azalea and hydrangea and beneath a rose-clad pergola, until they found themselves in a garden of sundials, urns and a ghostly population of Roman gods, emperors and vestal virgins.

Against the far wall they could also make out the faint outline of a summer house in the form of a Roman temple.

'Did you hear that?' whispered Algy. 'I though I heard something.'

Connie shrugged. Algy put a finger to his lips. 'Yes, there's someone in there,' he said, pointing to the temple.

They ran across the lawn. Algy arrived first and discovered Archer slumped on a marble seat, his head lolling like some flower on an old stem. In Archer's right hand he saw a cheese knife. His left sleeve was rolled up and his wrist lay exposed in his lap; in his hand was a silver keepsake containing what looked like human hair.

Algy stood there like one of the nearby statues: cold and lifeless; a spineless onlooker. If Archer was dead he would never forgive himself.

'Oh, God, what has he done to himself!' puffed Connie, as she brushed past him and knelt down to examine Archer's wrist. 'There's a mark here but the skin's not broken. And he has a pulse.'

She glared at Algy. 'What's the matter with you?'

He did not react. He was lost in a haze of recrimination and guilt.

'Don't just stand there!' she shouted, shaking the torpor out of him. 'Fred's eyes are open! Talk to him!'

'Fred!' Algy said at last, easing the knife from Archer's grip. 'Are you all right?'

Archer did not answer. His eyes were wide open, but so ringed by world-weariness that they resembled twin inkwells; he seemed in a complete trance. Behind the grey-blue stare he saw himself about to be reunited with his beloved Nellie. He could smell the rose-water she rubbed into her hair and feel the peachy skin that lined the dimple in her chin. Little Nellie Rose could live without him but he could not live without her mother. He was sure he could see her walking towards him, coming to join him, coming to take him away to a happier place.

Connie put her mouth to his ear. 'Mister Archer? Fred?'

'Nellie?' he answered with a sense of wonderment. 'Is that you? Is that my darling Nellie?'

He tried to sit up straight but needed Connie's assistance.

'No, but it is a friend.'

'Oh, I thought you were Nellie come to look after me.'

'No, it's Lady Constanza Swynford.'

Archer blinked, nodded and dredged up the outline of a crooked smile. 'Ha...the lady playing bad gin-rummy with Lord George at Rat's ...'

'No, I think not,' whispered Connie sternly before scanning Algy's face for any reaction. 'We met last February at a meeting of the Belvoir, don't you remember?'

'Ah...yes...is that so?' Archer said, starting to wonder where he was. 'I meet so many people...'

'Connie, what's that he said?'

'I can't make it out!' she answered tetchily, her cheeks flushing unnaturally in the cool night air. 'What do you expect? He's just rambling, hallucinating badly.'

'All right, Connie! I'm sorry!' Algy replied urgently. 'Stay calm! Don't make matters worse than they are!'

Algy removed his dinner jacket and draped it around Archer's shoulders. 'Fred, let's get you inside. It's getting chilly now.'

Archer looked up. 'Algy, is that you?'

'Yes. You'll be fine in a jiffy.'

Algy slipped one of Archer's arms across his shoulders and tried to lift him to his feet. Archer broke free and steadied himself against a column. He began to sob, huge body-racking sobs that he had been storing up for months and which now threatened to knock him off his feet.

'I can't go on!' he cried out. 'Life means nothing to me now. Nellie was my glory, my pride, my life, my all, and she was taken from me at the very moment that my happiness did really seem to me to be so great and complete as to leave nothing else in this world that I could wish for. I would gladly give up money, honours and everything else, even my life, in exchange for only one word from her dear lips.'

Algy was crying inside for his friend. 'It'll be all right, Fred. Just steady yourself down.'

'No, it won't, Algy. For God to take her away when she was only 23! Oh, if I could only love a woman half so well as I loved her, I would. But I could not. And I never will now.'

Connie chewed her lips, unable to hold back her own tears. She wanted to hug Archer and cuddle away his anguish but had enough presence of mind to tell herself not to.

'I am so thoroughly wrapped up in racing that I really never think of anything else, not even of where I am and of what is going on around me. It's my way of pretending everything's just like it used to be when Nellie was with me. It's the only way I know of getting through each day. I wake up tired in the morning, I ride work on the gallops, I sit in the turkish bath, I drink the "Mixture", I place bets, I go to the races, I play with little Nellie Rose and I try to sleep again. But all I see is my precious Nellie's face smiling at me all the time.'

He stared at the lock of hair and his chin dropped to his chest, tears beginning to puddle his dress shirt as he clutched at a square of trellis to hold himself upright. Connie sprang forward to support him, but then shied away, feeling powerless to help.

'Do you know what my only real consolation is now?' Archer mumbled.

He did not wait for an answer. 'I don't mind telling you that it is in prayer. I have, like other men, been careless about that sort of thing but since poor Nellie's death, when I am alone I spend most of my time on my knees in earnest prayer. I get out of bed in the night when everything is still, and kneel and pray. It is such a comfort. The only comfort I have now. I know that it is what she would like me to do.'

Algy felt as if he had been introduced to a new person.

'You're surrounded by friends, Fred,' he said. 'No one can possibly replace Nellie but you've many, many friends who are willing you to get through this and who will do anything in their power to help.'

'Don't you mean hangers-on?'

'No.'

'I don't mean you, Algy,' Archer added hurriedly.

'I…we,' said Connie, 'can assure you that you have countless real and genuine friends.'

'Really? Are you sure?'

'Yes,' said Algy. 'And, don't forget, there's also little Nellie to consider.'

Yes,' said Connie. 'She loves her father and she needs him.'

Archer sat silently, absorbing what they had said. He thought of his little daughter back in Newmarket and for a second or two it seemed he might buck up but then his expression faltered once more. Something else had crossed his mind.

'You know, the Duchess had a note sent to my room before dinner,' he said, an expression of donnish fretfulness creasing his brow.

'About St Mirin?' said Algy.

'And the other thing,' replied Archer, trying not to catch Connie's eye.

'Oh that.'

'The woman won't give me a minute's respite. She'll drive me insane, I'm sure of it.'

Algy assured him that the Duchess, for all her eccentricities, was far too worldly-wise not to recover her senses in due course.

'But it's not just her.'

Algy waited for him to continue. It took Archer a full minute to pluck up the nerve to do so.

'It's Fenner!' he cried out. 'He's here!'

'What!' exclaimed Algy. 'Mo Fenner down here? At Selhurst? He never leaves London!'

'No, at the racecourse. He cornered me yesterday during racing.'

'This thug's some brass neck! Whereabouts? I saw no sign of him!'

'In the racecourse stables.'

Algy scratched his head. 'How the hell did he manage to get in there! It's guarded like the Bank of England!'

'He must have bribed a gateman!' Connie blurted, wringing her hands and wandering off into the shadows. 'There's no other rational explanation!'

'You were dead right, Brusher' said Archer, perking up a liitle. 'He wants compensation for Sandown. And right badly.'

Algy felt happier now he had a tangible problem to target, the pain in his jaw forgotten. 'Then let's give it to him,' he said, jutting out his chin. 'Let's raise the cash and pay him off tomorrow.'

'You can't! He told me he was going straight back to London.'

'Nevertheless, we must get rid of the monster once and for all.'

'I can help out and would deem it a privilege,' volunteered Connie, edging back toward them.

'No, M'Lady,' said Archer apologetically. 'He doesn't want money. Not even my money.'

Algy and Connie knew what the other was thinking.

'Fred,' said Algy, 'is there something else you want to tell us?'

Archer knew there was, if he could only find the courage. It was enough that he already hated himself. He clenched his fists and forced out the words.

'He wants me in his pocket. He wants me to compensate him in kind.'

Algy felt like punching one of the stone emporers. 'Fred, don't tell me all this talk of a Jockeys Ring is true and you've been fixing races!'

'No!' protested Archer. 'One or two of us just sum up a race now and again, and if there's an obvious winner we make it known to all concerned so that they can profit.'

'You mean the other connections, owners, trainers - and jockeys?'

'That's right, yes.'

'And Fenner's in on this too?'

'Yes.'

'Bloody hell, Fred!'

Algy lent against a Doric column, his head against the cold marble. He felt like kicking himself. He had guessed something like this might be happening. But he had been too gutless to do anything about it.

'Now he says I'm to throw races to order,' said Archer, beginning to sob once more. 'I can't do that. What would my Nellie say?'

Connie put her arm round Archer but her attempts to calm him down were met by a dismissive wave of the hand.

'Look at me, Fred!' Algy said with a sudden injection of authority.

'Fenner can't touch you!' he said, locking onto Archer's eyes and willing fighting spirit into him. 'He can't afford to put the squeeze on someone like you! You've too many powerful connections. Isn't that right, Connie?'

Connie's mouth fell open but proved incapable of speech. Her mind was preoccupied with her fate to concern itself with Archer's.

'Connie!' barked Algy. 'Are you listening?'

'Yes, Algy,' she mumbled.

'I said Fred has powerful friends in the Jockey Club! Fenner can't touch him!'

Connie heard herself muttering some platitude in agreement; but the shrill voices inside her head were arguing otherwise. She wiped the perspiration from her palms on her velvet covered hips and lifted her head, focused on the brightest star in the galaxy and rolled her head round her shoulders. One voice had begun to grow louder and assert itself. It belonged to her conscience.

'I do think, though,' continued Algy, 'that it may be as well to have someone by your side every minute of the day. As for Fenner's demands, ignore them.'

Archer examined their faces and saw two friends willing to put themselves at risk on his behalf. He wanted to find the courage to join with them. If only he were braver. There was only one person who could give him that courage. What would Nellie say? He put the keepsake to his cheek and suddenly he heard her voice. Stop moping: start fighting back.

Archer looked at Connie and recognized Nellie's compassion. He looked at Algy and saw her backbone. He wiped away the last tear from his cheek, got to his feet and shook hands with each of them in turn.

'All right then.'

THIRTEEN

The following day there was only one topic of conversation at Goodwood among the fast set that gathered for luncheon in the half dozen marquees erected on the members lawn. It wasn't the threat of rain posed by a few clouds being tugged across a mackerel sky or the quest for the names of possible winners. After the events at Selhurst Grange the previous evening, it was talk of Algy's and Connie's betrothal.

Algy ordered Connie to deny catergorically any possibility of an immediate engagement, pleading the excitement of the occasion and intoxication for her outburst. If she did not, he would take it upon himself to make the situation very plain - whatever embarrassment ensued.

They took a corner table and rejected any company on the pretext they only had eyes for each other. This was half true. Algy could hardly keep still. His blue eyes kept scanning the room for potential tormentors. One glare was enough to see off Deek and Seger: that anyone might be foolish enough to intrude upon them and give him an excuse to release some of his anger seemed unlikely.

Connie identified the one man who would as soon as he entered the luncheon room: as did every other diner except Algy, who had his back to him. His upright posture showed off a once intimidating physique which the belligerent clack of his cane on the parquet floor was deliberately calculated to accentuate. Beneath the shock of mustard-coloured hair was a hawkish nose and mouth so large and well sculpted they resembled the bust of a military hero.

'What's this I hear about a forthcoming marriage?'

The words fell on the luncheon room like a dusting of frost, but one hard enough to make Algy's toes tingle for it was a hectoring voice he had been taught to obey which the pungent odour of the paraldehyde its owner took as a sleeping draught only served to reinforce and identify. He leapt to his feet, scattering cutlery noisily onto bone china like grapeshot.

'My business, not yours!' he snarled, squaring up to his father.

'There's no need to shout. You already have the ears of the room,' replied Lord Belton with the cold dignity of a Caesar unused to settling for anything less. 'I swear there are more gossips in here than at a fishwives convention.'

Bothering to check whether his observation had found its mark was beneath Lord Belton but his son could see that it had. A hunger for violence whetted the atmosphere.

'And you're intent on feeding them, I suppose?' he shouted.

Lord Belton narrowed his eyes, the better to focus on the inferiority of his interrogator who felt himself trembling with rage. Algy knew what his father was doing. Poking and prodding until he got the reaction he wanted. Just like he always did.

'Why should I?' Lord Belton intoned, picking an imaginary speck of dirt from his white linen jacket. 'I suspect your antics have done so already. They always have...'

'What are you insinuating?'

'Let's just say that I dislike the idea of officers bolting on horseback when their men on foot are left to die.'

Lord Belton's hitherto riveted gaze turned briefly toward Seger and the pair exchanged smirks.

Algy thrust his face to within an inch of his father's. A wild animal was running a-muck inside his chest which he was desperate to release. But why demean himself?

'Not the kind of behaviour in the face of the enemy we would have entertained in the Crimea!' Lord Belton added sniffily.

One more word, Algy promised himself, and his father would have his nose splattered all over his face. But why give him the satisfaction?

'Algy, please!' murmured Connie, staring down at her half-eaten salad. 'You're embarrassing us.'

'Then tell this meddlesome man to go away,' Algy replied, his fists clenched by his side, 'before I forget he's just an embittered old man behaving like some pathetic wasp in a jam jar!'

Lord Belton's expression, which had remained stitched in place throughout, now displayed traces of satisfaction in the down-turned corners of his mouth. He examined his watch, looked at his son's face as if it were no more than another dial and departed as he had entered: as imperiously as an ageing bull elephant. Only the keenly observant would have detected the slight tilt of the head as he passed Seger's table.

******

Over the next few weeks Algy hardly left Archer's side. They were denied Connie's company because once the latest gossip reached the Earl of Kesteven he promptly arranged for his daughter to visit her mother in Venice. She departed under protest.

A fortnight after Goodwood, Algy accompanied Archer to Kempton Park. The opening race on a lacklustre card was the Sunbury mid-weight Handicap over a mile, a mediocre contest that had cut up into a three-horse race involving animals called Cavalier, Edlington and Drakensberg to be partnered respectively by Archer, Charlie Wood and George Barrett. Archer was on the favourite.

Algy left Archer in the weighing room and had almost reached the grandstand when he recognized a flinty figure hustling his way.

'Bumbo, what are you doing here?' he laughed, pleased to see his godfather. 'I understood you had no runners today.'

'Quite so,' gasped Raper, 'but I wouldn't miss this race for all the whisky on Speyside!'

'I might have known you'd spot the implications!'

'Sussex is not the ignorant backwater you London Johnnies like to think! I've heard all the stories about this so-called Jockeys Ring! A three-horse race involving Archer, Wood and Barrett! This I want to see'

Algy frowned. Was it that obvious? Eliminate Archer on the favourite and the other two choose who wins? He had to admit it probably was. This was a race Fenner could not have organized any better had he been given licence. It was a race on which Fenner would want to make money. Lots of money.

They ascended to the top tier of the grandstand which was deserted. Raper produced a snuff-box and pinched some onto the back of his thumb for Algy to partake. He screwed up his face in horror. Raper shrugged, snorted the powder himself and then produced a hip flask from which he took a lengthy swig.

'Want some?' he said, proffering the flask enthusiastically. 'It's Burroughs!'

'They call it Beefeater now,' Algy replied.

'Do they! Well, they can call it whatever they like. I call it a bloody fine gin!'

Algy was saddened to see his godfather reliant on alcohol at this hour and declined to join him. Raper noted the down-turned mouth but disregarded the rebuke: no one told him when, where, or how much he might drink. At his age he would enjoy a dram or two at breakfast if he so chose.

He wiped his mouth with the back of his hand and let out a contented sigh of equal flourish. 'Your loss, my boy!'

'Have you taken a financial interest?' Algy asked, looking away.

Raper took a further tot and viewed him incredulously. 'My dear boy,' he said waving his flask, 'does Doris have fleas?'

Algy smiled. 'So? Where's your money gone?'

'On Archer, of course!'

******

Down in the weighing room Archer tapped his whip against his boot. He knew what was coming as Charlie Wood sailed alongside.

'Leave this to George and me,' Wood said. 'You find some trouble in running and we'll sort out the rest.'

'You think so?' Archer replied, staring straight ahead. He had gone over this scenario in his mind and had steeled himself.

'We'll see you're all right! You'll not lose out!' Wood continued.

'And Fenner's behind this?'

'Look, Fred,' Wood hissed. 'You've been making life very difficult lately for some of us! Fenner's running out of patience - which he ain't got much of in the first place!'

Archer marched onward, whip twirling.

'Just this once!' pleaded Wood with more than a hint of desperation in his voice. 'And then we're all in the clear!'

'If you say so, Charlie,' Archer said nonchalantly.

'It's just a matter of counting our winnings! Trust me!'

Archer assured himself. Do they think I'm stupid? Trusting Charlie Wood? And George Barrett? In a three-horse race like this? They can carve up this race with or without my help. I've done it enough times myself. They'll not be taking any chances.

So neither did he. His eyes never left the starter's arm and he had Cavalier in line and on the move when the flag fell. He had decided that out front and clear was the place to be if Wood and Barrett planned skullduggery.

He took Cavalier to the running rail and sensed Barrett on his outside, whip already cracking into Drakensberg.

'Fred!' Barrett shouted, 'Are you with us?'

Archer stared between his mount's ears and quickened the motion of his hips in the saddle. Cavalier fly-leapt in response. Good! His confidence in the horse rose.

'So far, so good, eh Bumbo?' Algy muttered.

Cavalier and Drakensberg were now racing side by side, the former shielding the latter from the view of the grandstand and enclosures. Barrett crouched low in the saddle and in one movement lent across and attempted to yank Archer's left foot out of its stirrup with his right hand.

'Did you see that?' cried Algy. 'I swear Barrett tried to put Fred over the bloody rails!'

Archer lost his balance, causing Cavalier to crash into the rail and only his long legs saved him from slipping sideways out of the saddle. Barrett urged Drakensberg past the stricken leader, lashing out at Cavalier's stifle with his whip as he did so, and cut across him toward the inside running rail.

Algy watched Archer take a firm grip of his whip and crack Cavalier back into stride. Wood reacted instantly and urged Edlington upsides Cavalier.

'Now they've boxed him in!'

'So we can guess what's coming next!' Raper called back.

Archer had guessed it too. He had to get out of the pocket or when Wood gave the signal that he was ready to go on and win the race, Barrett would cleverly ease Drakensberg so that his horse would fall back on Cavalier, causing him to lose all his momentum - and with it the race.

'He's going for the run up the inside!' shouted Algy.

'Helluva risk!'

The two men put down their race-glasses and exchanged knowing looks. They knew how dangerous a manoeuvre this was in an ordinary race. In the context of this particular race, Archer was poking his head in the mousetrap.

'For Christ's sake, Fred, be careful,' Algy muttered under his breath.

Archer sank his spurs into Cavalier's belly, deftly switched his whip into his left hand and administered three rapid-fire whacks across the animal's backside. At the same moment, he tugged hard on his right rein so that all the power he had generated from Cavalier was directed between Drakensberg and the fence.

'That horse is a brave bugger! He's going through with it!'

'Either that,' observed Algy, 'or the poor bugger's afraid of the mad bugger on his back!'

Archer saw the combination of Drakensberg's bay rump and the white fence start to intimidate Cavalier as he stuck his head into the gap. He felt Drakensberg was tiring and if Cavalier could maintain his run, he knew they had a chance of winning. He hit his mount once again and felt the pain of the running rail smacking his right boot. But he ignored it as Cavalier they fought their way along the fence, forcing Drakensberg to yield and drift away to the left.

Drakensberg was beat but Edlington wasn't. Wood had rousted him and was whittling down Cavalier's advantage.

'Cavalier's knackered!'

'Don't write him off, Bumbo! Remember who's on his back!'

Archer felt as exhausted as his horse but the feel of all his former confidence returning gave him extra energy. He stole one last glance at the winning post and then put his head down, willingd his emaciated body and the shattered animal beneath him to raise one final effort.

With 50 yards to run Cavalier's lead was reduced to a neck. Then the two horses were eyeball to eyeball. Ten strides from the winning post, Archer's metronomic rhythm of legs, hips, elbows and hands wavered. The tiny stutter momentarily distracted Wood and disrupted his own rhythm. The feint had worked. Then it seemed to Algy as if Archer picked up Cavalier and hurled him across the finishing line, his body thrust forward in a deliberate attempt to catch the judge's eye. It succeeded. He had burgled the race by a neck.

Although his body was limp with exhaustion, Archer's eyes danced like fireflies. He felt good. He heard the cheers and he felt like a champion again. Algy watched him dismount and acknowledge the applause by touching his cap with his whip instead of thrusting it under his arm and knew his old friend had resurfaced. He slapped him on the back without worrying whether the force of it would knock him off his feet.

'Some race, FA!' Raper rasped as they walked back toward the weighing room. 'Look, you've paint all over your right boot!'

Archer looked down. 'I didn't notice.'

'Your boot is ripped open from heel to toe!' said Algy. 'I suppose you didn't notice that either! And before you say anything, I saw what went on out there - and it wasn't accidental!'

'That's what I shall be telling them if they ask!' Archer replied matter-of-factly.

'Fred,' said Raper, 'don't you think it's time this scandal was exposed?'

'No, I don't.'

'I'm sorry but I can't agree,' said Algy. He nodded toward Wood and Barrett, now huddled in conversation with a figure that, even with his back to them, looked suspiciously like Cocky Arnull.

Archer halted.

'Look, Algy,' he said, raising his whip like an admonishing finger, 'I can't. Trust me, I can't!'

'I don't believe you're saying this! You might have been killed out there!'

'Algy's right, you know,' said Raper.

'You cannot ignore corruption like this any longer!' Algy continued. 'It's not right, Fred!'

'You do as you see fit, Algy. You've a job to do, a column to fill - I know that. But keep my name out of it. It'll all blow over. I shall square things with Fenner.'

'Are you sure that's possible?'

'Money's his game,' replied Archer, suddenly talking in measured terms. 'I'll see he's handsomely repaid. That'll do him!'

Algy shrugged. 'I hope you're right, Fred. I just hope you're right.'

'I'm sure I am,' Archer said proudly.

FOURTEEN

Archer's rehabilitation rapidly became a resurrection. Wood's lead in the jockeys' table was steadily whittled away over the next few weeks until Archer caught and passed him in the first week of September. He and Ormonde predictably trounced St Mirin in the St Leger but he repaid the Duchess's faith in the colt by winning on him twice at Newmarket and the colt's end of season target became the Cambridgeshire for which he was installed as one of the favourites.

The only drawback was the weight St Mirin was set to carry. Archer knew the punishment involved in boiling his body down to anything approaching the allotted 8st 6lb. But he told little Nellie it would be worth it. He might become a trifle short-tempered, he confessed, but a series of carefully placed bets could net enough to clear all his debts and still leave enough left to retire. Nellie merely gurgled but the very thought of retirement was all the incentive her father needed.

There was something else Archer wished to correct before he retired: he had never ridden in Ireland. So, with his thirteenth consecutive jockeys' championship now assured, he accepted an invitation from the Lord-Lieutenant, the Marquis of Londonderry, to partner Cambusmore in his own race at the Curragh on 21 October.

Algy would also travel. The Sunday afternoon before their departure found him in a quandary. He paced his rooms, tossing over in his mind the pros and cons of finally writing the short, sharp piece he had been eager to write for some months. Now seemed the perfect opportunity. But what would Fred say? Would he object? Probably: he wouldn't care for the rumpus. But he could be won round.

Algy stopped to admire the print of Bendigo humbling Caunt and studied the victor's face: what would he do if he were Archer? Would he fight till he dropped? Yes. He would see justice done. But would Fred? Had he the same fighting spirit? Algy walked to the picture of his friend riding Bend Or to victory one-handed in the Derby. He had his answer.

Algy sat down at his desk and quickly committed his thoughts to paper. He read the piece through a couple of times and having finally polished it to his satisfaction, he typed it out and, en route to the Turf Club, called in at the offices of *The Sportsman* at 139-140 Fleet Street and dropped the copy into the tray of his editor, Henry Downes Miles.

******

The only drawback surrounding St Mirin's participation in the Cambridgeshire as far as Mo Fenner was concerned were his mounting liabilities on Carrie Red's colt. Nevertheless, he reckoned he had everything under control.

In the meantime, nothing was going to put him off enjoying his usual breakfast of angels on horseback and a tankard of porter fortified with three raw eggs, the sort of repast he grew accustomed to eating during his prize-fight days - though nowadays thetankard was a prized solid silver 17th century example by Thomas Dare of Taunton.

Sat in the dining room of his splendid three-storied Georgian townhouse in Gower Street, he felt well satisfied with the long journey he had made from the dockside back-alleys of Wapping where he was born and raised as Nathaniel Fenner: he acquired the name 'Mo' during his years as an 'enforcer' when he regularly employed the phrase 'Half a mo!' to put unsuspecting victims off guard before kneeing them the groin.

He had made the most of what few gifts God had given him. If those gifts were a pair of lethal fists, so be it. All the pious humbugs who criticised men like him for the way they had made something of their lives out of nothing could rot in their own sanctimony. He had seized his limited opportunities and life had been good to him. It would continue to be so. No, there was no need to lay off any of this St Mirin money. He, Mo Fenner, had everything under control.

His moment of self-satisfaction was abruptly curtailed by the intervention of a jittery Cocky Arnull.

'Mister Fenner, you'd better 'ave a look at this,' he said as he almost tripped over the scraggy black and white cat that had followed him through the door. The animal looked as if it had been enjoying a night of fighting and fornication, its matted white fur now a filthy shade of grey. Arnull instinctively made to kick it away.

'You put your boot to that cat an' you'll feel mine up yer arse!' said Fenner. 'Yer more expendable than 'im, an' don't yer forget it!'

The cat sprang onto the table and shook its head, spraying blood, saliva and mucous in all directions.

'Here you are, Percy,' said Fenner, ignoring the animal's ill manners and tossing one of the bacon-wrapped oysters at its feet. The cat wolfed down the tit-bit before rolling over and exposing its pot belly in a bid for further attention: the stray had not so much been adopted by Fenner as it had adopted him.

Fenner dutifully stroked the cat's stomach until it began emitting a purr that would have done credit to a lion and then turned his attention to Arnull. 'Now, what do you want?'

Arnull laid that morning's issue of *The Sportsman* on the table and retreated a safe distance. He had folded it into a neat square to highlight an article printed in bold type and entitled 'Who Will Halt This Canker In Our Midst?'

Fenner dabbed his eye with a handkerchief and reached for his pair of half-moon spectacles which, once perched on his nose, rendered him more teddy bear than grizzly bear. He stared at the newspaper and ran a knife-tip along the lines as he read.

'Is it not right to ask the stewards of the Jockey Club whether they are aware that scabrous rumours abound to the effect that a conspiracy exists between certain influential jockeys and a certain so-called professional bookmaker to arrange the result of races for their own benefit?'

Fenner prodded the phrase 'so-called professional bookmaker' and snorted.

'It must be stressed, straight away, for the peace of mind of his legion of followers, that the most influential jockey of all is not involved. Any attempts to tar the champion jockey with accusations of skullduggery must be treated with the utter contempt they deserve. It is ridiculous to suppose for one single moment that a jockey so admired, revered and, yes, loved by his public would risk throwing throwing it all away by agreeing to be party to such calumny.'

'A jockey so admired': Fenner's mouth twisted and he motioned Arnull to replenish his prairie oyster with more porter.

'If the stewards have heard of such rumours, and believe such a "Jockeys Ring" exists, what steps have they taken to address and deal with the matter before the sport suffers incalculably? The supposed existence of planned frauds and robberies, the pulling of certain horses, the combination of certain jockeys are all tearing at the vitals of the Turf.'

Fenner's jowls darkened and he drained the tankard in one long draught. He told himself to remain calm: it was bad for his heart to get over-excited.

'*Spyglass* respectfully suggests to the stewards that they could do worse than commence their enquiries by emulating those Three Wise Men of biblical times who followed the star to "The Holy Land." The stewards may, however, find their journey leads them not to a stable but a "Rats Nest" of unimaginable proportions.

Or have matters sunk so low that the poor flies can demand nothing from the spider in whose web they are entangled?'

A 'Rat's Nest'? Fenner's knife ceased following the lines of newsprint and resumed its former position on the table. Its owner wiped his mouth, removed his spectacles and then wiped his eye. His head was beginning to feel as if it had taken an uppercut from Bendigo and he was sure his eyeball must be swollen up judging by it tenderness. His head throbbed and his hands began to shake. Who is this 'Spyglass'?

He raised the knife above shoulder height and brought it crashing down in a sweeping arc, pinning the offending article to the table and sending Percy scampering for cover.

'Enough's enough! It's time Mister Archer, was brought to heel,' he snarled. 'And this meddlesome journalist friend of his…whatever his real name is.'

'Haymer,' volunteered Arnull.

'Yes, him!' added Fenner, leaning back in his chair. 'That bastard's slicker than snot on a doorknob.'

Fenner watched the knife quiver in the table-top. He imagined it in Archer's throat where it belonged. Grabbing the hilt, he pulled it free and pointed the blade at Arnull.

'I want the pair o' 'em taught a lesson!'

FIFTEEN

Silas Mort read the telegram just delivered and lobbed it onto the back of the fire. He showed no reaction to its contents other than to pick his nose and add the outcome to the other stains on his shirt. Then he crossed to a rickety cupboard (by no stretch of the imagination could it be called a wardrobe) and pulled out a tatty brown overcoat fit only for a scarecrow, plonked a faded brown billycock on his head to hold down what little remained of his straggly hair and left at once for Manchester's London Road Station where he waited for the 'Irish Mail' which was due to arrive at 10.30 pm en route from Euston to Holyhead. He did not bother to take any luggage. He had no intention of lingering in Ireland even if his task were to take him that far.

Those unaware of his principal occupation would never have guessed it. Mort was short in stature yet possessed of long spiderly limbs which gave his movements an unenviable jerkiness suggestive of a complete lack of co-ordination. However, anyone who concluded this quirk must have constituted a physical liability for a man in his line of work was quite mistaken. Brute force was never Mort's metier. Fists and boots were not his weapons of choice. He preferred stealth. Silas Mort was a back-stabber who favoured a switch-blade.

The Irish Mail arrived within a minute or two of schedule. Mort boarded the first-class accommodation and began conducting a methodical search for his quarry. He found them in the fourth compartment. He took a seat in the fifth where he could cover their every move. That he had only purchased a third-class ticket did not trouble him. When he presented it to the ticket inspector it was punched without comment, for Mort radiated an aura that had a profound effect on people. One lazy eye may have had something to do with this; as might the pock marks that looked as if they had been made by a dull-edged chisel.

The train chugged into Holyhead at 2.30 in the morning and Mort followed his targets at a discreet distance on the short walk to the jetty. He had seen newspaper photographs of the two principals; if that had proved insufficient the attention and name-calling being directed toward one in particular - even at this time of night - would have sufficed.

He watched them negotiate the gangplank to the SS Hibernia and tailed them toward the first class cabins where they entered adjoining rooms 101 and 102. He heard keys turning in the locks. He glanced about him and spied a pull-down seat at the far end of the gangway. He sat himself down and waited. About 20 minutes later he felt the vessel lurch into life.

With each nautical mile completed beyond the Holyhead breakwater, sailing conditions worsened as the Irish Sea lived up to its choppy reputation, the vessel pitching and rolling like billy-o. He sat eating an apple, immune to the usual human responses; for as long as he could remember he had been devoid of feelings; freaks like him were told they were fit only for a circus. So he adapted: he slept a lot; he ate sparingly; he killed as often as possible. And he only truly came alive when busying himself with the last.

After an hour's vigil during which he lovingly rehearsed the forthcoming orgy of violence in his mind, he heard the sound of a door being unlocked. He slunk back into the shadows, mind and body suddenly enlivened with anticipation.

The door to cabin 101 opened and Mort observed its occupant emerge. The man looked haggard and pea-green: the front of his jacket was specked with dried vomit. He staggered to the nearest companion-ladder and began an unsteady ascent toward the deck. He was too preoccupied with negotiating stairs that seemed in perpetual motion to realize he was being followed.

Archer reached the top of the stairs and almost pitched full-length onto the deck. For someone with next to no stomach contents he had amazed himself by throwing-up repeatedly since leaving Holyhead. The cabin seemed air-less. He had to get some fresh air even if it did mean disregarding Algy's instructions to stay inside with the door locked.

He was instantly refreshed by a brisk sou-wester blowing a curtain of rain in his face, but the moon shone down like a bright white lamp and dazzled him: that and the motion of the boat almost toppling him over. He lent against a bulkhead and gradually inched his way toward the stern.

Mort was monitoring Archer's progress. He ran his tongue along his lip and reached into his pocket. Once Archer tottered out of sight the other side of a davit, he moved swiftly and nimbly to within three feet of him. He noticed Archer looked like death and thought how he would soon know what it felt like.

Mort heard Archer retch - followed by the unmistakable thud of a body falling onto wooden planking. He peered round the davit. Archer was lying face down on the deck. Mort clicked his switch-blade into life and raised it, ready to strike. The boat pitched violently and forced him to steady himself all over again. He licked his lips a second time and once again raised the knife high above his head.

'Fred! What on earth are you doing up here? You'll catch your death!'

Mort sucked his teeth and let his arm drop to his side as Algy zig-zagged across the rolling deck toward Archer. He watched Algy grasp Archer under the armpits, ease him into an upright position and lead him to the gangway. He cursed the interloper under his breath and pulled the billycock firmly over his ears until the rain ran down his back.

******

It was 5.50 on a dank Tuesday morning when the mail boat tied-up at Kingstown Pier. Waiting to escort them via train to Westland Row Station in Dublin city and thence the Shelbourne Hotel was Captain Patrick Joseph Fitzgerald, a ruddy complexioned and well nourished young official from the Irish Turf Club. This in itself suggested how important Archer's visit was to Irish racing, but they were soon made to realize just how important it was to the Irish people. Turning into St Stephen's Green, they caught sight of the crowd massed outside the Shelbourne Hotel which became increasingly animated and vocal once their carriage came to a halt and its passengers were positively identified.

The crowd swarmed round the carriage and a man in a voluminous blue cape with gold braiding stepped forward. He raised his right arm to reveal a heavy silver bell which he immediately started clanging. Then the town crier performed the civic duty which he had been rehearsing for two days.

'Gentlemen!' he boomed. 'This is to give notice that Mister Frederick Archer, the celebrated horseman, has arrived in this city, and that he *will* ride the winner of the Lord-Lieutenant's Plate on the Curragh on Thursday, the 21st day of October, 1886. Gentlemen! Come and see the wonder of the world! God Save the Queen!'

'Would you believe it!' said Archer, suitably awed.

'You should!' replied Algy. 'People don't just admire you. They love you.'

Archer stepped from the carriage, chin hiding on his chest nevertheless, and followed Fitzgerald into the hotel foyer. They sat down to breakfast - if Archer's tablespoonful of castor oil and half an orange qualified as a breakfast - before leaving for a photographic studio in Lower Sackville Street belonging to a Mr Chancellor where Archer sat for his portrait: copies of the photograph were on sale by tea time and soon in great demand. Then they boarded a train for Kildare and the Curragh, some 30 miles south west of the city. Archer had nothing to ride that afternoon but he was keen to familiarize himself with a new track.

His principal aim, however, was to locate a set of scales. He had not ridden for four days and he was anxious about his weight, fearing it may have ballooned. He gave his jacket and waistcoat to Algy, took a saddle and sat in the chair.

The mechanism jerked into action as Algy adjusted the weights.

'Fred, you're 9st 4lb!'

'Never mind! My old horse has only 9st 3lb on him, so I have only to get one pound off.'

'Are you sure?' said Algy, scrutinizing the list of runners pinned to a noticeboard. 'It says here that Cambusmore is set to carry 9 stone!'

'Nonsense!'

'I've half a crown that says I'm correct!'

'Go and fetch a copy of the conditions!'

'They're printed here!' said Algy. 'Four-year-olds and upwards 9 stone, 3lb allowed for mares and geldings.'

'Well then, Cambusmore's an entire, so that's 9 stone 3lb!' protested Archer.

'Fred, I think they mean it the other way - the mare's allowance of 3lb comes off the 9 stone!'

Archer felt like ending his aversion to profanity. The last few days had been so enjoyable. Now he must get back on the treadmill. 'I'll sweat it off tomorrow,' he said grimly.

They returned to the Shelbourne to find a note waiting for Archer from Mr Michael Gunn, the proprietor of the Gaiety Theatre, asking if he might be gracious enough to honour the said emporium with his presence at that evening's performance of *The Mikado*. Archer professed total ignorance of opera but Algy assured him that it was comic not tragic and he would thoroughly enjoy the experience. Archer received a standing ovation when he took his seat in the Royal Box and Algy calculated that there were more pairs of eyes concentrating on him than the stage. His own, however, were riveted on the delectable singer playing one of the three little maids.

Archer spent most of the next day either ensconced in the Shelbourne's Turkish bath or dosing himself with slugs of the 'mixture' in an effort to lose those four pounds. With him safely occupied, Algy accepted Fitzgerald's invitation to dine at his Dublin club.

Their departure from the Shelbourne did not go unnoticed. Mort watched them climb into the cab and decided to follow. The job was throwing up more obstacles than he had envisaged and if he could not reach Archer, the toff would have to suffice. Fenner was not an employer to be left long without good tidings.

The portly Fitzgerald - 'Just call me Padjo!' - proved convivial company at a dinner that was unassuming in its constituent parts but surprisingly pleasurable in their sum. Afterwards he suggested they adjourn to a place of 'private entertainment for gentlemen of discrimination and taste' that had recently opened in Merrion Square.

'Are you familiar with *poses plastiques*?' Fitzgerald asked casually while running a chubby finger round the inside of his collar as their cab turned out of Nassau Street.

'Naked models in classic poses? Of course!' Algy replied, suggestively raising his eyebrows. After the alarums of the last 48 hours he was in the mood for relaxation.

'That's settled then.'

'Living sculptures...'

'...paintings that breath! Shame they're not permitted to move!'

'Piccadilly and Mayfair are crawling with these "pleasure palaces" nowadays!'

'Dublin, less so, I'd say!' responded Fitzgerald, warming to the coming prospect. 'But we're catching up!'

Algy's imagination was already working faster than a piston. His libido was not far behind, fanned by thoughts of Connie: the touch of her fingers; her smell; her eagerness.

Fitzgerald jumped from the cab, straightened his tie and trotted up to the imposing portico of a slightly less imposing house. He knocked on the door which was opened by a liveried flunkey who, after greeting Fitzgerald like an old friend and accepting a sovereign, led them into a spacious *salon* whose tired drapes and furnishings suggested where the money might be well spent. Every chair and sofa was turned to face a curtain at one end of the room.

'Will you take a drink, Brusher?' said Fitzgerald, settling into a care-worn chair. 'I've every confidence you'll be in need of one! If only to cool you down!'

'Would this establishment run to calvados?'

The mock horror on Fitzgerald's face told him it would not. He accepted a cognac and sat down next to his host whose pudgy face now wore the glazed expression of the school glutton locked overnight in the school tuck shop.

The room was filled with the usual clientele for such 'entertainment': two old buffers sharing a worn leather chesterfield were lost in conversation; a group of rowdy young swells occupying a *chaise longue* were guzzling straight from bottles; a number of other individuals sat patiently in their wing-back chairs smoking cigars or sipping port.

'Ah, good-o!' Fitzgerald babbled when a dinner-jacketed man emerged from behind the curtain.

'Gentleman! May I present the first of our *tableux* for this evening. It is entitled "The Wonders of the Orient - The Japanese Tea Ceremony!"'

Algy shifted in his seat at the promise of oriental erotica and his blue eyes shone like shards of lapis lazuli. He prayed he would not be disappointed.

A hum of polite appreciation emanated from all bar the young bucks who yahooed instead. The *majordomo* stepped backwards, hauling the curtain with him to reveal a rather poor interpretation of a Japanese tea garden. Not that anyone in the audience was remotely interested in the authenticity or otherwise of the setting. Each pair of eyes was flicking from one figure to another in search of personal gratification: the *tableau* featured four girls, sporting white-painted faces in the geisha style, each in various degrees of undress and posture to satisfy every taste, be it for breasts or bottoms.

Algy's eyes were drawn to the girl pretending to be pouring tea. The flat, boyish chest and erect brown nipples were strangers to him but the cut of her jet-black hair and the crimson of her bee-sting lips were not. Her face reminded him of an illustration in a childhood history book that depicted the ecstasy of Joan of Arc tied to the stake. The image that gave him his first adolescent stirrings.

'Padjo,' he whispered. 'Who's the girl pouring the tea?'

'You mean the one with the fried eggs for breasts?'

'There's no need to be so ungallant! I think she looks splendid and she does look awfully familiar.'

'I've no idea - but I see what you mean. She's a corker!' said Fitzgerald, revising his opinion. 'Wait, of course! I've got it! She was in *The Mikado*.'

Algy studied her face with the concentration of the lovelorn. 'Damn me if you're not right!'

Despite her colouring, there was much about the girl that reminded Algy of Connie. She certainly had the same effect on him. But unlike Connie, this woman was within touching distance. And he positively ached for the warm comfort of a woman's body. However temporarily.

'Padjo, I must meet her!' he said, grabbing Fitzgerald's wrist. 'Can you arrange it?'

'You've been dipped in the Shannon and no mistake! There's no bashfulness in you, is there! Padjo'll see what he can do!'

Padjo Fitzgerald was the kind of man who could fix anything and forty minutes later Algy found himself standing outside the door of the room set aside for the use of the *artistes* as a dressing room. He knocked, waited, and entered when invited.

She was sat in front of a dressing-table mirror with her back to him, still in her flimsy costume, in the process of removing her heavy oriental make-up. She half-turned in her seat to greet him and he realized in an instant how it was that sirens lured mariners to their destruction.

'Good evening, sir,' she said. 'It's a pleasure to meet you.'

Her voice provided him with a second shock. It was soft, melodic, almost set to music.

'The pleasure is entirely mine,' he answered. 'My name is Algy Haymer. And you?'

'Maud Grace,' she answered. 'And it is me who should be thanking you, Mister Haymer…'

'Please call me Algy, Miss Grace.'

'If you will call me Maud.'

'Why, of course.'

'I just had to convey personally my congratulations on your performance…'

'Standing out there half-naked is not much of a performance!' she said amid laughter that tumbled from her as pure and natural as springwater.

Algy blushed. 'I'm so sorry! What I meant to say was your performance last night…at the Gaiety!'

'Oh, I see!'

'I never imagined I'd see you in a place like this! Someone as talented as you are…'

She interrupted him once again. 'Now, much as I appreciate your kind words concerning my performance last night, please don't get the wrong impression. I'm no star! I'm only the local understudy who just happened to get on last night because Yum-Yum went down with a touch of the Dublin vomiting bug!'

Algy's ignorance caused another bout of blushing. She blushed back.

'But you can't be expected to know all that,' she said, lowering her lids. 'The truth of the matter is that girls like me have to earn a pound where and when we can. Rent has to be paid!'

She took refuge behind an opulent looking *chinoiserie* screen constructed of bamboo and suitably decorated in a delicate oriental style that had Algy seen it anywhere else than a Dublin pleasure palace he would have thought a genuine work by Nesfield.

The tiny G-string that had been protecting her modesty was flipped over the top bar before she had realized it. He must think I'm a terrible flirt, she thought: but was she being too tarty? She stood there naked wondering what this handsome Englishman was thinking and then ran her hands down her body from neck to thighs pretending they were his.

'Are you in Dublin for long?' she asked.

'Not long,' answered Algy, picturing the scene on the other side of the screen whence he heard the rustle of garments being squeezed into.

'Here on business?'

'Sort of.'

'That sounds *very* mysterious!'

Algy pulled at his collar. He sensed he was floundering badly and fast making a fool of himself.

'May I treat you to a late supper by way of compensation for my crass behaviour?' he asked, fingers crossed behind his back.

'A late supper, you say?' she giggled. 'This is Dublin! You're not in London now! You'd be lucky to find a pie shop open at this hour!'

He tried again. 'Then please allow me to find you a cab and escort you home?'

She emerged from behind the screen in her street clothes, a coltish figure in a simple green gingham frock that revealed a glimpse of brown lace-up ankle boots. Though ordinary in the extreme, this outfit failed lamentably to dim her Celtic beauty. Thick black hair cascaded to her shoulders, framing a heart-shaped face of porcelain complexion and accentuating the redness of her lips - not so crimson as before yet still as kissable.

'Are you a man to be trusted?' she laughed.

Algy prayed his expression did not lay bare the dishonourable designs presently occupying his mind to the exclusion of all others and raging through his loins like a fire deep in the hold of a ship.

'You look like a man a girl can trust!' she said as if it were a line from a song. 'And a cab certainly beats walking!'

Maud Grace had already made up her mind. She was accustomed to fielding blarney from enough of Dublin's rich playboys to see through this Englishman's. But beneath the veneer of his dashing looks and gauche charm offensive she thought she recognized something more genuine. She was prepared to give him the benefit of the doubt. He looked to her as if he might be worth it.

She reached for her coat. Algy got there first and held it open for her.

'Why, thank you, kind sir!' she said.

There was, Algy was pleased to note, a distinct sparkle in her amethyst eyes. He searched in vain for her hat.

'I dislike hats,' she explained, halting his quest. 'I prefer to feel the wind in my hair.'

Algy's adoration soared: a free spirit, he hallelujahed, just like Connie.

SIXTEEN

They stepped out into a cool Dublin night. Algy hailed a cab and they clip-clopped up Nassau Street, across the River Liffey and on up Sackville Street, past the impressive facade of the General Post Office. They became so engrossed in each other's company that she failed to notice the cab had passed Blessington Street, where she had lodgings at number 53. The cabby grunted an apology, pulled the brown billycock down over his ears and turned his horse in accordance with her directions.

Algy waited expectently to see if she would invite him in. Maud Grace saw the tip of his nose and ears turning pink with cold and knew she wanted to warm him up. The corners of her mouth wrinkled as Algy paid the fare and she told the cabby he could go.

Algy followed her inside. Initial impressions confirmed Maud Grace to be a woman not exactly flushed with cash. Nevertheless, the few sticks of furniture demonstrated a woman of taste and she had clearly taken pains to personalize the room with numerous photographs that depicted her in various stage roles.

'That's my favourite,' she volunteered, as Algy examined the selection laid out on her dressing table. 'That's me as Buttercup in *HMS Pinafore*.'

'You look fabulous!' he said, moving on to the contents of her dressing table: silver-capped perfume bottles, an ivory comb and brush set, a jewel box decorated in mother of pearl and a collection of ornamental figures.

He picked up a small Japanese okimono of a geisha carved from jade. 'I saw the D'Oyly Carte production at the Savoy. I can just imagine you in the role.'

'Why, thank you again, kind sir!' she said with a theatrical curtsy.

'And I see you like all things oriental? All the rage at present! I'm rather partial myself.'

126

'Ah, you've found Maud-een!' she said, removing her coat and crossing the room to join him. 'I bought her only recently, as a keepsake of my time in *The Mikado*. I found her in a little shop called Quirke's in King Street.'

'In jade, too.'

'Yes. The rest are Connemara green marble but jade seemed more appropriate for *The Mikado*. They say jade brings love, wealth...'

'...and longevity!'

'I'll settle for the love and wealth!'

The warmth of a smile that began deep behind her eyes left Algy completely tongue-tied.

'Now, what can I offer you?' she said laughing. 'I've no alcohol in the house but I can make a pot of tea!'

'That's lovely.'

'A real one this time! There's nothing in that pot back there in Merrion Square!'

Algy felt in need of considerably more than a cup of tea. He studied every inch of her body as she stood there at the sink filling the kettle from a jug. The way her hips reposed to one side, thrusting out her buttocks for closer inspection, was mesmerizing him. He found himself mentally stripping her.

'That's strange,' she said. 'The cab is still outside. But the cabby's gone.'

Algy peered through the curtain. 'Yes, odd. I'll go down and check everything's all right.'

Algy opened the front door. The cab-horse looked up at the noise and snorted. He looked up and down the street but saw no sign of the cabby. He rubbed his chin: there was something familiar about that battered brown billycock.

Mort bared his teeth and brought the blade down toward Algy's neck but hearing his grunt Algy managed to knock Mort's knife arm upwards with his right arm while grabbing the wrist with his left. They slithered along the wall of the building entwined like a pair of mating serpents, Mort trying desperately to break free now he had lost the element of surprise. Algy sank his teeth into Mort's knife hand and gnawed.

Mort howled and dropped the chiv. Instinct made him keep squirming but he knew resistance was futile in the face of physical superiority. He begun to wonder what death would be like when Algy swung him round and delivered a vicious head-butt which flattened his lips against his teeth and broke his crooked nose for the umpteenth time. Algy smiled as the pain spread over Mort's face until the eyes rolled up into the back of his skull. He watched him slide down the wall to the ground; then he used Mort's jacket to truss his hands and feet, stuffing his muffler in his mouth to keep him quiet.

Algy's thoughts turned to Archer and the possibility that Fenner had sent two assassins. Then he looked up at the light in Maud Grace's window. No one could get at Fred in the Shelbourne, he told himself. He went back inside.

'Everything all right?' she said, pouring his tea.

He crept up behind her and wrapped his arms around her waist. She did not resist. She turned, her body rubbing against his.

''So, that's a "No" to tea, then?' she said, lingering open-mouthed so that he might be in no doubt what she wanted of him.

Algy cupped her face in his palms and gently kissed her on the lips. She answered his tenderness by sucking the tongue from his mouth and taking it deep into her own. She pushed open Algy's jacket, undid his tie and the top two buttons of his shirt.

'There, that's a start,' she said, sweeping a wayward lock of his blond hair neatly back into place. 'Now, you get yourself into bed! I shan't be a minute.'

She could not wait to see her athletic suitor naked for she was in as much haste to make love as he was. Algy reached for his wallet.

Her violet eyes shone. 'I'll have you know that I may not be wealthy but I don't sell my body!'

'I…I'm sorry,' he said. 'I wasn't thinking…'

'Now, you do as you're told and let's have no more talk of money!'

She disappeared behind a wooden screen which Algy took to be where she undertook her *toilette* leaving him feeling ashamed of his crassness. He got undressed and leapt into the brass bed that he discovered behind a curtain in the corner.

The sight of Maud Grace walking toward him moments later in the sheerest imaginable camisole and matching pair of French knickers - each tied at the side with ribbon - inflamed him. He could see her nipples straining against the fabric and the outline of the dark mass between her legs sent a tremor through his body that slammed to a halt in his groin.

She peeled back the linen counterpane and descended on him with the urgency of the famished. Her shock of black hair cascaded across his belly and he felt days of abstinence joyously drain away as she consumed him like custard, right down to the last lick of the spoon. He lay there and sighed.

Algy's respite lasted as long as it took for her to untie the bows and straddle him. She moaned as his tongue made moist contact. A relentless warmth gushed through her like rising mercury that induced a cry so intense she was unable to express it. She finished motionless, her hands gripping the iron bed-head, her red lips describing a perfect circle of silent ecstasy.

They fell asleep in each other's arms: she warm, secure and at rest; he feeling guilty and restless. He had definitely abandoned Archer and he had probably betrayed Connie.

And when he awoke after a disturbed night, it was Connie's body he saw nestling beside him on its stomach.

SEVENTEEN

The cries of hawkers and costermongers drifting in from the street insisted Algy had best be on his way if he was to reach the Curragh in good time. He sneaked out of bed, dressed and enjoyed one last peek at Maud Grace. This was the *tableau* he would remember her for.

Algy rushed back to the Shelbourne to spruce-up and was soon at Kingsbridge Station boarding one of the three lengthy 'specials' put on to ferry race-goers to the Curragh. There had been horse-racing on this broad plain for a thousand years but it is doubtful whether anything like the events of Thursday, 21 October 1886 had ever been witnessed in all that time. A hot butter-yellow sun beat down on a vast crowd that would have challenged Irish Derby day: a funfair was enjoying a brisk trade and judging by the hundreds of uniforms in evidence, almost every officer and soldier from the nearby headquarters of the Irish Army had been granted temporary leave of absence. Everyone had come to see Fred Archer.

At least Algy hoped they had. This multitude might conceal any number of Fenner's thugs. There was no reason to presume Fenner had settled on just the one. His ear began to ache as he ground his teeth. If there was a killer out there he would be powerless to stop him.

Cambusmore and Isidore were backed off the boards and won easily enough, both pulling themselves to the front well before the line, but at odds of 6-4 on and 4-1 on respectively they hardly repaid Archer's band of supporters. Nevertheless, they still cheered Archer wildly as the Marquis of Londonderry led Cambusmore through the advancing crowd toward the winner's circle. Algy's eyes went from one excited face to another, looking for the unexpected, seeking the benign mask that hid malevolence. But there were just too many faces.

Archer dismounted and the crowd moved forward to mob him. Algy's collar stuck to his neck. He panicked and dived among them, swearing and lashing out at anyone who even attempted to lay a hand on Archer, even resorting to a headlock to quieten one noisy protester.

'Steady, man!' shouted Padjo, prising them apart. 'That's only a Kildare magistrate you've got by the throat!'

Algy relaxed his grip and grovelled an apology. 'Jesus, I'm sorry, Padjo! I must look a fool! But I'm so wound up about Fred's safety. You never know who's out there.'

'You're right about one thing!' said Fitzgerald, shaking his head. 'You are a fool! Anyone harming Fred Archer this day would have to be mad! He would likely find himself lynched on the spot!'

Algy reddened at the thought of his own stupidity.

'Your friend had no need of an English bodyguard because he has thousands of Irish ones!'

'Of course, Padjo. I should have realized,' said Algy shamefaced. 'And before I go let me say thanks for everything. And I do mean everything.'

Fitzgerald shook Algy's outstretched hand and eventually twigged. 'Ah, yes, the oriental maiden!'

Algy took out his wallet. 'I hesitate to ask, but will you do me one further favour?'

'Anything, just name it.'

Algy counted out the banknotes he had remaining. 'I've £100 here. Will you find a nice piece of jade, a figurine, perhaps a little Japanese boy, something like that? I believe there's a shop in King Street - goes by the name of Quirke's, I think - and see that it reaches a young lady called Maud Grace at 53 Blessington Street.'

'Easily done!' said Fitzgerald. 'Any message or note?'

'No. Just see that she gets it. I think the lady will know who it's from.'

******

The party returned to the Shelbourne to collect their luggage. They had a good three hours to kill before the Royal Mail steamer sailed for Holyhead.

Algy found a sofa in a quiet, pot-planted corner of the lobby and sat down to wait for Archer. A waiter immediately appeared at his elbow and enquired whether he wished to take tea. The sandwiches being consumed elsewhere looked deliciously inviting and he was indeed hungry but out of consideration for Archer he confined himself to a pot of Earl Grey.

'Goodness me, FA,' he said when a ripple of applause signalled Archer's eventual arrival, 'you do look beat!'

'And I feel it!'

'Sit down and have a cup of tea.'

'No thank you. Just a cup of hot water and a squeeze of lemon.'

'Are you positive?'

'I've got to do 8st 12lb tomorrow.'

'Tomorrow?' queried Algy, non-plussed. 'Are you quite mad?'

'I'm going straight down to Sandown. I'm riding a colt for Bob Peck in the first. He's got 9 stone but I've another in the 2YO seller with 8.12. What with the travelling tonight and in the morning I don't want to put too much weight back on. It was hard enough getting it off yesterday!'

Algy replaced his cup in its saucer and pushed them aside. His eyebrows joined in one long worry-line. This continual talk of weight was starting to prey on his own mind, so what it was doing to Archer's?

'Fred, your every waking hour seems plagued by pounds and ounces,' he said, studying his companion's hollow cheeks and sunken eyes. 'You can't continue torturing your body in this way, it's just not natural. You looked washed-out! What did you scale today - 8.12? That means you lost 6lb in 48 hours!'

'Yes.'

'So is it any surprise you look like death!'

Archer cleared his throat and decided to be mischieveous. 'If I look bad now, how shall I look next Tuesday!'

'Good God, man! You don't seriously mean to say you are going to try to ride St Mirin at 8.6 in the Cambridgeshire?'

'I am sure to ride St Mirin 8st 6lb, or at most 8 7.'

'Be reasonable, Fred! When was the last time you weighed out at 8.6 for God's sake!'

Archer pondered. 'Not this year.'

'You're damned right not this year!'

'Ah, now I remember!' Archer suddenly said triumphantly. 'The day Saraband made his debut at Kempton! Last May it was.'

'There, last May! That's a good 18 months ago!'

'He won 12 lengths, pulling a cart!' added Archer, recalling the sort of information that tends to stick in a jockey's mind for future reference.

Algy folded his arms. 'Nor is 8.7 realistic!'

'I drew it for Candlemas in the Eclipse!'

'Yes, and that was the last occasion!' Algy said, springing forward like a self-satisfied barrister. 'Three months ago!'

'That's right,' Archer conceded reluctantly. 'I suppose it was.'

'Lately you've struggled to do nine stone! And you've just said yourself what a struggle it was to make the weight yesterday.'

Archer sipped his water. He hated the thought of angering Algy and he felt sure he knew where this conversation was leading. He swallowed another mouthful of water. 'I made 8.8 for Ormonde the other week at Newmarket!'

'St Mirin is not Ormonde and the Cambridgeshire is not the Champion Stakes!'

'I can sweat and purge myself.'

Algy shook his head in exasperation. 'Please, Fred, I implore you not to even contemplate such a thing! Wasting like that at this time of year has been the ruin of many a jockey. You need a more strength to combat the elements, not less.'

Archer examined his finger-nails, as usual immaculately manicured. There was something he wanted to say and Algy deserved to hear it first.

'Algy,' he said eventually, 'you're the first person I've mentioned this to, but this will be the last time I do anything like this. Next season I've promised myself I'm not going to do less than 8.10. The only reason I've agreed to ride St Mirin is because I've never won the Cambridgeshire.'

Algy beamed. 'That's splendid news, Fred. But why bother to wait till next year? Quit now! Let's not fool ourselves, wasting's been the death of some jockeys!'

'Never mind if I go out or not,' replied Archer, sticking out his chin defiantly. 'I shall do it this one last time!'

Algy inhaled deeply and drummed the arms of his chair in frustration. 'Can't you cheat the scales a bit?'

Archer laughed. 'What, by "toeing"?'

'It can be done.'

'Not by me it can't! Others might get away with it but the clerk of the scales watches me like a hawk! Old Dorling would spot my toes on the ground in no time! And enjoy shouting about it!'

'Well then, make up some excuse for not riding St Mirin!'

'Fat chance of that! And, anyway, I think St Mirin can win.'

Algy picked up a teaspoon and began tapping it on the table.

'I have it!' he exclaimed. 'Melton's in the race with top weight?'

'Yes, I know.'

'Well, inform Her Grace you should ride him for Lord Hastings. Good God man, you did win last year's Derby and Leger on the horse, so she can hardly object!'

Archer smiled at Algy like a kindly uncle about to disappoint his favourite nephew.

'I see,' said Algy meekly, 'you've already thought of that and dismissed the idea?'

'Melton's the biggest thief in England these days. He'll not always put it in, you know.'

'Fred, surely, if any jockey can make the blighter run, it's you!'

Archer squeezed a weak smile. 'After what the Duchess has paid to take sixth call on me, she'll not let me off St Mirin in hurry!'

'So it's true?' Algy said, getting to his feet. 'You have accepted a retainer from her?'

'Yes'

'How much?'

'I can't say!'

'A considerable sum, then!'

'Impossible to refuse!' said Archer cheerfully.

Algy ran a hand through his hair, deperately seeking inspiration from somewhere. But he knew now he was fighting a lost cause. He slumped back into his chair.

'You never know, perhaps she'll scratch him,' he said half-heartedly. 'There was talk of it in this morning's paper.'

'He'd have to be half dead before she'd even think about it! She's backed him to win a fortune!'

'You as well, I suppose?'

'I've invested,' said Archer, pausing between the two words.

The hesitation unsettled Algy. He sensed the worst. He lent forward and looked Archer in the eyes.

'Not with Fenner?'

'Certainly not,' replied Archer, throwing back his head. 'Undo all the recent good work? No, the Duchess's agent has put some on for me in her name.'

He shuffled his feet as if hoping to sidestep Algy's likely next question. Precisely how much had been wagered on St Mirin in his name he was not prepared to divulge. Acknowledging the figure reminded him that it was a sum he could ill afford to lose.

Their attention was diverted by a telegram boy in a bright green uniform who had marched into the foyer crying Archer's name.

'Fred!' said Algy. 'It's a telegram for you!'

'Oh, I didn't hear.'

Archer was turning the colour of the boy's uniform. He prayed it was not one more telegram from a creditor.

Algy called the lad over, tipped him a shilling, and passed the telegram to Archer who immediately sliced it open with a finger.

'Who's it from?' Algy asked, casually pouring himself another cup of tea. 'Anyone important?'

'It's from the Duchess,' Archer answered, relieved.

Algy ceased pouring, teapot hovering in mid-air. 'What's it say?'

Archer continued staring at the message, screwing up the nerve to tell him.

'Well?' said Algy.

'My horse runs in the Cambridgeshire,' Archer said with the solemnity usually associated with the reading of a will. 'I count on you to ride it.'

'Bugger!' exclaimed Algy, spilling tea over the tablecloth. 'Some people won't be content until they see you in the ground!'

EIGHTEEN

One man totally indifferent to Fred Archer's fate was Herbert, First Earl of Kesteven. Profligacy and tardiness, on the other hand, were subjects guaranteed to provoke him, and his mind was currently preoccupied with both as he paced the dining room of Denton House.

Kesteven was unaccustomed to being kept waiting. Only three people had ever dared. All three were women. He could hardly take issue with Her Majesty the Queen. He did complain to his wife Ginetta that the Italian attitude to time-keeping was intolerable but their divorce had eliminated unpunctuality from that source. The third, however, was a continued source of irritation: his daughter Constanza. It was now 26 minutes past twelve and he had expressly told her to be at Denton by noon, for luncheon at 12.45. He took out his watch and checked it against the walnut-cased longcase clock by Thomas Tompion that stood in the corner.

Herbert Swynford had made his immense fortune in the Leicester hosiery trade, making fine socks and stockings that were worn from Leicester and London to Montreal and Melbourne. He threw his considerable wealth behind the Conservative Party and was rewarded by being created the First Earl of Kesteven when it was returned to power in 1858. Thus, Denton was not a traditional country mansion in the style of Selhurst or Haverholme but a sprawling turreted folly built with 'new' money by a man who chose to ignore contemporary opinion that 'a Gentleman's house ought to be not merely substantial, comfortable, convenient and well furnished, but fairly adorned and free of ostentation.'

That he had spent a small fortune on Denton never gave him a moment's concern. What did alarm him was the conduct of his spendthrift daughter. That he had been the architect of this predicament by spoiling the girl rotten did not escape him, but this 'engagement' that had filled the gossip and society columns of late had finally dragged him to his senses. Constanza was out of control. He had to act.

Kesteven's impatience with his daughter's tardiness had run its course and he was half-way through his cream of leek soup when she eventually breezed through the doors of Denton's dining room.

'Ah, you've arrived at last!' he said, putting on the warmest welcoming expression he could manufacture, never an easy feat given his naturally lugubrious features but harder still now the large beaky nose and jowls sagged with age and worry. His eyes were immediately drawn to his daughter's choice of outfit: the thick tweed suit in a shade of russet was ideal for the inclement weather but the fox stole draped around her shoulders was totally unacceptable. He suspected this vulpine trophy was only being worn as a means of taunting him with its connotations to that day with the Belvoir he preferred to forget.

'Here you are daddy!' she gushed, holding out a parcel neatly wrapped in gold paper. 'A present from Venice! Some of that marbled paper you like so much from Legatoria Piazzesi in San Marco.'

She placed the package on the table beside him, not waiting for him to take it from her hands or inflict a paternal kiss. He paid it a cursory glance and continued eating.

'What news on the Rialto?' he said eventually, chuckling at his drollery.

'When are you going to revise your script! Same worn-out joke for as many years as I've been going to Venice to visit mama!'

Connie strode round the room, avoiding eye contact. She knew the sparring had begun and sensed her father thought likewise. She had spent so long rehearsing this encounter in her mind yet she was already feeling lost. She began to wish she had never come.

'Well, how was your stay in Venice?' asked Kesteven, fiddling with his soup spoon.

Connie's eyes remained fixed on the oak tree at the bottom of the drive. 'Absolutely divine, since you ask!'

'How did you pass the time?' he continued in a monotone that suggested the question was asked out of force of habit rather than genuine interest. 'I found the place dreadfully dull.'

Connie scowled. 'Only morons could possibly find Venice "perfectly dull."'

Kesteven normally loved leek soup but was finding it increasingly difficult to enjoy the bowl presently before him. He wondered whether it might be best if he said what he wanted to say without further ado.

He watched his daughter casually pick up the porcelain figurine of a lute player that stood on the window sill. 'Do be careful with that ornament! It's Minton!'

Connie tensed. 'If anything's likely to make me drop it, it's the sudden roar of your voice!'

She obediently put the figurine back where she had found it and recalled how she had planned the course of this conversation: put him at his ease: talk about her holiday; soothe him; lull him. Above all, lull him.

'Now, as I was saying…the high point of my stay was undoubtedly the season of Verdi at La Fenice, especially *Rigoletto*!'

'How lovely,' Kesteven replied, between slurps.

'Oh, you should have heard *La donna e mobile*!'

'Why? What is it?'

'Well,' she smirked, 'it's an aria sung by a Duke, a notorious womanizer, who explains his belief that all women are flighty, simple creatures, to be enjoyed but not taken too seriously.'

Kesteven thought he got the point. 'Like your mother?'

'Or even me!'

He refused to be amused. He took another spoonful of soup. 'And the weather? Hot and sticky as usual? Windy?'

'The sirocco was comparatively mild this year. The odd thunderstorm, of course. But what would northern Italy be in high summer without a torrential storm to clear the air now and again?'

'Damn mosquitoes everywhere, I'll be bound,' he droned. 'And that stink coming from the canals!'

'Inescapable, as usual!'

Her father blew out his cheeks. He had got something right at long last.

'We escaped the worst of the heat by taking step-papa's boat out to the islands.'

Kesteven's eyes narrowed and Connie turned away to hide her grimace: alluding to the Count's wealth was sure to alienate him.

She turned back with her sweetest smile in place. 'Daddy, I'm *so* sorry I was late. That beastly train from Leicester to Grantham! Stuck in Melton for absolute ages!'

'Sit down and have some soup. How was your mother? Well I trust and enjoying Venetian society?'

'No soup for me, Gilbert, thank you!' she said, smiling angelically at her father's butler. 'What's the fish today?'

On being informed it was fillet of turbot in a dill sauce she rubbed her hands together gleefully and said that would be grand. Then she proceeded to enquire about Gilbert's wife, son and daughter - and even the well-being of the family spaniel - as if her father had left the room.

Kesteven had observed his daughter perform many little pantomimes like this in the dozen years since her mother's return to Italy and treated this one with equal indifference. He appreciated that for a teenage girl to be deprived of her mother at the onset of puberty could be problematic, but he believed the flounces, the petulance, the surliness and the general antipathy subsequently directed at him merely amounted to a passing phase. He had not, however, envisaged this to be a phase capable of lasting 12 years.

'Mama is keeping well, as you've asked,' Connie eventually condescended to reply as she placed a small piece of turbot in her mouth.

'Please don't talk with your mouth full, Constanza! It is most unbecoming of a lady.'

Connie controlled her temper by gripping knife and fork ever tighter and succeeded in grinding out an answer. 'She did go down with a summer cold while I was there but seemed to be on the mend by the time I left.'

'Is there anything she needs?' asked Kesteven urgently. 'Did she send any word?'

'No,' his ex-wife's daughter replied with barely concealed satisfaction. 'Nothing at all.'

Connie's lie had the desired effect. Kesteven cleared his throat and wiped the back of his spoon on the lip of the bowl. He had long suspected that the exotic Venetian beauty Ginetta Lorenzon, whom he met and married after a whirlwind courtship during his Grand Tour of 1859, had been a gold-digger. Now she had no further need of his money. A handsome divorce settlement and a second marriage to a Venetian count, who ran the city's biggest bank and resided in the 16th century splendour of the Palazzetta San Lio, had seen to that.

'No fish, Gilbert,' he said, summoning the butler. 'I'll have the lamb shank.'

'Far too heavy for lunch!' his daughter admonished. 'Swimming in all that red wine sauce! You'll give yourself a heart attack! Mark my words!'

Kesteven snorted. 'I'll not be missed,' he said. 'And, just for once, you mark *my* words!'

Connie struggled to retain her composure at her father's perceptive remark. He was plainly angry. And why shouldn't he be? She had done precisely what she had told herself repeatedly not to do. She had failed to control her silly tongue. She had annoyed him. Everything was going wrong.

'Gilbert, that will be all for now,' said Kesteven, as Gilbert served him his lamb shank. 'You may leave us until called.'

The only noise disturbing the silence was the plink of expensive Sheffield cutlery on equally expensive bone china boasting the mark of Josiah Wedgwood's Etruria factory.

'I've not brought you here to bore me witless with tales of your holiday,' Kesteven said at length. 'Let's cease this charade, shall we?'

'If you say so, daddy, then we must!' Connie replied churlishly.

'What's all this balderdash about you and Haymer?'

'I think...'

'Let me finish!' her father interjected, his voice rising noticeably.

'I thought I had made it abundantly clear on any number of previous occasions,' he enunciated pedantically while neatly positioning his knife and fork on his plate at half past six, 'that you were to stay well away from that man! He's no good! He's a thoroughly bad influence! A waster! Hanging round racetrack riff-raff. Gambling! And, I don't doubt, whoring!'

Connie threw up her hands in protest. 'Daddy, if you'd just give him a chance!'

'He's bad lot! Even his own father says so. If it had not been for that soft mother of his he would have been cut-off without two happennies to rub together - and serve him right too! '

'Algy is...'

Kesteven banged a fist on the table, causing the cutlery to jump off his plate. 'I'll not have the name of that libertine, that lecher, mentioned in this house!'

'What are you talking about?'

'Any man who takes advantage of an immature and vulnerable girl of fifteen is a lecher in my book. I only wish I'd taken a horse whip to him at the time and had done with it!'

Kesteven mopped his brow. He had said what he wanted to say. Not exactly as he had planned, but it had been said. It grieved him to see the tears in his daughter's eyes but she had to be told.

His onslaught had taken Connie unawares and blew away any vestige of her carefully calculated strategy. She screwed-up her napkin and flung it in his face.

'But I seduced him!' she announced haughtily and any amount of pride.

Kesteven's bulbous nose started to resemble a split damson.

'What did you know of...'

He could not bring himself to broach the subject. Where he came from sex was something confined to the bedroom in the dark. It was designed for, and confined to, procreation not pleasure and was not mentioned in polite conversation. And it most certainly was not an excuse for a romp in the hay between an innocent girl and an acknowledged lothario.

'Probably a lot more than you imagined! And in any case, when did you ever care what I knew about anything. You were only ever interested in making socks!'

Connie heard herself speaking and realized her visit had turned into an unmitigated disaster. She took a moment to settle herself.

'Father, when were you ever interested in me?'

'I always...'

'When did you ever show any interest in what I was doing or what I wanted to do?'

'Your future was...'

'You were only ever interested in making me into something you wanted me to be. You treated me just like mama!'

'Constanza! That is simply not true!'

Connie's complexion now matched the colour of her outfit and was not the result of hours spent lazing beneath the Adriatic sun on the Lido. She was fighting mad and refused to yield.

'I was nothing more than a chattel, a trophy to be exhibited in front of your cronies wearing the finest new frock from Paris or wherever.'

'But you were a girl...'

'Yes, you made it pretty plain I was a disappointment!'

'Constanza, I didn't mean it like that.'

Connie felt her eyes begin to prick with tears. 'You wanted a son, so I tried to become one for you. But that wasn't good enough for you either.'

'You were such a sweet little girl and I was unsure of myself.'

'Please, no excuses!'

Kesteven had lost one woman dear to him and was reluctant to lose the other. 'Remember, I was an only son,' he said in a tremulous voice. 'I had no sisters and until I met your mother my life had been devoted to my business.'

'If only mama had had another child!'

'If only,' echoed Kesteven, the note of genuine remorse in his voice passing undetected by his daughter.

'But I can understand why she did not! She rightly refused to bring another innocent human being into this house for you treat like one of your chattels!'

'You will not speak to me like that!' he shouted, head rocking. 'You will pay me some respect! Whatever you may think, I am still your father, this is my house - and it is your home.'

'But not for much longer!'

Connie felt the words come into her mouth that were guaranteed to enrage her father: 'Algy has asked me to marry him!'

'What!'

'And I accepted, naturally.'

Connie looked at her father's face growing bluer and wondered whether he would drop dead of a heart attack.

'Stuff and nonsense!' he roared.

'We love each other. You can't stop us and neither can Lord Belton!'

'So be it!'

'We shall survive!' she said, making for the door.

Kesteven was going to have the last word, as he always intended he would. In the circumstances he saw no reason to dress up what he had to say in fancy language.

'If you think for one moment that I shall continue to bankroll your frivolous life of debauchery and its merry-go-round of gambling and drinking and partying,' he said, puffing out his chest, 'then you may think again, young lady! You are 25 years of age. It is high time you grew up!'

Connie's bottom lip trembled. She knew what was coming next: she had heard it all before.

'It is about time you married and settled down! Suitors are queuing up to ask for you hand! Lord Seger, for one. First class material!'

Her father had rendered her absolutely speechless.

'There's absolutely no call for you to entertain a reprobate like Haymer!'

Connie's face was wet with tears and quivering from brow to chin.

'Crying will not help you out of a jam this time!' Kesteven declared with a decisive stretch of the neck. 'I have waited a long time for a grandson!'

'And you shall have to wait a little longer!' she yelled, suddenly finding her voice again. 'If I have anything to do with it that's something you'll never have!'

'It will be your loss more than mine!'

'Even so, I'll have something you never had nor ever will.'

'And what, pray, is that?'

'I have love! I don't need you or your money!'

'Then you shall have your wish and have neither!' he bellowed and turned his back on her.

Connie flounced off. After taking half-a-dozen steps she paused, turned and walked sedately over to the window sill. She picked up the lute player and, coughing to gain her father's attention, held the figurine out at arms length before allowing it to drop onto the floor. She watched it smash into fragments as numerous as the horror lines on Kesteven's face and felt a surge of rapture at his devastation. Then she swept out of the room without a backward glance. She was not about to let her father see her eyes brimming with tears. He might get the wrong idea. He might be foolish enough to think some of them were for him.

Connie slammed the carriage door of the 5.07 Leicester to St Pancras train and banged her fist against the window. She had been so determined to keep her latin temperament in check. There was too much at stake. She only had herself to blame for leaving Denton empty-handed.

And right now she needed every penny she could get.

NINETEEN

Connie spurned a detour to Mays Court and went directly to Liverpool Street Station and thence Newmarket for the running of the Cambridgeshire the following afternoon. She spent every mile of the journey twiddling with her hair and worrying about the outcome of a race on which all her hopes of financial salvation were now pinned.

She found Newmarket as depressingly bleak and cheerless as herself, buffeted by an easterly wind so bitter it might have come all the way from Siberia. Her mood darkened further at the sight of Seger and Deek alighting from the adjoining carriage and she retreated into her compartment until they had gone. After waiting ten minutes, she asked a porter to find her a cab and went straight to The Rutland Arms where she took dinner alone in her room. When the waiter came to collect her tray he found her lamb cutlets virtually untouched and the bottle of chianti still two-thirds full.

Connie retired to bed knowing it was going to be a long and sleepless night.

******

Algy had travelled up from London the previous evening and stayed the night at Falmouth House, Archer's red-brick pile on the Fordham Road named in honour of the noble patron he especially admired and respected.

This was Algy's first opportunity to assess Archer's domestic lifestyle. Its cluttered abundance of furnishings was a hallmark of wealth but its lavishness still came as some surprise and helped explain why Archer's finances were so strained. He concluded the upkeep of the house alone had to be enormous and, in addition to temporarily hosting Mrs Coleman and

Captain Bowling, the permanent staff comprised a cook, two housemaids, a nursemaid and a gardener, plus Archer's groom and personal valet Harry Sarjent.

Archer was still in his custom-built Turkish bath when Algy came down to breakfast, which had been laid out in the morning room. Just a couple of coals lay in the grate and the room was too cold to sit and eat breakfast: in part because of that and in part out of sympathy with his host's regime of self-denial, he restricted himself to grapefruit, toast and coffee but he made a mental note to call in at the Rutland Arms for bacon and eggs before racing.

Algy folded his napkin and gazed around the room. Besides the fine oak table at which he sat, the room contained a matching oak bookcase and a piano; on each side of the mantelpiece were photographs of Archer and his formidable rival of old, George Fordham. Every item, however, was overshadowed by two large oil paintings of Archer's parents that graced the walls.

It was while Algy was studying the latter that Archer came in, grey-faced and brushing the last drops of sweat from his face with a towel he proceeded to wrap around his neck and tuck into the top of the heavy, quilted dressing gown he had put on after completing his sweat.

'They're fine likenesses, I like to think,' he said, joining Algy in front of his parents' portraits. 'You've not had chance to look round the house properly, have you?'

'No.'

'I'll go and dress and meet you in the dining room. There are some lovely paintings in there by Harry Hall you'd like. Dutch Oven...Wheel of Fortune.'

The dining room Algy entered was papered in dark green and once again handsomely furnished with a magnificent table that could easily seat a dozen guests. Along one wall was a huge mahogany sideboard that sagged under the combined weight of silver plate and numerous racing trophies in gold and silver.

Archer caught-up with his guest and led him into the drawing room which was guarded by a seven-feet high German long-case clock presented to him as a wedding gift by Count Festetics. For such a huge instrument it was surprisingly quiet. Algy looked at the dial, hummed and drew his hunter to corroborate the time.

'Do you know this clock's fast, Fred? It says 11.54.'

Archer blinked. 'No. It doesn't work.'

'Shame.'

Though smaller than the dining room, the opulence of the drawing room nonetheless made Algy whistle. At one end of the room was a stunning gilt-mounted mirror that stretched from floor to ceiling; facing it at the opposite end was a display cabinet packed with yet more memorabilia from Archer's career. It was surprisingly devoid of equine portraits and dominated by an imposing mantelpiece in variegated black marble inlaid with pink and yellow flowers. On the mantelpiece sat a French ormolu clock that Algy noticed also seemed to be stuck at 11.54. Come to think of it, he thought, nor was the clock in his bedroom working properly.

He took a closer look at the fireplace and surreptitiously rubbed his hands together: despite it being mid October there was no fire lit and the room felt as cold as all the others. It was this omnipresent cold, Algy decided, that was at the root of the mustiness he had detected on arriving the previous evening. It reminded him of the day his father took him to Rumbelow's, the Lincoln undertakers, to view his grandmother's body.

'You must see this,' insisted Archer, motioning toward a large picture of the Prince of Wales hanging above the door. 'His Royal Highness signed it for me!'

Algy studied the engraving minutely and it occurred to him that the man beside him possessed so much yet so little of what he truly craved. But at least these reminiscences seemed to be cheering rather than depressing him, which had not been the case of late.

'I'd just ridden his very first winner on the Flat. Counterpane. The filly's dead now, poor thing.'

Algy sighed inwardely. It seemed that death had got his companion by the throat and would not let go. He wondered how any man with all this, and the love of so many people, could be brought so low.

'FA, you've certainly done yourself proud!' he said, trying to change the subject and offer some cheer. 'I doubt whether we've anything better than this room at Haverholme.'

'I deserve no praise,' said Archer gloomily. 'This is all Nellie's work.'

Algy mentally kicked himself for being so stupid. If he needed any conclusive evidence that death did indeed permeate every square inch of Falmouth House, its owner had just provided it. The place reeked of death: it was eerie; unhealthy; unsettling. It was in the ceiling; in the floor; in the furniture. Everywhere. When he had gone up to bed the previous evening the creaking stairs and the wind moaning through the trees outside had been enough to make even he glance over his shoulder in search of ghouls and spectres. He must persuade Archer to move somewhere else and start afresh before this suffocating atmosphere choked the life out of him.

'Did you see the portrait of father?' said Archer, eyes twinkling at last.

'Yes, I did.'

'They say I follow after my mother in looks and build, but thank God I followed after father when it came to riding!'

Algy swallowed hard and thought even harder, trying to decide whether this was Archer's way of sending him a message.

'It's not many men who can say their father rode the winner of a Grand National!'

'Yes, indeed,' said Algy, somewhat flustered. 'What was the animal again?'

'Little Charley!'

'Of course it was.'

'Fancy you forgetting!'

'Unforgivable!' said Algy, accepting the rebuke graciously even though he had more important matters on his mind than the names of Grand National winners.

'He taught me well, Algy,' said Archer, picking up a small silver-framed photograph of his father and smiling.

'Self-evidently!'

Archer held up the photograph and tapped a finger on his father's face. 'He put me up on a little dun-coloured pony with a black stripe down its back. I named him Chard and if I did not ride as I was told father threw bits of turf at me as I went by and cursed me something awful!'

Algy forced a smile. If he were honest, he envied Archer his sense of belonging and his deep and genuine love for his father.

Archer's smile broadened as a host of childhood memories fought for possession of his tongue. 'Father soon had me winning pony races at the back of The Plough in Prestbury! And hunting over Cotswold stone! I think I was more afraid of him than any horse he or pony he put me on! He always told mother I'd make more out of my riding than I ever would out of book-learning.'

Algy played with the buttons of his waistcoat. At this moment it seemed to him impossible for his host to contemplate ever being the son of any father bar William Archer. He felt jealous: why couldn't William Archer have been his father also?

'Oh, I'm my father's son all right!' Archer volunteered proudly, replacing the photograph.

Algy suddenly felt the need of a drink to release his tongue which was stuck to the roof of his mouth.Was there ever a better time and place to put the question he had long wanted to ask?

TWENTY

Algy prayed he was not about to make the greatest blunder of his life. He could sense his heart pattering faster and faster.

'How well did you know your father?' he asked guardedly.

'Not half so well as my mother.'

Algy tugged an ear and then pinched his eyebrows together.

'I suppose you've heard all the rumours?'

'What rumours?' replied Archer defensively.

Algy hesitated, but having come this far he could not show the white feather now. 'The tittle-tattle about my father…and your mother.'

Archer curled his top lip over his two front teeth and looked away. Of course he had heard the 'tittle-tattle' and he preferred not talk about it, even in the privacy of his own drawing room.

His discomfort communicated itself to Algy, who began shaking his head and wishing he could take back his question.

'I'm so sorry Fred, you've enough on your mind as it is without me making insensitive remarks!' he gabbled, banging a palm against his forehead by way of an exclamation mark.

'No, it's all right, Algy. I heard the rumours long ago. Impossible not to hear them on a racecourse. You know as well as me that there's no finer place for spreading gossip!'

'That's a fact!'

'Anyway, they must have affected you as much as me,' continued Archer, without thinking. He paused, realizing where the conversation must lead but he surprised himself by feeling less disconcerted than he had anticipated. 'It's time we talked about it.'

'I can't deny it, yes they have,' answered a relieved Algy. 'Many's the time I've wanted to broach the matter with you but lost my nerve at the last moment.'

'At Epsom, before I went out to ride Bend Or in the Derby, I suspect?'

Algy went weak-kneed with embarrassment. Had he been that transparent?

'Don't look so surprised!' said Archer. 'I may only be a jockey, who doesn't read fancy books like you do, but I can read a man's heart and mind! There I was, about to risk all by riding in the Derby with one arm useless! And you were worried for my safety. We both knew I could have been killed that day!'

'That's right enough!'

'So, it must have seemed like your last chance to sort things out, clear the air. It was only natural for you to want to know if we were brothers - well, half-brothers - before it was too late.'

'Well, I never...'

Archer cut him off. 'I know that father and me are hardly matched bookends, what with him being so short and squat and me so tall and slim like mother, but she was a striking woman and I obviously take after her.'

Algy stood slack-jawed at Archer's eloquent explanation.

'You know what they always say, the dam is more important than the stallion!'

Algy manufactured another weak smile at Archer's apposite use of the bloodstock breeder's credo. 'Quite so, Fred.'

'I've always admired Lord Belton and he's been very good to me down the years but I think it's just a matter of some of your chums in the newspapers wanting to create a story where there really isn't one.'

'But, Fred, as a journalist, I know this sort of improbable story often does have substance.'

'Not this time, Algy.'

'Are you positive? Has your mother - or your father - never referred to the stories in any way?'

'No, as God's my witness, never.'

'No mention of my father visiting or lodging with you when he was down hunting with the Cotswold or the Beaufort? The merest hint of any liaison?'

'None whatsoever,' replied Archer emphatically.

So that's that, thought Algy, his breath starting to come in gulps. He felt the need to seek refuge at the window but as he crossed the room he could barely muster the will or the strength to put one foot in front of the other and he caught his foot in the carpet. He swore under his breath: he had embarrassed himself and his friend and now he could not even walk straight. It annoyed him just thinking what kind of an idiot he must appear. He looked out into the garden but saw no trees.

'And I've the highest regard for your father. If there was any truth in the story that I was …'

Archer struggled to complete his sentence.

'His son,' Algy volunteered.

'Yes…his son… I'm sure he would have told me - or you - by now.'

Algy snorted loudly. 'I doubt very much whether he'd deign to tell me! We barely exchange words!'

'Still?' replied Archer, who had heard the racecourse rumours. 'That's sad.'

'Yes, it is. One lives in hope but we seem farther apart than ever.'

'I sincerely hope the two of you can patch things up.'

'Thank you, Fred.'

Another uncomfortable silence descended.

'I lost my brother William a few years back,' Archer suddenly exclaimed, 'and I swear on the bible that if I were able to choose a replacement I'd look no further than you.'

Algy grappled with similar emotions. 'My sentiments entirely. I could wish for no finer fellow as a brother.'

The two men hugged each other. At that moment Algy sensed his dream had been finally extinguished. Their embrace had warmth and affection but it felt more like clutching a comfort pillow in bed instead of a loved one. He gently freed himself and diplomatically enquired about the function of the adjoining room.

'Oh, that?' replied Archer vacantly, as if the preceding five minutes had never happened. 'That's the conservatory. We can get into the grounds from there if you like.'

The two men walked through a flourishing kitchen garden and then past a tennis court and some paddocks until they stopped to inspect a carriage house containing a dog-cart, pony trap and a particularly smart brougham. Finally they reached the stables where the head of a chestnut hunter poked out from one of the loose boxes.

'He's an intelligent gleam to his eye,' Algy observed brightly.

'This was Nellie's mount, her pride and joy,' replied Archer haltingly as he stopped to caress the animal's nose and ears. It was obvious to Algy whom he was caressing in his imagination. 'She loved to hunt. Did I ever tell you that I had dressed up in my hunting togs to cheer her up the day she…'

Archer's hand slipped from the horse's muzzle and the sentence remained unfinished. Algy patted him on the shoulder.

'I see you've a hot-house over there,' he said raising his voice with false enthusiasm but genuine sympathy. 'Show me your plants.'

They found the gardener tending to a row of pots containing violets.

Archer ran his fingers beneath the purplish-blue flowers. 'They're beautiful aren't they? They came from Dillistone and Woodthorp's nursery over at Haverhill. They're a new one from France called *Patrie*, bred from the wild violets of the Crimea. It's these red streaks that make them extra special. And they flower every month, you know.'

Algy raised his eyebrows. 'Fred, you sound a proper gardener!'

'No, tis all Nellie's doing…'

'Tomatoes and grapes too, I see,' said Algy quickly.

He helped himself to a grape and, without thinking, offered one to Archer.

'I probably shouldn't.'

'Not one grape! What harm can one grape possibly do you?'

'Algy, I can't afford to eat anything.'

154

'Poppycock! One grape won't hurt!'

Archer folded his arms and gave Algy the kind of penetrating glare brooking no nonsense that he used to get from his housemaster.

'I can assure you just three bits of dry toast and two half-bottles of champagne are the only things to have passed my lips these past 24 hours and I still won't make 8.6 on St Mirin this afternoon.'

Algy buried his hands in his pockets to stop himself from shaking some sense into Archer and merely voiced his dismay. 'Fred this is utter madness!'

Archer persisted regardless. 'I might be able to squeeze 8.7 if I wear nothing under my silks and use my smallest saddle.'

Algy's patience snapped; he grabbed his elbow and led him to the hot-house door.

'Do you not realize how bloody cold it is today?,' he barked. 'Feel that air! You ride with next to no clothing on your back and you're asking - no, begging - for trouble! You'll sweat during the race and the perspiration will have frozen to you by the time you get off St Mirin.'

'But I must ride him!' said Archer even though Algy's anger had frightened him.

'Rubbish!'

The Duchess is counting on me!'

'Ignore her!'

'Impossible! Since she's been up here at Sefton Lodge I get daily re-minders! Her money's down!'

'She can afford it.'

'But so's mine - and I can't!' Archer shouted.

'What does money matter set against your health?'

By now the two men were glaring at each other. Archer studied Algy's wide-footed stance and tensed forearms: he knew Algy would never strike him but he sensed Algy was not going to back down.

'I've never ridden the winner of the Cambridgeshire,' he said after some deliberation. 'If I don't succeed this time I shall never try again.'

'Fred, don't be a blithering idiot! *That* matters even less!'

'It matters to me!'

Archer's head wobbled from side to side and Algy realized this was a discussion in which logic was never going to prevail. It was an argument he was not going to win.

'And you've no obligations to Fenner?' Algy queried softly. 'No bets… or anything else?'

'No! I told you before we went to Dublin that I was having nothing more to do with him – and I meant it.'

Algy sighed. 'I'm really glad to hear that.'

Archer began to speak, then paused. 'Can I be blunt?' he said eventually.

Of course.'

'That article of yours did me no favours.'

'In what sense?' Algy asked in an aggrieved voice. 'The exact opposite was the intention!'

'A lot of people have obligations to Fenner, you know. Some of the names would surprise you. Villiers wasn't alone.'

'You mean Francis Villiers isn't the only member of the Jockey Club so deep in hock that flight to the continent is the only recourse?'

'There are plenty more in debt up to their eyeballs.'

'I should have thought I'd have known!'

Archer heard the air being sucked through Algy's teeth and watched him take a measured pause before levelling the inevitable question

'Fred, why don't you name names? Surely it's time someone did?'

'I can't. It would be more than my life's worth.'

'But you're untouchable!'

Archer permitted himself a thin smile. 'You think so?'

'There's no question!'

'I don't know about that. There are some powerful people mixed up in all this.'

'I appreciate this is a delicate situation,' said Algy adopting a conciliatory tone, 'but I'm sure I could put together a piece for *The Sportsman* that succeeds in exposing this infamy without exposing you personally to any danger.'

Archer adjusted the towel round his neck. He reckoned he had already gone far enough. 'As I've told you before, it's been mentioned to me that it would be in everyone's interest if you let the matter drop.'

Algy thought he detected the look of a wounded, cornered animal in Archer's popping eyes and reluctantly agreed to do just that for the time being. But he refused to back down when it came to the Cambridgeshire.

'I hope you're doing the right thing and all this effort proves worthwhile, because all the touts are adamant that St Mirin can't even be assured of finishing in front of his stablemate.'

'I heard all about that trial he ran with Carlton down at Manton,' chuckled Archer, happy to be back on safer ground.

'I'd have been stunned if you hadn't!'

'I know Carlton won easily but the Duchess's colt only had a boy on him. It'll be different on the racecourse. Carlton's a tricky ride and Woodburn's not very experienced, you know.'

'Edward Somerset is convinced Carlton will confirm the form of the trial and has backed him accordingly,' countered Algy with equal confidence.

'His Lordship is entitled to his opinion. But I intend to win this race. Then I shall take a nice long holiday during the winter.'

'Back to the United States again?'

'No, I'd rather like to see India.'

'Really? Never been myself - although my father was rather keen to send me there indefinitely a few years back!'

Algy laughed heartily but Archer failed to see the joke.

They returned to the house. If only he was setting sail today, Algy thought as he watched Archer swallow a tablespoonful of the 'mixture' before once more seeking refuge in his sweatbox. The previous afternoon he had ridden at 8st 10lb to win the last race. It defied comprehension for him to lose a further four pounds inside 24 hours. Algy did not want to think of the consequences and buried his head in a book.

He resigned himself to losing a brother. But he did not want to lose a friend.

TWENTY-ONE

Upon arriving at the Rowley Mile, Algy watched Archer sit on the check-scales to discover he had lost only three of the four pounds. Both men tried to put on a brave face.

Archer went straight out and won on a two-year-old belonging to the Prince of Wales, who was on hand to congratulate him, but he looked ashen and did not stop to talk with Algy on his way to the weighing room. Even Solomon, who had seen his master don silk on many days when he ought to have been home in bed, felt moved to speak out when Archer discarded the thin woollen singlet he had worn beneath his jacket on the Prince's filly. He fought to stop his teeth chattering, waved aside Solomon's protests and, picking up his lightest saddle, went through to the Clerk of the Scales to weigh-out for the Cambridgeshire. His walk to the chair was watched closely by a crowd of interested onlookers. He sat down, heard the balance click to a halt and Manning announce 'Archer- 8 stone 7 pounds; one pound over', and registered the 'told-you-so' mutterings that followed. He, however, showed no emotion.

Solomon implored Algy to make Archer see reason. Although he could well imagine the wind that howled across the Heath scything his friend's fragile body clean in two, Algy knew he was incapable of changing Archer's mind and told Solomon so. He loitered outside the weighing room wrapped up in the tweed overcoat he had recently purchased from Gieves & Hawkes for the winter jumping season and wished Archer the best of luck when he eventually emerged. The jockey's wrinkled grey skin might have belonged to an elephant were it not turning pale blue at the lips and earlobes; the fingers gripping his saddle were as white as an Alpine snowfield and, Algy thought, likely just as cold. Algy asked how he was feeling: Archer tutted and said he thought Melton was his only worry. Algy began to tell him that was not his meaning but stopped short: he nodded and returned Archer's half-hearted smile. There was nothing he could do to reach his friend now: Archer's mind was in race mode.

Algy climbed the three flights of stairs to the top of the grandstand, went through the tiny wicket gate in the wall ignored by all bar racing journalists, and hauled himself up the iron ladder on the other side that gave access to the roof thankful for the woollen gloves protecting his hands against the stinging temperature of the metal guard-rail. Although the wind tried its damndest to blow him off the ladder, he eventually stepped out onto the roof where the polar conditions were more than compensated by the spectacular view. This was the only vantage point on such a vast flat racecourse like Newmarket that yielded an uninterrupted view of the Cambridgeshire, the start of which lay exactly one mile and 240 yards away, a course dead straight from start to finish.

Monty Blackwell was already on the roof, holding down his hat with one hand while attempting to focus his race-glasses with the other. Algy fastened the top button of his coat and turned up the collar as the wind pricked into his face like a dozen needles. He wished he'd had the foresight to bring a scarf and hat, though he guessed the latter would not have stayed in place long.

Blackwell grimaced and waved his glasses. 'I'm off! It's colder than a polar bear's arse up here today!' he bellowed. 'If it's anything like this down there, poor old Archer will be turning to ice by now!'

Algy was already thinking along similar lines. He stamped his feet in search of warmth and braced his body against the wind to train his glasses on Archer, who was defying the temperatures and going down to post early as usual. He watched him zig-zag from one side of the track to the other and suspected he was assessing where the ground was faster. He hated to think what manner of freezing ordeal his friend was enduring and was grateful to find the conditions prevented him from forming any conclusive visual impression. For once, the market seemed to have no confidence in Archer's judgement: Carlton, carrying just 6st 13lb, was favourite; St Mirin only sixth-best, Algy having invested £900 to win £10,000.

Archer sat hunched over St Mirin's neck, trying to pretend he was warming himself on the hot air snorting from his mount's nostrils. His teeth still chattered like castanets and he could hardly feel the whip in his right hand or his feet in the irons. He stuck the whip under his arm and repeatedly blew on his fingers. One or two jockeys passed the time by teasing him with questions as to where he thought the best ground lay; he ignored them. He would never divulge his tactics and they knew it. But he was gambling on them taking note of his position and following his lead. The starter raised his flag.

Archer pushed and shoved St Mirin straight into the lead along the far-side rail, glad to get his circulation flowing and feel some heat in his limbs. Then he restrained him so that he might look around and gauge what everyone else was doing. He grit his teeth and cursed loudly. He counted a group of four or five horses racing up the near side rail, a dozen yards away to the left of his group.

Algy saw this bunch separate too and it unnerved him as much as it did Archer. Two groups divided by the width of a track as broad as Newmarket could be troublesome. It resulted in two distinct races. A jockey might win the race on his side of the track but lose the race proper to a rival on the other side; even the judge had been known to announce the 'wrong' winner on occasions. This was not a race in which Archer wanted to leave anything to chance. There were only 16 runners and he wanted them to race as one so he might keep each rival under close scrutiny.

Algy's arms cramped as held the glasses steady but what he was able to discern cheered him. Archer had dropped St Mirin into mid-field with the aim of shielding the colt from the worst of the wind. He was being asked to concede weight to every one of his rivals except Melton and every pound carried and every ounce of energy saved might just prove crucial.

After completing threequarters of a mile, Archer no longer felt the biting cold nor remembered his personal problems. His blood was up and he was as contented as any man could be who was riding to stave off financial ruin. His racing brain had taken over. Only the race mattered now, and it was a race to be won like any other. He pushed St Mirin into the front rank alongside his stablemate Carlton. He noted young Woodburn's arms pumping furiously and knew he had the favourite beaten. He glanced to his left for dangers. Which jockeys were sitting still? Which were rowing away?

Archer saw the brown jacket carried by Arundel leading a group of three that had drifted into the centre of the course. They were also toiling. Archer dug his heels into St Mirin's belly: he felt the reflex he wanted. The Duchess's colt jolted like a departing express train and sped clear. Archer's body temperature rose along with his spirits: he was going to do it.

Archer growled and kicked. He reminded himself not to break either of the cardinal rules of jockeyship in a situation like this: don't look round; don't celebrate victory prematurely. Had he broken the second commandment he might have visualized the happy expression on the Duchess's face as he came back victorious and the miserable faces worn by bookmakers who now owed him; imagined refreshing bubbles of vintage Krug going up his nose as he sat in front of a blazing log fire; and even tasted a slice or two of his favourite Wiltshire-cured ham.

Up on the grandstand roof Algy began to bounce up and down: against all the odds, it seemed Archer's sacrifices were going to pay off. He saw Carlton and Melton giving chase but neither was making any impression on St Mirin. If anything, St Mirin's advantage seemed to be growing. Algy put down his glasses, now unnecessary as the leaders entered the final furlong.

Then he groaned and punched the air with his glasses. Now able to appreciate the whole picture, he could plainly see that one horse was reducing the deficit. The 22-1 long-shot Sailor Prince, coming up the near side rail, was gaining ground - fast. He yelled a warning to Archer.

Archer, as Algy knew all too well, could not hear his plaintive cry: nor could he see the challenger because Sailor Prince was obscured by the group in the centre. But he did hear the crowd roaring. His body tensed. He instantly identified the high-pitched racket for what it was: a unique racecourse message. It denoted a fast-finishing horse getting to the leader.

He glimpsed a flash of violet silk far away to his left. He raised his whip and lashed St Mirin like Bligh's bosun applying the cat o' nine-tails. Something immediately felt wrong: his arm flapped as if its tendons had just been slashed. He tried to kick St Mirin in the belly but his boots seemed empty. He grimaced for this had happened to him once before: lactic acid was flooding his muscles and corroding their strength. Pretty soon they would cramp and lock completely. He started to panic. This could not be happening to him. He felt as deathly cold as the day Nellie died. Once more he was reduced to the power of prayer.

Algy tumbled down the ladder with no thought for his safety and barged his way through the milling crowds, fearful of Archer's reaction should the judge's verdict go against him. His first brief glimpse of Archer did not auger well for he was swaying in the saddle and in danger of falling off St Mirin. He eventually slid off the animal's back and lent against its flanks as Alec Taylor undid the girths and removed the saddle.

Archer raised his head in search of the Duchess. She stood impassively amid the plumes of steam drifting off St Mirin, waving away the routine mix of post-race congratulations and commiserations that carried more style than substance. At her elbow was the dark figure of Seger, black-hatted, black-coated and black-jowled.

Archer mumbled a few words to her that Algy could not make out but she had none for him in return. She merely wrinkled her nose as if she had the stench of a Holy Land gutter in her nostrils. In fact, she had pre-empted the judge's verdict: St Mirin had been caught, which meant it was her jockey's one pound overweight that had made the paper-thin difference between victory and defeat; and the vast difference between landing a massive coup and sustaining a huge loss.

Archer saw no sympathy in her mortuary eyes, only the sin of letting let her down. He took the saddle from Taylor and went to weigh-in.

'Here, give me that,' said Algy, appearing at his side. 'You're all-in!'

'Do you think I held on?' he managed to say between gasps.

'Save you breath, Fred! There's nothing you can do about it now.'

'I think I may have just won,' he wheezed before sneezing so violently that Algy had to hold him upright.

Algy removed his coat and wrapped it around Archer's shoulders. 'Make way there, please. Stand back!' he shouted, shepherding Archer through the crowd. 'Can't you see the man's exhausted. Give him some room!'

Archer's head began to roll and his efforts to speak disintegrated into fits of coughing.

'It was that pound overweight that made the difference!' he croaked. 'It's all my fault!'

'Who knows? Let's just get you inside before you die of exposure.'

'I hadn't the strength to lift him home!'

Sweat pockmarked Archer's blue skin like hoar frost and Algy could feel his body shaking even though it seemed to him as if he was walking alongside a furnace.

They reached the weighing room just as the result was being announced: Sailor Prince by a head.

Archer's chin dropped onto his chest, saliva and phlegm congealing on his scarlet silks. His breath came in short gasps and he seemed to be shrinking right in front of Algy's eyes. There was nothing he could do to ease Archer's suffering. He knew how he must be feeling because his own chest was tighter than a drumskin. At times like this solitude became your only ally. Algy could not bring himself to linger on such a pitiful sight and stumbled away.

Solomon begged Archer to take a sip of hot sweet tea. He tried but it only made him nauseous. His limbs felt as if they had been racked and his head thumped from the disturbing truths that were crashing around inside his skull like so many marching bands. It had all been for nothing. He had failed the Duchess. She had lost her money. His friends had lost their money. He was deeper in debt.

Paranoia was neither a word Archer would use freely nor a concept with which he was especially familiar. But as he sat with his head in his hands seeking the strength to go out for his next ride he did think the world was closing in on him. And he reckoned he was running out of options.

TWENTY-TWO

Connie also departed the Rowley Mile feeling wretched and resigned to facing up to the consequences of her own actions alone.

She had remained incognito by watching the Cambridgeshire from the Silver Ring instead of the Grandstand and had screamed with unladylike ardour as St Mirin passed her in the lead. The judge's verdict caused her to scream just as loud and her cheeks still showed evidence of tear stains when she caught the late train back to London. At Liverpool Street she took a hansom for Mays Court: this, she decided, was her penance.

She soon began shuffling in her seat as she wrestled with her problems and, although the process was not without some lip-biting and head-tossing, she finally prioritized them and reached a decision. Running away from them was no longer an option. The solution was obvious. It would be awkward but she had no choice. It must be implemented.

The cab had got no further than jolting down Cheapside before she had regained her poise. She tapped twice on the roof and instructed the cabbie to forget about Mays Court and take her to the Cafe Royal.

Connie sat back and began patting her hair in anticipation of the attention her arrival would engender.

******

Archer put back the three pounds within 24 hours but the damage was irreversible. He was coming down with a very heavy cold and constantly snapped at Bowling and his sister whenever they suggested he confine himself to bed. Instead, he roamed the house or the garden talking to himself, asking himself how he could have lost the Cambridgeshire and how he was going to recover his losses. The answers he came up with only made him bang a fist to his forehead. He pleaded with Nellie to help him find the answer.

Ill or not, he was determined to get through the remaining three days of the Houghton meeting because he had a hatful of fancied rides. Algy watched him win the opening race on Wednesday's card and was shaking his head in awe when he felt a dig in the ribs.

'I see your man has been up to his old tricks!' Seger drawled, top lip dripping with contempt.

'Seger, what are you prattling about now?'

'Common knowledge!' he said sniffing the pink carnation in his lapel. ' It's all round the racecourse! Everyone's talking about it!

'Whatever it is, it's passed me by.'

Seger took out a handkerchief that matched his button-hole and caressed each nostril in turn. 'That, I must say, would be a surprise, given that the pair of you are as thick as *thieves*!'

Algy's fists clenched as he felt, the bitter taste of bile beginning to clog his throat.

'Edward Somerset is putting it about that Archer paid young Woodburn to ride Carlton a loser!' continued Seger with the arrogance of someone confident such a public place assured his safety.

'That's utter drivel!' Algy replied peevishly. 'There was no need! Carlton's not in St Mirin's class even at those weights!'

'Well, you know what they say, and they *are* saying it, there's no smoke without fire!'

'Rubbish! And I have Fred's word on it!'

Seger's nose twisted as if he had inadvertently wandered into a pig sty.

'You'd take the word of a jockey!' he snorted. 'I thought you possessed more insight, Haymer. Jumped-up johnnies with brains no bigger than their bodies! Can't be trusted! They'll tell you one thing and then do another! Not one of them is worth a button if truth be told!'

Algy squared up to him. 'Some, perhaps! But not Fred Archer!'

Seger, to Algy's surprise, stood his ground: chest puffed out, chin jutting forward, dark skin stretched to breaking point across his jowls, mouth rotating as though crammed with fighting words. Algy had never seen him so animated.

'Archer's probity is so assured if you must know,' Algy continued, voice rising in response, 'that there have even been attempts on his life by the scum behind this so-called Jockeys Ring!'

'Death would be too good for the man!' Seger spat back like a cobra. 'I've found him to be little more than a crook! Devious and self-serving! A living disgrace is what he really deserves!'

Algy grabbed Seger's lapels and lifted him clean off the ground.

'I'd be careful what you do in public, Haymer,' said a suprisingly calm Seger. 'You surely don't wish to draw attention to yourself - or Archer.'

Algy knew he was correct, relaxed his grip and Seger's heels slowly sank back into the turf alongside the crumpled carnation dislodged from his lapel. 'What are you driving at?'

'I suppose because that's the precisely the kind of defensive kneejerk one has come to expect from you whenever Archer's reputation is impugned.'

Seger slowly ran the tip of his tongue along the underside of his moustache, stealing every possible second to relish what he was about to say.

'Haymer, I've never taken you for a fool but surely you're not telling me that you're the only man on this racecourse who isn't aware that you and he are brothers!'

Words that in any other context would have filled Algy with joy now made him blush.

'Or should I say half-brothers?'

Algy could not decide whether to hit Seger or walk away. Instead he did neither. If Seger had proof, he wanted to hear it.

'It's as well you don't live in Gloucestershire! No-one within ten miles of Prestbury disputes it for one moment! Everyone knows you father had the sexual appetite and morals of a goat!'

Seger felt a cuff-link cut into skin as Algy squeezed his wrist and frogmarched him away from the paddock toward the saddling boxes.

'Look here, Haymer...'

'Shut up, Seger! I'm not going to hurt you, though God knows I'm tempted,' hissed Algy. 'Let's talk over here where we won't be disturbed.'

Algy backed Seger against a wall. 'Let's hear what you've got to say! And for your own sake I hope you are not going to waste my time.'

'Look,' replied Seger in the act of looking about for assistance should he need it, 'remind yourself when Archer was born...'

'January 1857.'

'That's correct. And did your father not have a penchant for hunting with the Cotswold in the '50s?'

'Yes, you damn well know he did. Everybody does! He went down every year until he broke his leg in '59 and could no longer sit a horse.'

Seger drew a deep breath and hoped we would not have to use it calling for help because he was beginning to enjoy himself.

'Well, so did my mother,' he continued deliberately. 'She told me how she often saw your father in the King's Arms in Prestbury of an evening - but seldom any other.'

'So what?'

'And who owned that inn? Emma Archer's parents, that's who.'

'Everyone knows that too!' said Algy, jabbing Seger in the chest. 'Get to the point!'

Seger noted the anxiety beginning to pinch Algy's handsome features. He began to feel safer, and even rather excited: both at the thought of the power he was exerting over a man whom he had always feared and the revenge he was taking against the son of the man who had seduced his mother and then ditched her for Emma Archer. Her subsequent plunge into chronic alcoholism had never failed to remind him - the slurred speech, the slovenliness and unacceptable rudeness to old friends, the sheer ugliness of a woman out of love with life - of the vow he had made and repeated to himself on every one of those lonely, tearfuyl nights in his Uppingham bed like an avenger's mantra: to make the entire Belton family suffer for what they had done to his own.

Now he had it within his power to toy with the emotions of the Belton he despised for coming between himself and the woman he craved. The very thought of these contaminated seeds he was planting in his rival's brain eventually germinating to devastating effect brought a genuine smile to his face and a renewed swell to his chest.

Seger flattened the ends of his moustache with thumb and forefinger and prepared to conclude his case with the practised panache of an Attorney General.

'My mother saw her and your father together throughout Easter 1856, huddled together in one of the little alcoves in the old smoke-room upstairs,' he said with a sage-like nod of the head. 'That's roughly nine months before...'

'Yes, I see what you're getting at!'

'Ask yourself this. Does Archer look anything like William Archer? No, he most certainly does not!'

'He follows after his mother...tall, dark,' Algy spluttered.

'You may think that but not many people in Prestbury agree with you!'

Algy did not want to think that at all. He felt totally elated. Yes, the evidence was circumstantial but there were eye witnesses of sorts, enough to convince him to visit Prestbury and delve deeper. And quite possibly enough to persuade him to interrogate one other.

Had the bearer of this information not been Seger he might have given him a hug. As it was, he glowered at him and stood aside so that he might leave.

Seger smirked, touched his top-hat with his silver-embossed cane and walked away. He sensed that his revelatory card could not have been played to finer effect. The farther he walked, the cheerier he felt.

The altercation left Algy tingling. He felt fired-up. He jauntily strode off, whistling as he went. There was someone he wanted to speak with.

******

Algy knew where to find him. He walked into the cramped subterranean bar beneath the Grandstand and immediately caught a whiff of him.

'I'd like a quiet word with you if I may,' he said to his father.

Lord Belton eyed him suspiciously and apologized to his drinking cronies for his son's interruption. 'If you must,' he replied having assured himself there was no aggression in his son's demeanour. 'So long as you are brief.'

Algy led him to a dark corner of the bar. 'I want to talk about Archer...'

'That scoundrel! Just cost me a packet...'

'No! Listen!' Algy interjected. 'You asked me to be brief and I shall.'

Lord Belton placed his champagne flute on the bar and answered his son's glare with one of his own. 'Very well.'

'Is there any chance that he might be your son?'

Algy felt a rush of air fill his lungs as the words tumbled forth. He no longer cared how his father responded. He was prepared to cope with fists or words. He waited patiently, betraying no flicker of emotion.

His father's mouth rotated slowly as if it were chewing a particularly gristly piece of meat.

'A simple question,' said Algy. 'A simple one-word answer will do.'

'You damned impertinent...'

Algy's raised eyebrows were sufficient to make Lord Belton swallow the remainder of his sentence. He looked around to check if he had attracted any attention and lowered his voice.

'Absolutely not.'

'So the people of Prestbury are mistaken?'

'Pack of liars!'

'You never drank at the King's Arms? Never spent evenings in Emma Archer's company?'

'Of course I drank at the King's Arms - we all did when we were hunting in that part of Gloucestershire...'

'But never alone with Emma Archer?' Algy persisted.

Lord Belton straightened his back and contemplated for a moment the significance of what he felt he was obliged to say. He knew he had been ambushed but he thought he had regrouped and he knew he was an accomplished liar.

'Don't you think I'd acknowledge a son like Archer if he were mine? Why, I'd be proud to call him my son!'

Algy's face broke into a slow smile.

Lord Belton gathered the remnants of his essence and his upper lip twisted until it almost touched his nose. 'Far better a bastard like him than a wastrel like you!'

'Thank you, father,' said Algy softly. 'That's all I wanted to know.'

Algy turned and walked away, the smile on his face growing broader with each step. He reckoned he knew when his father was lying.

******

One man who had rejoiced in St Mirin's defeat was Mo Fenner: it also reminded him there was some unfinished business to attend to.

Unlike the news from Newmarket, the news from Ireland had been less welcome. Mort's telegram from Dublin, full of excuses, merely re-inforced what he had read in *The Sportsman*: namely that Archer's Irish excursion had been a resounding success both on and off the racecourse. He had wanted to read details of some unfortunate accident on the boat that had left Mister Archer injured or crippled.

Fenner downed the last of his porter and eggs and shouted for Arnull. After instructing him to arrange for Mort to meet 'a little accident', he sat back to ponder Archer's fate as Percy vaulted into his lap, coat now exhibiting a healthy sheen. The cat began purring as Fenner toyed with its leather collar, bearing a suitably inscribed gold disc, as he ruminated. In truth, he had already made up his mind what to do. And had taken immense pleasure in the process.

'Would you agree, Cocky,' said Fenner through pursed lips, 'that Mister Archer, for whatever reason, doesn't seem to care what happens to 'im?'

Arnull's features contracted as he gave the rhetorical question some thought before replying in the manner expected of him. 'I reckon so.'

'So, what shall we do about 'im, then? 'Im, an' 'is shadow, 'Aymer?'

Arnull's blank expression suggested this was a more taxing question but, eventually, he was more than equal to it.

'There's only one course of action left,' he ventured cautiously.

'Which is?'

'If we can't hurt Archer' Arnull said, growing more confident, 'it could be "The Policy" is the only thing that'll work?'

Fenner creaked in his chair. 'Good lad, Cocky! I'm pleased to see you've learnt somethin' these past few years!'

Arnull also relaxed. Praise from his boss came rarely.

'Now, what do you suggest?' continued Fenner. 'Who is there?'

More rhetorical questions for Arnull to recognize.

'There's 'is mother an' father, an' 'is sister, that Mrs Coleman,' he replied.

'Wrong!' shouted Fenner, sunny disposition vanishing. His eyes narrowed to slits beneath the gnarled brows, squeezing a trickle from the rheumy one that demanded immediate attention. He stopped stroking Percy and dropped him on the floor.

'That cat'll be lickin' its ears before you can think straight!' he ranted, hammering the table. 'I want Archer in a livin' hell! An' you talk of mothers...an' fathers... an'sisters!'

Arnull's moon-face began to grey. 'Sorry, boss, I wasn't thinkin' straight.'

'No, Cocky! You weren't thinkin' at all!'

'Yes, boss.'

Fenner regained self-control, dabbed his eye one last time and placed his palms on the table in front of him.

'Who does 'e live for?' he said calmly. 'Not 'is father or 'is mother or 'is sister. Who is the most precious person in 'is life these days?'

Fenner waited. 'Well!'

Arnull's lips began to move, and then stopped. Perhaps he had misunderstood. What he thought his boss was proposing might be taking things a bit too far.

'Come on! Spit it out!'

'You mean...'

'Yes?'

'...the little kiddie, 'is daughter?'

Fenner folded his arms. 'There, knew you'd work it out eventually. Now get away with you an' see it's carried out! An' no slip-ups or you'll wind up like Mort!'

'Yes, Mister Fenner.'

Even as he had given Arnull the order, Fenner was joyfully envisaging the agonies he had condemned Archer to suffer. To Archer it would, he assured himself, be akin to losing every race by a short head. He smiled as Percy jumped back into his lap and poured himself another glass of porter.

'Boss...' Arnull had returned.

Fenner reluctantly put down his tankard. 'I thought I told you to sort out "The Policy"?'

'Yes, boss, but there's some 'oity-toity woman at the door askin' to see you.'

Fenner turned up his nose. He was baffled. He was not expecting anyone answering to that description.

'Is that right? Well, a mug is born every minute an' it's lucky for me some of 'em live!' he chortled. 'What's 'er name?'

'Says she's Lady Constanza Swynford.'

TWENTY-THREE

Around the same time as Silas Mort's right arm was being shattered by one swing of a stonemason's mallet, Algy and Archer left Falmouth House for Newmarket Station. Despite his deteriorating health, Archer had ridden 11 winners during the in the course of the previous week yet they meant nothing compared to the defeat of St Mirin. He determined to fulfill his forthcoming obligations at Brighton and Lewes, and nothing Algy said could dissuade him. It seemed as if he had lost the mental capacity to think straight.

Accordingly, they were catching the Monday morning train out of Newmarket for the long journey via Cambridge, Liverpool Street and Victoria to the south coast where they would put up at the Albion Hotel in Brighton. As their departure coincided with Nellie Rose's morning outing in her perambulator, Mrs Coleman set off ahead of their carriage so that father and daughter might say their goodbyes at the station.

The little girl squealed when she spied her father and toddled over to clasp his leg. Archer stooped to stroke the curls poking out from beneath Nellie's woollen cap while she set about untying his bootlaces, the only sure way she knew of keeping him at home. Algy afforded them some privacy by walking to the edge of the platform. But he could not help overhearing.

'Be a good girl for your Aunt Emily, and remember, daddy loves you more than anything in the world and he will be thinking of you all the time he's away,' Archer said, dropping onto his knees and kissing the child on both cheeks. 'Now, give daddy a kiss.'

The girl puckered her lips and planted a sloppy wet kiss on her father's mouth. Archer stood up and led Nellie Rose back to her aunt. Then he went to join Algy but kept looking over his shoulder and waggling his fingers just to make her giggle and cry out 'Da-da.' He watched the tiny body bubbling with laughter and imagined her bouncy curls tickling his skin as she snuggled her head under his chin at bed-time, an infant's scent of milky breath, warm soap and fresh linen filling his senses. He tried to swallow his emotion by yawning but his chest began heaving uncontrollably with the heartache of being parted from this tiny incarnation of his beloved wife.

Tears glistened in Archer's eyes when he and Algy took their seats in a first-class compartment. Algy had hoped their journey would provide him with the opportunity to divulge the essence of his conversation with Lord Belton but one glance at Archer slumped lifelessly in the corner seat, cheek smudging the window, told him that any discussion would have to wait for another day.

Algy chewed his lip and immersed himself in a pocket edition of Tennyson poems.

✱✱✱✱✱✱

Archer's sister sat her niece in the shiny black coach-built Hutchings perambulator and began the push back to Falmouth House.

Emily Coleman's thoughts, like Algy's, were dominated by consideration of her brother's health and well-being. She knew him better than anyone alive and she could not recall him ever being so wretched and dispirited. What with his recent physical decline and the harrowing prospect of the second anniversary of Helen Rose's death to negotiate in two weeks time, she wished he had curtailed his season and gone on the projected holiday to India where sunshine and relaxation offered hope of reinvigoration.

On reaching the top of the High Street, she crossed the Moulton Road to show Nellie the horses exercising on Long Hill, which stretched away to the Bury Road. She knew third lot would be out, mostly slow-maturing two-year-olds who had not yet seen racecourse action. Knowing how skittish these youngsters could be, however, she deliberately kept a good 50 yards between them and her niece. She pulled down the canopy of the perambulator so the child might enjoy a better view and pointed out the horses belonging to her uncle George.

George Dawson's string of unraced juveniles were filing out of Heath House in readiness for solo half-speed canters up Long Hill as part of their gradual education. There were around a dozen of them, mostly bays with a couple of chestnuts and one grey, the colts at the front of the line and the smaller, flightier fillies at the rear. They were all well rugged-up against the cold of a November morning in their Heath House brown and orange livery that sported a GD in the bottom corner; their partners were equally smart in regulation kit of brown boots, jodhpurs, jerkins and flat caps.

All that is except the dark brown horse who had detached himself from the rest of the string, or so it seemed to Emily Coleman when she first noticed him. Horse and rider stood out, she thought: while those in front merely jig-jogged with excitement as their turn to canter approached, this particular animal grew increasingly fractious - a waywardness which his conspicuously scruffy rider seemed unable or unwilling to correct.

Suddenly, for no reason Coleman could fathom, she saw the horse break ranks completely and gallop headlong in their direction.

Coleman took a firm grip of the handle and frantically tried to turn in a tight circle to evade the runaway. The wheel locked. With its one front wheel making steering one of its lesser attributes, the Hutchings was notoriously unwieldy under pressure and even more so on wet November grass. The more she pushed and pulled, the more it stuck in the turf and appeared likely to tip over.

The frightened Nellie Rose began to scream as the galloping hooves rumbled louder and louder like an approaching thunderstorm. Coleman looked up to see the horse just a dozen strides away, its rider making a bee-line for them, his tight-lipped expression stating he had no intention of taking evasive action. She scooped up the terrified Nellie Rose and shielded the infant with her body, prepared to take the full brunt of the impact.

Then the horse dug in its toes and reared up onto its hind legs, whinnying and snorting at the punishment it was receiving from spur and whip. Its rider continued to shout and urge the animal forward. Again and again he drove his spurs into the horse's belly, drawing jets of blood. Once more the enraged beast reared, squealed and pawed the ground, its neck now lathered in sweat, saliva spraying off the bit being pulled farther and farther up into its gaping mouth. But it refused to budge another inch.

Above the screams of her niece, Mrs Coleman pleaded for their lives. She tried to run but she felt hollow-legged and too faint to move. One rider metamorphosed into two and she heard them both laugh. Then, as she collapsed on the ground, the rider wheeled the horse around and galloped away at full tilt up Long Hill.

All this had occupied barely half a minute. By the time George Dawson rushed to their aid the mysterious horseman had disappeared from view.

'Good God! Are you all right Emily?' he shouted. 'Is Nellie Rose hurt?'

'We're unharmed!' she replied haltingly as Dawson helped her to her feet. 'What was he doing!'

'He must have been crazy! I'll find out who he was! I'll get to the bottom of this, don't you worry about that!'

Coleman grabbed his wrist. 'Please, George, whatever you do, please don't tell Fred about it.'

'He must be told!'

'He has enough worries. I don't think he can cope with much more!'

Dawson breathed deeply and then nodded. He knew she was right.

******

Nellie Rose's good fortune on Long Hill was not shared by her father on the south coast. He failed to partner a single winner at the Brighton fixture. All he achieved on the wind-battered Sussex Downs was to invite his fever to strengthen its hold and on returning to the Albion Hotel on the Wednesday evening he informed Algy he was taking straight to his bed.

To his surprise, Archer found his room in complete darkness. He had expected the curtains to be drawn but through some oversight the gas-lamps had not been turned up; what light there was came from the fire in the grate which showed signs of being damped down rather than banked-up for the evening. He felt for the knob on the lamp nearest the fireplace and after some fiddling managed to increase the flame.

Archer shrieked. As the yellow flame gradually filled the bowl, he thought he saw a ghost sitting in the armchair by the window.

'Why, Mister Archer, yer back at last!' said the pale-faced occupant of the chair.

Archer lent on the corner of the table and peered into the semi-darkness. 'Who are you?' he said huskily, wondering whether he had wandered into the wrong room.

'My name don't matter!' the intruder barked.

'But what are you doing here?'

'Now, sit or stand, it don't matter to me, but not another peep. Just keep yer mouth shut an' listen.'

Archer's flopped into the chair opposite like an injured bird looking for a safe place to roost.

'That's good. Make yerself comf'table.'

The intruder waited a moment or two for the fear of the unknown to begin working. 'Mister Fenner wonders what you thought about the little kiddie's accident t'other day?'

'God! No!' sobbed Archer, gripping the arms of his chair. 'What accident? Is Nellie all right?'

'Stop babblin' like a baby! I thought I told yer to keep shtumm!'

In the half-light Archer's eyes were reduced to looking like two large wet saucers. Behind them, his brain was whirling faster than a ship's propeller but to far less purpose. He must return to Newmarket right away.

'So you 'aven't 'eard then?'

The only sound was the squeak of cloth against leather as Archer fidgeted.

'Well, I'd better tell yer. She was out for a nice walk in that posh new baby carriage of 'ers when I'll be damned if she didn't nearly get'erself run down by a runaway 'orse!'

Archer pitched forward, panting like a snared rabbit. All he could think of was that if anything had happened to little Nellie he may as well be dead. And he would see to it himself if he had to.

Some seconds elapsed before he managed to ask whether she was safe.

His torturer grinned maniacally. He enjoyed his work and it was his job to make Archer suffer. Mister Fenner would not want it otherwise.

'Please God, don't say something has happened to my little Nellie?'

'The 'orse missed 'er! Lucky, were'n it? Thought they might 'o told yer.'

'Thank God!' cried Archer, clasping his hands together in prayer.

'They prob'ly thought it best not to worry you, what with things goin' badly this week. Got beat on 'ow many favourites this meetin'? Four ain't it?'

Archer sobbed into a handkerchief. All he wanted to do was see his daughter and hug her.

'On t' other 'and, it might not 'ave been the grace o' God that caused the 'orse to miss 'er. That 'orse could have missed 'er by the grace o' Mister Fenner.'

Archer looked up: his moist eyes and quivering lips indicated that he did.

His visitor rose from his seat and advanced toward him. He bent down and placed his forefinger under Archer's chin, slowly raising it until Archer's watery eyes were level with his own.

'Now this is what's goin' to 'appen,' he said, nastiness dripping from him like saliva. 'Yer havin' a bad run. Anyone can see that! Some people reckon yer've gone for the season. Couldn't even ride the winner of a one-'orse race!'

He giggled at his humorous aside even though it was hardly original.

'Now yer got two rides t'morrow at Lewes. Correct?'

Archer was right under his nose but could only see Nellie Rose.

'Pay a-ten-shun, *Mister Archer*!'

'Yes.'

'Yer ride two horses t'morrow! Right?'

'Yes,' replied Archer, 'Luctretius and Tommy Tittlemouse.'

'Well, Mister Fenner reckons there'll be plenty o' money on horses to beat 'em. So, *Mister Archer*, yer a clever fellow! Worked it out yet?'

Archer blinked.

'That's right! Mister Fenner's goin' to back those nags to win! So, yer'd better win.'

Archer shook his head violently as the reality of his situation struck him with the force of a revolving door.

'Be sensible!' he said. 'No one can guarantee a winner! You might be able to guarantee a loser but not a winner! Anything could happen!'

'Well, yer'll just 'ave to see that nothin' does happen! They're goin'to win! Or else another little accident might befall yer precious kiddie that turns out a bit more serious.'

'No, please no!' Archer had dropped to his knees.

'Well, Mister Fenner would like you to know that the matter is in yer own 'ands. Get the picture?'

'Yes, I think I do.'

'See as you 'ave. Mister Fenner don't want any mistakes!'

Archer began to mumble, wishing he was dead so there would be no more decisions to make.

'What's that yer sayin'?' Arnull asked. 'I can't hear! Now, whisper in me ear.'

Arnull leant over Archer, placed his ear to Archer's mouth and nodded as the jockey muttered a few hesitant words.

'I see,' he said, standing up again. 'Right you are, then. I'll be off. Mister Fenner likes to 'ear good news as soon as possible.'

With that Cocky Arnull slid up the window and climbed out the way he had come in by demonstrating all the nimbleness of the thieving little snakesman he once was.

His news would not make an happorth of difference to his boss who wasn't bothered whether Archer won the races or not. His money was staying in his pocket. He just wanted to make Archer squirm.

Archer watched Arnull go and then rushed across to lock the window. He lent against the window frame trembling like the last leaf on a branch: alone, exposed and vulnerable to the slightest disturbance.

******

Algy took one look at Archer's unsteady gait on Thursday morning and shook his head.

'Fred, that's it! You can't possibly ride today! There's not an ounce of strength in you!'

'I'm fine...I've taken a walk...'

'You've been out walking! In your condition?'

'I had some business to conduct in the town.'

Algy was not listening and raged on regardless. 'You can't possibly ride today...'

'I must ride today. I must!'

'Why?'

'Don't ask me to explain. I have my reasons but I can't tell you.'

'Let me fetch a doctor?' Algy pleaded. 'Perhaps he can hammer some sense into you!'

'No!' replied Archer in a voice loud enough to attract the attention of other residents sat in the Albion's lounge. 'I don't want to see any doctor and should one come I shall refuse to see him! Is that clear?'

Algy thrust his thumbs into his waistcoat pockets and shrugged. He was startled by Archer's vehemence for despite being palpably too weak to blow out a candle, he appeared full of fight. Enough to fight his own corner perhaps.

'Because you know he'll sign you off!' Algy eventually responded, throwing his newspaper on the floor.

'No doctor, do you hear!'

'All right, FA,' said Algy, angrily. 'If you say so.'

For the first time, Algy was sorely tempted to let Archer sort out his own problems. Archer's anguish was becoming contagious. All this continual aggravation was making him edgy and he was starting to wonder how much more of it he could absorb before he said things he knew would be as instantly regretted.

Archer brooded throughout the journey to Lewes, snuffling under a scarf and heavy overcoat, the sweat dripping from his brow. Normally such sweating, however uncomfortable, would have been something worth celebrating. On this occasion, he sat motionless and speechless. His thoughts were preoccupied with what he must do. It made him feel sick with self-loathing but he had no choice.

Once he reached the track, Archer excused himself and Algy observed him having a separate word with the riders of Ludlow and Indian Star, the only opponents that might feasibly beat Lucretius and Tommy Tittlemouse. Archer said little but whatever the words both jockeys listened to them grim-faced before shaking their heads.

Ludlow trounced Lucretius by six or more lengths and Algy returned to the weighing room to find Archer lying down on a bench with a towel over his face.

'Please stop this now, Fred!' he begged. 'Before you kill yourself!'

'No, I'll be all right!' Archer replied to the familiar voice.

'Good God, Fred! I've never seen you lying down between races! You can't possibly ride in the next!'

'I can and I will.'

'You're not right! It wouldn't surprise me if you were to fall off him before you got to the start!'

'My mind is made up! I shall ride!' Archer said angrily, removing the towel and sitting up. 'It's only a five furlong sprint. He'll not need much pushing - and he'll win!'

Algy walked out behind Archer ready to catch him in an emergency. He legged him up onto Tommy Tittlemouse wondering what was going on inside Archer's head. Had he known, Algy would never have permitted him to leave the paddock.

Too much was going on and too little of it made any sense to Archer. He allowed the horse to find its own way out onto the track while he sat virtually comatose in the saddle and eventually faced the starter with his thoughts not on winning a race but preserving his sanity. He felt like a dead man riding.

Indian Star beat Tommy Tittlemouse out of sight with Archer giving his mount as little assistance as he had Lucretius. Archer almost fell into Algy's arms when he dismounted and told him to cancel his rides for the rest of the week and accompany him back to Newmarket.

On the train back to London, the worry lines on Archer's face looked like they had been cut with a knife. Apart from that one brief request to Algy, he had not uttered a single word since sliding off Tommy Tittlemouse. His limbs felt like lead weights and he shivered and sweated alternately but he could not sleep. His mind would not allow it. He must think of a solution by the time he reached home or it might be too late.

At Liverpool Street, Algy persuaded him to sip a basin of arrowroot containing a tot of brandy which enabled him to sleep during the onward journey and he awoke as the train slowed entering Cambridge, pronouncing himself much better. Algy did not believe him: he was slurring his words and swaying against the rhythm of the train.

Before the train finally juddered to a halt Archer reached into his breast pocket and fumbled for a piece of paper which he eventually pressed into Algy's hand.

'Algy, take this.'

'What's this?' replied Algy, unfolding it.

It was a cheque. A blank cheque.

'What's this for?' he said, totally bemused.

'Thank you for all that you've done these past months.'

'But there's absolutely no need!' said Algy, getting to his feet and staring out of the window, not so much grateful as offended by the gesture. 'We're...'

He knew the term he wanted to use but felt as if some unseen hand had tied his tongue down. He cursed God for being so obstructive: how could he risk adding to Archer's agony now?

'We're...friends!' he blurted out. 'You don't have to pay me!'

'Even so, it would give me pleasure.'

'Well, if that's the case, then of course I shall accept it.'

Algy refolded the cheque and put it in his pocket, though he had no intention of filling it in let alone cashing it.

When they reached Falmouth House, Archer was put straight to bed. The following morning his condition had deteriorated further. He was feverish and restless to the point of delirium. Doctor Wright was called. The symptoms had worsened by the afternoon and Wright was sufficiently alarmed to seek a second opinion and summoned Doctor Latham from Cambridge. Latham came out on the Saturday and at 6pm the two medics signed and released a bulletin: 'Mr F Archer has returned home suffering from the effects of a severe chill followed by high fever.'

The bulletin told only half the story.

TWENTY-FOUR

'Brusher,' Captain Bowling called up the stairs, 'It's Lady Swynford to see you.'

Algy dropped the book he was reading, checked Archer was still sleeping soundly and hurried downstairs into Falmouth House's drawing room to find Connie in such a state of high excitement that she almost jumped into his arms.

'Algy, you must come down to The Greyhound tonight!' she babbled, cheeks flushed, thrusting a hand-bill under his nose.

'Well, it's good to see you, Connie,' he said, eyes shining. 'Someone said they'd seen you the other week but I told them they must be mistaken because you were in Venice.'

Connie flicked a lock of his hair back into place and paid no heed. 'These are going up all over the town! Bill Riley has organized boxing for tonight. Anybody who's anybody will be there! Do say you'll Come!'

Algy frowned. 'Oh, I don't know, Connie. The doctors have diagnosed FA as having typhoid fever. I really should remain here.'

'I've always wanted to see "The Fancy"!' she gushed. 'And I can hardly go on my own! Don't be such a stick-in-the-mud!'

'Riley does put on a grand show!' said Bowling, who had followed Algy into the room and overheard Connie's news.

'I didn't realize,' said Connie.

'Oh, yes! They're regular and popular. There are always plenty of down-and-out ex pugilists touring the country, fetching up at one tavern after another where a welcome might be found, prepared to step into a ring in return for free bed and board.'

'I see.'

'The landlord might even arrange to fight a main of cocks.'

'How marvellous!'

'One thing I'll say for Riley, though. He's not like some of the publicans in the villages outside the town. He does draw the line at dog fights!'

Connie cringed. 'I should jolly well hope so!'

'His bar takings will be boosted enough,' added Algy. 'The place will be packed because the fighting's just an excuse.'

'For what?'

'Don't be so naïve, Connie. You know very well. In a place like Newmarket any excuse for gambling is good for business.'

'I'm getting more excited by the minute!' she squealed.

'Don't get too excited. There'll be no show at all if the maw-worms have their way!'

Connie pulled a face. 'Maw-worms?'

'The opposite of your good self,' Algy answered.

Connie stood open-mouthed.

'Those who detest "The Fancy" and see it as their mission to ensure that fights are raided by the authorities,' he explained.

'Boxing's not really illegal is it?'

'No, but cock-fighting is,' Bowling interjected. 'Has been for 40 years.'

'Technically boxing is illegal because it's considered akin to an affray or a riot,' Algy explained.

Connie waved her arms. 'So, how can Riley...'

'Enforcement of the law is arbitrary,' Algy continued, 'especially if the boxers wear gloves.'

'Gloves! Not bare knuckles?'

'Sorry, Connie! But they are only flimsy chamois leather.'

'I can't see Riley being put off!' said Bowling. 'He can be assured of a carriage or three bursting with free-spending students from Cambridge. The University has plenty of young swells and bloods who love nothing better than to pit their fists against an over-the-hill bruiser!'

'Better than duelling I suppose!' said Connie.

'Yes, the lure of PR is like a rite of passage,' confirmed Algy, sarcastically.

'PR?'

'The Prize Ring, old-style bare-knuckle boxing.'

'The Noble Art!' exclaimed Bowling.

'Algy,' said Connie with mischief written all over her face, 'didn't I hear you say once that you had indulged in "The Fancy"?'

'Long time ago,' he said abruptly. 'I was still at school.'

'Perhaps you'll be seduced tonight!' she said, pouting provocatively.

'I know *one* of the racing fraternity who'll be under the ropes like a shot!' volunteered Bowling in the act of lighting his pipe.

'Who's that?' asked Connie.

'Our esteemed neighbour across the road at Bedford Lodge,' said Algy.

'You can be sure "The Squire" will need no second invitation!' added Bowling.

'George Baird?' piped Connie. 'That weed?'

'Most certainly.'

'But he's 25 going on 55! He spends all his inheritance on boozing, gambling and ...'

'Whoring!' added Algy quickly to save her blushes. 'But there's nothing Baird loves more at the end of an evening's carousing than to don the gloves.'

'However, Lady Swynford, you may be certain,' Bowling intervened eagerly, 'even in his cups, The Squire retains enough sense to avoid mixing it with Brusher here! His Uppingham reputation has gone before him!'

'Then we must go tonight if The Squire's going to make an ass of himself!' said Connie, clapping her hands in delight.

Algy threw up his own hands, but in refusal. 'No, Connie, I really can't. I should remain here.'

'Nonsense! You cut along!' interjected Bowling. 'Doctor Wright has been in to check on FA this morning, and Doctor Latham, and they're both happy with his condition. They say the fever is subsiding.'

'That is good news!' said Connie, though whether she meant Archer's health or Algy's release was open to question.

'Mrs Coleman, Sarjent and I have everything under control.' continued Bowling. 'FA will be safely tucked up in bed, we'll see to that! You go off and enjoy yourself. You could do with a break. And I know FA would say the same.'

'There!' said Connie. 'You have your *exeat*!'

Algy had to admit to himself that he did feel in desperate need of a respite from the daily grind of watching over Archer. What better relaxation could there be for a lifelong devotee of 'The PR'? And then there was the added incentive of an evening of unlimited possibilities with Connie. He required little in the way of persuasion.

He glanced at Bowling, who smiled and nodded enthusiastically. Algy returned the smile and agreed to collect Connie from The Rutland Arms at around 8 o'clock.

Connie left Falmouth House snuggling into her fox-fur stole, her eyes emerald bright and her freckles ablaze. Everything was going so smoothly.

******

The courtyard at the rear of The Greyhound, located at the bottom end of the High Street opposite the Jockey Club Rooms, was chock-full when Algy and Connie arrived that evening. People were standing on carriages, carts and wagons, with yet more spectators ringing the galleries and hanging from all the windows of the pub's upper floors. Likewise the adjacent buildings, which had the result of creating something of an amphitheatre. Connie was entranced: she thought the scene replicated all the dubious charms of Tyburn Fair on the morning of a public hanging.

The 24-feet square ring, bounded by two ropes twisted around the four corner-posts, was already set up in the middle of the courtyard and liberally spread with sawdust to soak up the blood; that is apart from a small area at its centre where a line had been marked out in chalk. Algy explained to Connie that this was the line of 'scratch' which fighters must toe at the start of each round in order to continue the bout.

'A round ends with a knock down,' he explained further. 'There is no limit on the number of rounds. Contests tend to be decided by the exhaustion of one fighter rather than through any clean knock out.'

'Then what happens?'

'The beaten fighter's second will "throw up the castor".'

'The what?'

'His hat - to concede defeat!'

Connie was as spellbound as the day she heard her first fairy tale. 'Tell me more! This sounds so thrilling!'

'The greatest virtue a prizefighter can demonstrate is gameness,' continued Algy. 'In genuine championship bouts, fighters have to be half blind with blood, their fists swollen like sponges, ribcage and stomach aching fit to burst before capitulation even becomes an option. These contests can last for ages. Bendigo and Ben Caunt fought 93 rounds lasting over two hours back in 1845!'

Algy's enthusiasm was catching: Connie made a fist and swung at his chin.

'Steady on, Connie! Calm down!'

'Put 'em up, Haymer!' she said, dancing around him. 'Let's see what you're made of!'

Algy enveloped her fists in his until she stood still.

'That's serious boxing, championship boxing. You'll not be seeing the like of that on tonight's bill!' he laughed.

'Why ever not?'

'Tonight's just a lot of half-drunk swells who ought to know better being cajoled into sparring against some has-been. Just a splendid excuse for gambling on how long the poor stupid beggar might last before he's carried out!'

Algy pointed toward the ring. Riley was ducking under the ropes. To great applause, he rang the bell he was carrying and called for order above the tumult.

'Gentlemen! Please!' he bawled.

The jeering and catcalls that his request incited was accompanied by much gesticulation in Connie's direction and a chant of 'Lady Present! Lady Present!'

Riley begged the lady's pardon.

'Make room for the lady, please! Let her through!' he shouted.

Connie smiled regally and made toward the ring.

'Why it's Lady Swynford! I might have known. And she's keeping the fine company of the one and only Brusher Haymer! Who knows, perhaps the Honourable Mister Haymer will *honour* us with his presence in the ring some time this evening?'

The crowd parted reluctantly to allow Algy and Connie passage ringside where two beer barrels were rolled into position for them to sit on. The roar of approval that met Riley's last suggestion had, however, filled Algy with foreboding: he knew the mob had an awful habit of getting what it wanted at fight nights.

'Gentlemen…and Lady!' Riley began. 'Welcome to another evening of pugilism at The Greyhound!'

Another roar, much louder than the first, rent the air. Another clang from Riley's bell.

'We invite any brave Corinthian gentleman to share the ring with our visiting pugilist for a maximum of *five rounds*! Thirty seconds rest between rounds and a further eight seconds to come up to scratch!'

Yet another barrage of cheers. Yet another series of clangs.

'We shall be fighting under the London Prize Ring Rules of 1838! Rules for real fighters not the Marquis of Queensberry's Rules for namby-pambys!'

Now the cheers were boosted by much stamping of feet.

'There will be no kicking! No gouging! No butting! No biting! No low blows!'

Boos, hisses and cries of 'Shame!'

'Now, let us give a warm Newmarket welcome to our visiting pugilist!'

'Who? Who? Who?' came back the chant.

'Standing just 5 feet 6 inches and weighing nine stone two pounds we have the one and only Charlie Hannan, the …'

Riley's next words were lost in the ensuing pandemonium.

'What did he say?' shouted Connie. 'Who is this Hannan?'

'Charlie Hannan, "the Pink of the Holy Land,"' Algy shouted back.

'Pink?'

'That's his nickname!'

Algy could not fathom what was going on. Hannan was not the usual ex-pug who propped up these occasions. He was still in shape. He still took serious contests

The noise crescendoes when Hannan entered the ring. He looked as mean and wicked as the tarantula spider to which he was often likened. His scarred and disfigured features remained frighteningly impassive as he strutted round the ring, resplendent in his white knee breeches, stockings and shiny black shoes, the bones of his ribcage gauntly prominent and the muscles on his torso and forearms standing out like miniature hams.

'Why is his face so dark?' Connie enquired.

'It's all the astringent they've put on him! It pickles the skin. Toughens his eyebrows and cheekbones and minimizes the bleeding. Protects him against cutting too easily. He'll have had it all over his knuckles as well. Gloves or no gloves!'

Clang! Clang! Clang!

'Who'll be the first brave man to step into the ring with the Holy Land Pink?' cried Riley. 'Think, Gentlemen, of the tales you'll be able to tell your grandchildren! The night you shared a ring with Little Pink! Gloves may be rented for one penny! So, who will get us started?'

An appreciative hum began to run through the crowd as it became clear someone had volunteered to be the first sacrificial offering of the evening.

'Why, who's this I can see making his way toward the ring?' boomed Riley to a cacophony of boos. 'It's none other than "The Squire"!'

Baird's omnipresent gang of camp followers cleared a path through the crowd. Their leader eventually reached the ring and virtually slid under the ropes on all fours, though whether by design or from the effects of over imbibing earlier in the evening was unclear. One of Baird's lickspittles removed the coat from his shoulders to reveal the puny physique befitting a man who subjected his body to every vice imaginable. Skinny though he was, Baird carried a roll of puppy fat around his midriff and there was no muscle definition whatsoever on his shoulders or forearms. A soppy grin spread across his flabby face, highlighting a chin that seemed transparently of the glass variety.

'I'll give you 5/1 "The Squire" goes the distance!' shouted a lone voice.

'He'll not last two rounds!' screeched Connie.

Baird was already gloved-up. Knowing him, thought Algy, he's got some bullets jammed in each fist for insurance. Hannan donned his gloves in the opposite corner and the two men came up to scratch for the first time. Riley shook his bell for the bout to commence.

The two fighters drew back and circled, first to the left and then back to the right. Baird was the first to throw a punch, a telegraphed straight left which The Pink accepted flush on the chin by parting his gloves at the last moment. He dropped straight to one knee, shaking his head as if he had been struck by a steam hammer. Riley clanged the bell to end round one.

'He's fibbing!' yelled Algy along with nearly everyone else. 'Come on, Riley! He's fibbing and you know it!'

Connie was tugging at his sleeve. 'What the deuce is fibbing?'

'Cheating, of course! Dropping onto one knee is meant to be involuntary! It's a foul if a fighter does it purposely to end the round. Baird's punch wouldn't have knocked you over!'

'This is rather disappointing! When are we going to see some proper boxing?'

Algy guffawed. 'Connie, this bout is nothing but a farce, a fix, an ego-booster for Baird. There'll be nothing for you to get excited about in this fight!'

Even though the crowd howled its increasing displeasure at the antics of the two fighters, precious few blows were landed in the remaining four rounds. At the end of the fifth Baird's seconds dragged him back to his corner, and by the copious application of smelling salts managed to drag him to his feet just in time to come up to scratch - and therefore claim to have lasted the full five rounds.

Baird's cronies chaired him round the ring amid volleys of jeering and whistling while The Pink sat sullenly in his corner. Someone hurled a beer pot into the ring and a half-eaten meat pie thrown from an upstairs window splattered on the back of Baird's head to huge applause.

Baird grabbed Riley's bell and began ringing it vigorously.

'Gentlemen…and Lady Swynford!' he cried, looking directly at her. 'The Squire did his best and offers his apologies for not winning your favour! You deserve better! And there's one here who I know - we all know - is well capable of putting on such a display! Friend and counsellor to the champion jockey himself! A moral guardian of the Turf! A man utterly fearless with the pen! But, is the pen mightier than the sword?'

Baird may not have been much of a boxer but during his brief studies at Eton and Cambridge he had read enough about Citizen Robespierre's techniques to know how to work a crowd and whip it into a rabble. The tumult gathered strength.

'Yes! The hero of Isandlwana, Brusher Haymer, is the man to give The Pink a good fight!'

Algy felt as cold as if it had just received the noose from the hands of hangman Berry.

TWENTY-FIVE

'Oh, go on, Algy!' beseeched Connie. 'Show them how it's done!'

Algy tried to think of a viable excuse but knew perfectly well there wasn't one available. The fact that he had been warned years ago in the strongest possible terms of the possible repercussions of another blow to his ear counted for nought in his current predicament. He knew he would never be able to walk down Newmarket High Street again if he ducked this challenge.

He stood up and stretched out his arms in acceptance. The crowd bayed its approval: 'Brush-er! Brush-er! Brush-er!' He removed his jacket, handed it to Connie and slipped between the ropes. Unbuttoning his braces, he peeled off his shirt and tied the braces around his waist. One of Riley's pot-men, who was acting as second and bottle-holder to all the evening's volunteers, fitted him with a pair of gloves and he alternately thumped one clenched fist into the open palm of the other until he was happy with their fit. Then the second took out a large tub of goose grease and proceeded to smeared generous dollops onto Algy's eyebrows, cheekbones and chin. Lastly, while Algy executed some practice jabs and swings to loosen-up, he applied liberal handfuls to his shoulders and arms. The stink made Algy's eyes smart but he consoled himself with the hope that the grease might deflect the odd blow or, at least, minimize their impact.

Algy sought out Connie. One look into her vivid green eyes now shimmering as big as half-crowns told him she was already getting an enormous sexual charge. His toned body glistened in the glare of the torches and lamps placed around the ring and the sight of his pectorals rippling in the chill of a November night was taking her breath away. She was unable to sit still, the sinuous gyrations of her bottom, hips and bosom resembling a charmed cobra as she anticipated the spectacle of two grown men stripped to the waist and knocking six bells out of each other for her entertainment. This was foreplay new to her but one that did not suffer by comparison.

Algy shuffled his boots in the sawdust beneath his feet, rolled his shoulders one last time and turned to confront The Pink. Connie bit her bottom lip.

'One hundred guineas says Brusher won't go the five rounds!' offered a top-hatted gent leaning out of the carriage to her right.

'Done!' she declared. 'But I'll give you 200 if he doesn't!'

Algy came up to scratch, right foot forward. A knowing mutter went round the crowd. He was a southpaw. He fought the wrong way round. He led with his right. Southpaws were rare: often ricky customers for even the wiliest and most experienced fighter.

Algy needed every advantage because he knew he was not going to be given an easy passage like Baird. He calculated he had six inches in reach and a good three stone on The Pink and he had to capitalize on them. His longer reach might keep The Pink at arm's length. If not, his best chance of survival lay in wrapping him up when he came inside before he could use his superior punching power. Landing some telling blows of his own would be a bonus.

But up close, The Pink looked as big and as strong as a Hereford bull: his shoulders sloped in and then thickened up high, a sure sign of power, and his eyes were alert and full of craft. Algy's stomach tightened, tickled by countless butterflies - which reminded him of one final thing: show no fear or you're done for.

The Pink declared his intentions from the bell. He feinted to his right with a roll of the hips and threw a succession of straight lefts into Algy's face, his hands as quick and sharp as razors. Algy had hunched his shoulders and forearms to ward off the rainstorm of blows but he was caught flat-footed and reflexes dulled by years of inactivity failed to cope; his right arm parry was a fraction too late, the sideways movement of his head just too slow. The blows caught him full on the nose and sent him reeling.

Algy had forgotten just how painful a decent punch on the nose could be: it felt as if he now had a nose on each cheek. The Pink bobbed from side to side and clubbed him with a right-hander, forcing Algy to grab him around the shoulders and hold on tightly. He felt the warm stickiness of blood spreading across his face and watched it drip onto The Pink's shoulder. There was nothing for it. Algy gathered his strength and shifting his grip to The Pink's waist, picked him up and grappled his lighter opponent to the ground, thereby ending the round.

Algy's satisfaction at surviving one round against The Pink was soon tempered by the pot-man's voice telling him there were four more rounds. The blood was washed from his face. His neck was massaged and a towel waved in his face. Neither removed the cold hand of fear from his shoulder. The bell sounded. Never had Algy wanted 30 seconds to last longer.

This time he was ready for The Pink. When he dummied and tried to come in behind the jab, Algy sidestepped and had a right uppercut waiting for him. The timing was not quite perfect but it caught his opponent full in the solar plexus under the ribcage: The Pink's eyes flared with the upswing of his head and a crown of sweat was knocked from his brow, the blow lifting him clean off his feet. The crowd went wild as he dropped down onto one knee, his mouth working like a goldfish.

It was Algy's round. He returned to his corner, jigging up and down on his toes, stirred up by that surge of primal satisfaction with which he was once so familiar.

His second was equally ecstatic. 'Lovely punch, sir! Who taught you that one?'

'William Thompson,' replied Algy with a puff of the cheeks.

The bottle-man blinked.

'Did I hear you right, sir? Did you say *William* Thompson?'

'Yes.'

'*The* William Thompson of Nottingham?'

'Yes'

The second's mouth fell open. 'You were tutored by the great Bendigo himself?'

'Yes. He was a friend of my father.'

'Well, I never did!'

The bell sounded for round three. Buoyed by his inside information, Algy's second rushed off to place a bet on his fighter.

The Pink could not wait to get cracking. His pride had been hurt more than his ribs in the previous round. He went after Algy, circling him like a hunting kestrel, firing a series of lefts and rights which skidded off the well-greased forearms Algy crossed in front of his face for protection. Having forced his opponent onto the back foot, The Pink pulled off his trademark move against larger men, truly a masterstroke. He sprang high into the air and chopped a slashing right-hander down his left cheek.

Algy swore he had been cut with a red-hot chiv. The round finished with him sat in the sawdust, sucking back the pain from the ugly two-inch gash pumping thick gobs of blood onto his shoulder. Out of the corner of his eye he glimpsed Connie standing on her beer barrel exhorting him to 'knock the little bleeder's block off!'

His second helped him back to the corner. 'Go for the clinch, sir!' he whispered, giving Algy a swig of water.

Algy didn't hear him. The advice was being proffered into his left ear. He swilled the water round his mouth and spat it out, turning the wood shavings at his feet to crimson slush.

What Algy did hear was the little voice in his head telling him he could not afford another round like the third. His right hand was throbbing from the impact of that punch to The Pink's midriff in round two and his squashed nose was impairing his breathing. He would have to rely on his left hand to ward off The Pink until such time as he could either wrestle him, or throw him, to ground.

Algy shuffled up to the mark and snaked out a couple tentative right leads. The first one grazed The Pink's shoulder as he ducked but the second caught him on top of his head when he corked back up. The jar of knuckles on bone reverberated right back to Algy's shoulder socket like the kick-back from a poorly held Purdey.

But after five or six minutes of action, the lessons instilled in Algy by Bendigo in the gardens of Haverholme Priory all those summers ago began to flood back. 'Young sir, if you please,' he heard himself being told, 'once you land a jab on the bully's button, you hit him with a cross!'

Algy did what the master had taught him. He arced a peach of a left cross into The Pink's face that stopped him dead and brought full-throated roars from the crowd. Though hurt, The Pink refused to go down. With everyone egging him on, the thought crossed Algy's mind that he might actually stand a chance of finishing off The Pink. He got careless, opened up his stance and telegraphed his intentions by dropping his left arm.

The Pink was faking. As Algy shaped to throw the uppercut, he thought someone must have sneaked up behind him and smashed his forearm with a hammer. The Pink had beaten him to the punch with a mighty right hook of his own. The air whooshed out of Algy as a river of flame scorched up his arm. He resorted to the clinch and made The Pink bear all his weight so that they inevitably fell to the ground in an undignified heap.

Algy was hauled back to his corner, looking a real mess. He was covered in gore from the open wound on his cheek and the damage to his nose; his left arm hung down by his side, and his right hand felt as if it had been plunged into a wasps nest. Most ominously, he felt blood seeping from his left ear. Common sense told him to quit.

Connie had seen enough. Her head was spinning, though no longer with sexual excitement but a troubled conscience: the handkerchief she had clutched to her cheek to mask her passion was now wringing wet with tears, for what had begun as a titillating game was turning into a sadistic inquisition. She jumped off the barrel and ran to Algy's corner.

'Algy!' she cried, sticking her head through the ropes. 'That's enough! You must stop this now!'

Connie's intervention was all the incentive he needed.

'Go away, Connie!' he sniffed, trying to suck in as much air as his mangled nose allowed. 'I've come this far, I shall see it through!'

She grabbed Algy's second by the arm. 'Throw up your hat!'

'What?'

She made a lunge for his headgear. 'Throw up this bloody hat!'

'Connie!' shouted Algy. 'I shan't tell you again!'

The bell clanged for the fifth and final round. Algy pushed Connie away and staggered up to the line of scratch. The Pink was there waiting for him, a lascivious grin pinned to his dusky pickled features which, though puffy from Algy's best punches, remained unbloodied. He tucked his chin carefully between the hillocks of well-muscled shoulder, right hand cocked like a matador preparing to finish his adversary with an *estocada* between the shoulder blades.

'Mister Fenner sends regards!' he growled out of the side of his mouth. 'This'll be a long round, *Mister* 'Aymer! Yer'll be lucky to crawl out of 'ere with yer balls in yer 'ands!'

Algy's jaw tensed from chin to ear as all his earlier misgivings found a home. He had been set up. He had seconds to conjure an escape. He had to end this round quickly. Otherwise The Pink would use every dirty trick in his repertoire to prolong the torture until he had reduced him to a shambling hospital case.

The Pink darted forward, pouring lefts and rights into Algy's abdomen, designed to inflict damage but only to soften him up, not take him out. Then he switched upstairs with a double-fisted attack which ended with a rabbit punch to the back of the neck that became a hold; while he had Algy immobilized, The Pink slipped his other hand under Algy's guard and Algy felt as if a giant wasp had stung him in the eye. The Pink had thumbed him.

Algy howled and retreated to the ropes, pursued by his gurning tormentor. He tried to absorb most of the blows on his elbows that were tucked in as tightly as Bendigo demanded. However, he knew he had neither the strength nor the technique of Bendigo to soak up such punishment for much longer. If he was to finish this fight in one piece he had to think of something fast, very fast. If he did not, and his senses became scrambled, The Pink would take great delight inflicting as much pain as was humanly possible before forcing him to quit. But neither quitting nor 'fibbing' appealed to him.

In the face of The Pink's relentless onslaught, Algy had no alternative but to retreat. Somehow he had to turn this to his advantage. Keeping his elbows tucked-in and his gloves in front of his face, he took The Pink's punches on his arms and slowly back-pedalled toward his corner until he felt the wood of the corner post against his back. Algy knew he was about to take a big risk but he also knew this was his last chance.

Algy counted to three. On three, he let his gloves drift apart slightly to expose his chin, inviting The Pink to throw a right to the head. The Pink intuitively launched a clinical right hook.

Algy was already in the process of executing his next move before The Pink's punch had travelled two inches. He ducked; though crouched would be a more accurate description. The Pink's right fist sailed over the top of his head and thudded into the corner post exactly as he had hoped it would.

The Pink screamed with pain and shook his head like a stunned bull in a slaughter-house when the hammer has only wounded. Algy rounded on him and rained a brutal series of right-handers into the side of his face until he sank to his knees and capsized. Algy watched the darkness slip over The Pink's eyes, felt a fatigue born of relief consume his body and let his arms fall to his sides.

Spectators were going berserk, hurling hats and beer in the air, paying out grudgingly or accepting winnings joyously. Algy's bottle-man jumped into the ring and helped him stagger back to his stool. He removed Algy's gloves as gently as he could but stil caused Algy to flinch. He tried to flex his fingers: they were as black and stiff as burnt sausages.

Connie had hidden her face behind her hands throughout the last round, only peeking through them when an extra roar suggested the fight might be over at last. Thanks to The Pink's guile and Algy's resolution she was being given plenty of practice.

'Oh, Algy! Just look at you!' she cried, palms to his cheeks, tears streaming down her own.

'I'd rather not, if you don't mind!'

'Let me clean you up!'

She began sponging away the blood.

'Look at the state of your poor eye!'

'You should see it from my side!'

'Algy, this is no time for joking! Look at your knuckles! They're like a row of black grapes!'

'What do you expect them to look like after they've been hammering iron?'

'Oh, this is no good! I'm taking you back to the Rutland!'

She tied Algy's shirt round his neck and draped his coat round his shoulders.

'Let's go!' she said, demanding a safe route through the crowd and ordering all well-wishers and back-slappers to stay back and keep their hands to themselves.

Algy was in no position to argue with her. She curled an arm around his waist and, supporting him as best she could, led him, slowly and gently, out of the courtyard and into the High Street just as the police swarmed into the yard.

'Bloody maw-worms!' she muttered in their direction.

'M'Lady!'

Connie looked round and saw someone giving sedate chase. It was her friendly gent in the top hat.

'M'Lady! Here's your winnings!'

'Keep your hundred guineas! I've no need of it!' she said quietly, gazing at Algy as if he was Michelangelo's David made flesh and blood for her personal pleasure. 'I have all I need.'

And she planned to make the most of it.

TWENTY-SIX

Connie removed Algy's jacket from around his shoulders, sat him on the edge of her bed and eased off his boots. His only response was to emit a low moan each time an arm or leg was obliged to move through more than 45 degrees.

'Now, don't be such a big baby!' she scolded. 'Just stay there while I run you a warm bath.'

'No! I'm beat. I just want to sleep.'

'Well, I'll fill a bowl with some lukewarm water and clean you up a bit. Is that all right?'

'Yes, that'll be fine.'

She disappeared into her bathroom and came back armed with bowl, flannel and towels to find Algy flat on his back, fast asleep.

She smiled. 'There's no avoiding it!' she trilled maternally. 'It's a bed bath for you, Algy Haymer whether you like it or not!'

Connie moved the oil lamp closer to the bed and saw for the first time the true extent of the cuts and bruises marring Algy's handsome face. She sat down beside him, swept the matted hair off his forehead and untied the shirt from around his neck. His chest was covered with angry red welts the length and breadth of a pocket comb and was caked with sweat and blood, the sight and smell of which made her heart quicken like a lover's rather than a mother's. The urge to kiss him proved irresistible and she tenderly planted four kisses on his face in the sign of the cross.

Soaking the flannel in the warm water, she slowly lifted his chin and began delicately bathing each bump and cut. She began with the nasty gash on his cheek which, thankfully, was not so deep as she had imagined. It might, she thought, leave him with a manly scar. She switched to a cold compress for the two purplish lumps the size of quails eggs on his forehead but they were so sensitive that his feet jerked involuntarily off the bed when she touched them. Having cleaned up his face, she slid a towel behind his head and after rinsing out the flannel, started to run some water through his tangled blond locks that were pink in places from the matted blood. When he flinched while she was drying his hair, she lent forward and kissed his forehead. Yet still he did not stir.

Next she turned her attention to unbuttoning and removing his trousers, no easy task for even such an experienced practitioner as herself owing to the complete lack of co-operation, for once, of the male concerned.

Removing the final items of Algy's clothing held no such fears. No matter how many minutes it required to leave him lying there as naked as a new-born babe, every one of them would, she assured herself, be a sensual feast. She took as much time as she dare to caress each and every part of him before sealing the successful bathing of each and every part with a lingering kiss.

Connie eventually stood back to admire her work. 'Poor Algy,' she cooed, looking down at a body resembling an painter's palette restricted to blacks, blues, reds and pinks. 'But at least you're clean!'

Then she departed to complete her own *toilette*, returning in a diaphanous robe the colour of pearl and loosely tied at the hip. She slid her finger through the slip-knot and let the robe fall to the floor.

'Algy Haymer,' she whispered. 'You don't know what you're missing.'

At the sound of her voice he sighed and turned on his side. Connie climbed gingerly into bed and snuggled up behind him until his buttocks sat neatly on her thighs and her breasts flattened against the warmth of his back. She stroked his hair, kissed his shoulders and the nape of his neck, and gradually fed her right arm around his waist until she was able to snuggle up nice and tight. She watched the rise and fall of his shoulders and listened to his breathing. She had never felt so content. She was where she wanted to be; where she had planned to be.

'But you'll find out in the morning!' she promised before falling sound asleep.

******

Newmarket's Clock Tower had just struck eight when Connie awoke on the Monday morning. She had slept well and she knew what she wanted for breakfast. The proximity of Algy's body did not so much re-ignite her desires of the previous evening as douse them with kerosene.

Algy was still sleeping, face buried in the pillow, his breathing shallow, even and rhythmical. Connie blew on the little blond hairs on his neck, but still he refused to stir. She switched her attention to his earlobe, which she began kissing and nibbling. Algy's hand flicked out to swat away the intruder. She took it and sucked his fingers one by one. His body twitched and stretched, eventually causing him to roll over onto his back. Connie's hand went to her mouth at the sight of his blotchy pink face but she was soon swallowing a laugh once she realized it reminded her of a freshly spanked bottom.

'Algy,' she purred, her hand continuing to amuse itself beneath the sheets. 'It's time to wake up.'

She slipped her leg over Algy's hipbone, across his belly, and slowly mounted him. Then something caught her eye.

'Algy!' she cried out. 'You're bleeding!'

He woke with a start.

'Connie! What's the matter?' he said, holding a hand to his head. 'What the hell's happening? Where am I?'

'You're bleeding! Look! There's blood on the pillow!'

Algy sat up, and made himself giddy.

'Oh, that!' he said, propping himself up and spying the red patch where his left ear had rested.

'You must see a doctor! It's a bad sign to bleed from the ear! Something terrible may be happening inside there!'

'It's only a perforated ear drum!' Algy said as if he was referring to a split nail.

'Only a perforated…' Connie spluttered, sitting down on the bed beside him. 'You shall go to Doctor Wright as soon as you're dressed!'

Algy placed his hands on her shoulders. 'Look, Doc Wright knows all about it. The ear was perforated years ago. Sometimes it bleeds, that's all.'

'Years ago! But you never told me about it!'

'Why should I?'

'Because…' she began but could think of no good reason.

'Connie, it's nothing.'

'But how did you do such a thing?'

He was uncertain whether to laugh or not. In the end he kept a straight face.

'Boxing.'

'Boxing! And you got into that ring last night knowing that!'

'I might remind you, Connie dearest, that you were party to my entering that ring!'

'You could have refused!'

Algy gave her a look which told her not to be so naïve. 'After being introduced as a war hero? Baird knew what he was doing…'

Algy fell silent and a tear trickled down his cheek. Connie stroked his hair in the vain hope it might soothe him.

'No-one holds that against you,' she whispered. 'It's long forgotten. Bowling says so…'

'Not by me it isn't!' Algy said, voice rising.

'Oh, Algy, don't!'

'I should have died alongside Jimmy and the rest!' he continued, the words coming faster. 'It would have been better for everyone!'

'No! What's the point of one more dead man! The battle was lost!'

Connie felt Algy's entire body tense with an anger that made her flinch.

'You don't understand, Connie, and you'll never understand! We weren't mere men! We were soldiers! Do you realize what that means?'

He did not wait for an answer and she was too frightened to give one in any case.

'Soldiers…do…their…duty!' he enunciated slowly in a mock authoritarian growl of which his father would have been proud. 'They…fight…to…the…end!'

Connie suddenly found her voice. 'But you had done your duty! You had fought! It was every man for himself!'

'Real soldiers don't bolt! Only cowards run!'

Algy jabbed his blood-encrusted ear until it began bleeding again. 'And this thing is a constant reminder!'

'What do you mean?' Connie asked, eyes and mouth pinched with bafflement.

'The gunshot aggravated the perforated ear and left it completely buggered-up!'

'How?'

'*Tic douloureux* they call it.'

'Algy, don't play games with me. This is too serious.'

'To simpletons like you and I, facial neuralgia,' he explained. 'The damage affected the nerve in my jaw and every now and then it flares up. Exposure to cold air, a visit to the dentist…anything like that can trigger an attack.'

'How bad is it?'

'Pretty grim, like having a mad blacksmith hammering my jawbone into my brain!'

'Aren't there drugs you can take?'

'Not really. Just deaden the pain the best you can until the attack passes.'

'And how long's that?'

'Can be months!' he said, forcing a laugh.

'And it's a constant reminder of South…'

'Yes,' he interjected, 'it acts like a bloody great white feather!'

Connie embraced him and kissed him on the lips. 'Oh, my poor Algy!'

Algy stared vacantly at the ceiling. He began shivering - and at last noticed they were both naked.

'Connie, who undressed me?' he said, lowering his voice and permitting the crows feet of a smile to crease the corners of his eyes and mouth.

She pouted. 'Why, me of course! I saw nothing I've not seen before!'

'Don't tell me you had your ...'

'As a matter of fact, no, I didn't!' she said, unable to disguise the disappointment in her voice. 'But we spent a lovely night all the same.'

Algy's blank expression demanded she continue.

'We spooned and it was wonderful!'

'Spooned?'

'Slept fitted together like a couple of spoons in the cutlery drawer, you imbecile!' she giggled. 'Have you never slept like that before?'

Algy was forced to admit that he had not.

'More importantly, last night was the very first night we have ever slept together.'

'Oh.'

'And we didn't even make love!'

'Never mind!' Algy said. 'I had best take a bath and get back to Falmouth House.'

Algy slowly eased himself out of bed and shivered as his feet encountered the parquet flooring. He limped into the bathroom and shielded his sore eyes against the glare being transmitted by the best in contemporary enamel, brass and tiles.

Connie heard the bath filling and when the taps fell silent she tripped across to the bathroom door. She ran her tongue around her lips, pinched her cheeks and then her nipples.

'Do you need any help?' she said, leaning against the doorframe like some Venetian tart advertizing her wares on the Ponte delle Tette.

'Connie, why don't you put some clothes on?' replied Algy in the act of sponging his shoulders.

'Why, does it bother you? Don't you like what you see?'

She cupped her breasts in her hands and thumbed her nipples.

'Dotty! Behave yourself, please!'

'Algy Haymer,' she said, arms now harmlessly akimbo, 'there are times when I truly despair of you!'

'Stop whining, then, and come over here and wash my back!'

Connie glided over to the bath and began to soap his back. She rinsed it off by squeezing water from the sponge onto one spot at a time in exaggerated squirts that sent water spurting over the roll-topped edges onto the floor.

'How's that feel?' she murmured.

She dropped to her knees and peeped over the top of the bath at him like a small child eyeing up sweets on the counter that are getting tantalizingly closer.

'That's divine,' Algy moaned. He slid down the length of the tub until he was floating and then submerged.

While he ran his fingers through his hair to remove any traces of the fight, Connie lent over and began soaping his chest and belly.

'Now,' simpered Connie, 'tell me how *that* feels?'

Words were superfluous. She knew what it felt like. He had told her often enough: a warm, wet, velvet mitten. Algy lay back in the bath while she lathered every receptive inch of him before sponging him down. His eyes glazed over.

He opened his eyes to watch Connie climb into the bath and shifted his feet so that she might kneel between his legs. She straightened her back, causing her breasts to jut out flagrantly, each nipple pointing perkily upward, and when she knew he was suitably transfixed she circled the soap round her breasts one at a time until they resembled a pair of heavenly cream cakes topped with a bright red cherry. Then she took the sponge and, holding it between her breasts, squeezed it so that the water washed over them and cascaded in a foamy torrent onto her belly before flowing into the gully that hid her womanhood.

'Come on top of me!' he gulped.

'Are you sure?'

'Dotty, don't be so bloody stupid!'

'Then I'd best be *very* gentle.'

'I don't give a damn! Just come here! Now!'

Despite her primal instincts, she was true to her word. She rode him tenderly, for even though his grip on her buttocks made the urge to quicken almost irresistible, her rapture went beyond the physical: she felt Algy was all hers at last.

She felt she could go on for ever when Algy suddenly swung her over and came on top of her. He felt full enough to burst. His urgency took Connie's breath away and she gripped the rim of the bath as the water lapped against their writhing bodies. Algy looked down at her head thrown back in ecstasy, her red hair rubbing against the pearl white of the bath, and could not hold himself back any longer. Connie dug her fingernails into his neck and begged to be finished as the burning in her belly began verging on pain. Algy sent one final wall of water crashing all over the floor, mouth feeding on mouth, limbs knotted, one heart thumping against the other.

They lay enfolded in each other's arms, united at last, living the moment for as long as they could, swapping endearments. Could such joy last for ever? Connie was convinced it could and would; and she promised him she always got what she wanted. Algy was less sure. His emotional life seemed littered with disappointments. A permanent relationship with Connie had all the ingredients for another.

******

Half a mile away, Archer was trying to escape from the two men chasing him. Yet the faster he ran, the closer they got. Every time he looked over his shoulder he saw them gaining on him. He tried to make out their faces but they remained blurred: when he concentrated even harder to identify them it made his head spin and they only became fuzzier. He asked himself who his pursuers might be and decided they must have mistaken him for someone else. Now they were right behind him and starting to frighten him. He felt their hot fetid breath on his cheeks and ough hands grabbing his shoulders. He flung his arms across his face to protect himeslf, shouting at them to go away.

Finally Archer screamed himself awake. He sprang upright, panting for breath, his night-shirt saturated with sweat, his legs coiled in the bed-sheets. He kicked out to free himself and then ran to the window, hiding behind a curtain and peering from bush to tree and stable to coach-house, convinced he would spot the two interlopers in the gardens. He whooped with glee: there they were skulking behind the greenhouse.

What to do? He shuffled around the bedroom, hands clamped to his temples until the glint of a solution came to his eye. He wrenched open the pedestal beside his bed and found what he was looking for: it was a Webley revolver. He picked up the pistol, which seemed heavier, more cumbersome and infinitely more deadly than it had been as a mere trophy, and spun the cylinder with his thumb to check the chambers. He rummaged around in the pedestal for the tin box of cartridges and pressed one into each of the Webley's six chambers. He grinned. Nobody could touch him now.

He slouched on the bed and gathered the sheets around himself like white ramparts until he felt secure and perfectly safe inside. Then the broad grin turned lop-sided as he realized his stupidity: he freed his trapped left hand from beneath the sheets and shook the revolver in the air.

'If they're coming,' he chuntered, 'I'm ready.'

TWENTY-SEVEN

It was past three in the afternoon when Algy lent out of bed and examined his watch. There was some kind of commotion in the street. He left the half-covered Connie embracing a pillow and scrambled out of bed to find out what it was.

'There's been a shootin' at Falmouth house, mister!' a young stable lad called back to him in answer to his query. 'Someone's a goner, they say. They reckon it's The Tinman hisself!'

Algy felt his guts shrivel. He frantically pulled on his shirt and trousers, fumbling with the buttons, and shouted at Connie to wake up.

'Algy! Please don't shout!' she sighed. 'Come back to bed.'

'Connie, you don't understand. Something's amiss at Falmouth House. There's talk of a shooting.'

Connie's brain slowly cleared of sleep and she sat up. 'What did you say?'

'A shooting!' Algy repeated, searching for his socks. 'At Falmouth House. It sounds as if it could be Fred!'

He stamped his feet into his boots and dashed out of the door.

Connie watched her lover leave and then buried her head in the sheets, her world disintegrating faster than her father's Minton figurine.

'God!' she shrieked. 'What have I done?'

******

Algy dodged between two carts crossing the High Street and ran to Falmouth House. Although only a few hundred yards it left his mouth bone dry and reduced his legs to string, exhausted by the thought that something had befallen Archer while he had been making love with Connie.

210

He found an ambulance outside the front door and police everywhere. Constable Scarlett recognized him at once and let him through as far as an Inspector Reeve, who directed him to the morning room. Algy thought he could smell the mustiness of death. He sniffed again and changed his mind. It was not death but the faint whiff of washing: it was Monday, laundry day.

Algy burst in to be met by Captain Bowling; Mrs Coleman, Sarjent and Doctor Wright sat round the oak table as if they were awaiting the start of an inquest - which in a way they were.

'Brusher, good to see you,' said Bowling.

Algy went directly to Archer's sister, being comforted by the two nurses from the Cambridge Nursery Institution, Hornidge and Dennington, who had been brought over to tend her brother. 'Emily, what can I say?' he said in a faltering voice. 'I am so dreadfully sorry.'

'It's not your fault, Brusher. He was just so depressed! He missed Nellie so very much!'

'Of course he did.'

'And you know what this weekend was, don't you?'

There was no need for Algy to answer. Everyone in the room knew it was the second anniversary of Nellie's death. He had hoped the fact that it also marked little Nellie's second birthday might make it easier for Archer to cope. But he was wrong. He should have realized and acted accordingly. He felt as if he was no better than Somerset and the rest of Archer's fair-weather friends who had put their own interests first and abandoned him.

'It was just too much for him,' she sobbed.

'But I should have been here, by his side.'

'Don't punish yourself, Brusher,' said Bowling, spreading his hands in a gesture of regret. 'I wasn't here either when he needed me.'

'I suspect no-one could have helped him in the end,' added Doctor Wright.

Part of Algy wanted to embrace Wright's consolation. It was no empty hypothesis: there were five people in Falmouth House at the time of Archer's death, all of them powerless to prevent it. But another part of

Algy refused to believe he could not have saved his friend, his brother in spirit if not in blood.

'Perhaps,' he said thunderously.

'He appeared so much better,' said Bowling with a shake of the head. 'I thought he was on the mend.'

'When did you last see him?'

'I left him around noon. I had no idea what he must have been planning or I would not have departed.'

'Fred's mind did seem to wander during these last few days,' said Mrs Coleman. 'He seemed to forget things. He did seem better this morning but I had a long conversation with him and he said he was anxious about his recovery. Then, just after two o'clock, he asked Nurse Hornidge to leave us alone.'

'Was that unusual?' Algy asked.

'Not really,' she answered. 'I went over to the window and was looking out when I heard him say something.'

'What did he say?'

'He said, plain as day, "Are they coming?"'

'Are they coming?'

'Yes. It'll haunt me till the day I die.'

'Nothing more?'

'No.'

'Did he say who was coming?' asked a perplexed Algy.

'No.'

Algy looked toward the others but the response was similar.

Coleman wiped the tears from her eyes and blew her nose. 'Then almost immediately afterwards I heard a noise and I looked round to see him out of bed and he had something in his hand. I ran to him and when I saw it was the revolver I tried to push it away. The revolver was in his left hand, and I hurt my own hand trying to push it away. He then threw his right hand round my neck. Put the revolver in his mouth…'

'There's no need to carry on,' said Algy, taking hold of her hand.

'...and fired the revolver with his left hand. I saw him doing it but could not stop him. He seemed awfully strong.'

'Mrs Coleman, I do think you should go and rest awhile,' interjected Wright, walking round the table to where she sat. 'You've endured a terrible ordeal.'

'He then fell flat on his back close to a chair,' she continued, between huge sobs. 'I was screaming, but he never spoke. The door was always kept ajar but in the struggle he forced me against it, closing it, and so my screams were not heard. I had no idea there was a revolver in the room.'

Algy ran a hand through his hair as he tried to make sense out of what he had heard. But he could not. He turned to Nurse Hornidge.

'Charlotte,' he said softly, 'did you suspect anything at all? Did Mister Archer say anything that suggested his mind was in such turmoil that he might take his own life?'

'He had been in low spirits,' she replied after some thought, 'and when I got to his room at 11.30 this morning he did tell me during the course of a conversation that he thought he was going to die.'

'Did he explain why?'

'No, that was the odd thing.'

'It's that gipsy!' exclaimed Bowling.

'Gipsy?'

'Stuff and nonsense really,' said Bowling, his expression crumpling. 'He crossed her palm with silver as we were going into the track at Chelmsford a few years back and she told him he would die by the hand that gave it to her.'

Algy stared at Bowling and shook his head disbelievingly. He felt there was a clue to be found somewhere in all this but not in the form of a gipsy's curse.

'I told him to cheer up and that he was certainly not going to die,' continued the nurse. 'He said he wished he could agree with me. I asked him if he was comfortable, and he said he was. I was with him until about a quarter past two when Mrs Coleman sent me to dinner. I was only out of the room for a minute when the bell rang.'

'You didn't hear a shot?'

'No, nothing. Only the bell. The housemaid went to answer it but the bell kept on ringing, so I followed her upstairs.'

'And?'

'That's when I heard the cries of "Help!" I smelt powder as soon as I entered the room. Mister Archer was lying on his right side on the hearth-rug and I could see that he was bleeding from the mouth.'

Algy walked over to Sarjent and placed an arm on his shoulder. The valet raised his eyes and sniffed away tears. He could not shed any light on his master's state of mind.

'I was in the house at the time and heard the bell ring violently, but that's all,' he replied. 'Nurse Hornidge was turning Mister Archer over when I got to his bedroom and I saw the revolver fall from his hand onto the hearthrug.'

'How long had he had the damned thing?' Algy asked angrily.

'It was given to him by Tommy Roughton...' said Sarjent, eyes fixed on the floor.

'The trainer?'

'Yes,' confirmed Bowling. 'It was presented to Roughton after he won the Liverpool Cup with Sterling back in '73.'

'How could he be left with a revolver given his state of mind defeats me?'

Sarjent looked up. 'He brought the gun here after he and Mrs Archer were married because he thought that she and the house might need protection, what with it being known to be full of valuables.'

'I see.'

'Then only a month back he had it repaired after Mr Jewitt, over the road at Bedford Cottage, had been broken into by burglars.'

'And it was loaded?'

'He loaded it himself and instructed me to put it in the pedestal by his bed when he was at home and when he was away, and I stayed in the house, I was to move it into my room in case of emergency. The pedestal was never locked, you see. I put it back in his room last Thursday evening after he had telegraphed to say he was returning from Lewes.'

Algy felt like weeping himself at the very thought of Archer not only having access to a deadly weapon but also by the fact that Bowling and Sarjent knew of its whereabouts. He continued to patrol the room, looking fit to explode.

'Why on earth didn't you tell me about it?'

The valet blinked like a rebuked schoolboy and Algy felt like ripping into him but the sight of the his head sagging onto his chest made him think again. The sound of the valet's sobbing was drowned by Count Festecic's wedding present striking four.

'Did you foresee any of this, Doctor?' he asked, looking toward Wright. 'You've been his physician for...'

'Fourteen years.'

'Did you ever imagine he might become suicidal?'

'No, not at all.'

'So, it was a shock to you also?'

'Yes, absolutely. He was in a high state of fever when I was called in to see him on Friday morning. He was extremely restless and when I called again at two o'clock the symptoms had worsened. He'd always been in pretty good health - apart from that time his arm was savaged.'

'Muley Edris back in '80,' said Bowling automatically.

'But he was never a very strong man,' continued Wright. 'He was convinced that the dinner he had eaten in Brighton on the Wednesday was still in his stomach.'

'I dined with him that evening,' said Algy. 'He ate two oysters and one prawn and washed them down with a glass of your physic. I doubt whether the meal stayed in his stomach for more than an hour or so.'

'He refused any medicine other than his wasting mixture once he returned here. As you know, I called in Doctor Latham on Friday, and on Saturday we diagnosed typhoid fever.'

'Do you now think the news must have affected him more than we originally thought?'

'Obviously it depressed him. It was a setback. He was not delirious in his fever but disconnected in his thoughts. He kept saying he was going to die. It was a form of depression that drove him temporarily insane. But he had begun to improve by noon yesterday and his temperature began to fall in the afternoon.'

Algy thrust his hands in his pockets and stared up at the ceiling. He was becoming more and more convinced that the key to unlocking this mystery lay in Archer's last words.

'Doctor,' he said, 'did he ever mention to you who it was he thought were coming"?'

'No, never. The next time I saw him he was dead.'

At Wright's last few words Mrs Coleman finally succumbed to her grief and, on the verge of collapse, was helped from the room by Nurse Hornidge.

'I found the bullet that killed him on the dressing table,' said Wright once the two women had departed.

'Death would have been instant?'

'Yes. The bullet must have passed through the spinal column, between the two upper cervical vertebrae, dividing the spinal column. It would have caused instant death.'

'Thank God!' said Bowling.

'Amen to that,' added Algy.

The three men stood silently, each nursing their own recriminations. Algy's eyes had seldom been moist with adult tears and it embarrassed him to feel them awash. His thoughts returned to that evening in the garden at Selhurst Grange. He knew Archer had suicidal tendencies. He blamed himself. If only he had been in Falmouth House it would have been he and not Mrs Coleman in that bedroom. He could have subdued Archer.

Algy walked out of Falmouth House vowing never to forgive himself until the day he joined Archer in the ground. His friend was only 29-years-old. His own age, for God's sake. He had so much to live for. His daughter. Taking her hunting. Telling her stories of her mother. He could lead a normal life at long last. One where he might enjoy eating lashings of cake and blackberry jam if he so wished, instead of existing on fresh air and physic. He could travel. He could make that trip to India he'd always hankered after. Go back to the United States. The future offered him so much that he deserved.

Fred, Fred…why did you do it? Algy kept repeating the question until it almost drove him crazy. The answer must be hidden in that last phrase. Was Fred rambling, demented, delirious?

By the time he re-crossed the High Street, he had begun to wonder whether the explanation was simpler than that. Was he really expecting visitors? And if so, were they unwelcome visitors?

TWENTY-EIGHT

The weather for Archer's funeral four days later suited the town's mood. It was wet, cold and dismal. Shops and businesses closed their doors and put up the shutters. Crowds lined the entire route from Falmouth House, winding up the Fordham Road and down the High Street, to the flint-walled cemetery which looked out onto the Heath and the racecourse. Every stable boy and apprentice in the town turned out, hats off, in final tribute to their hero and role model.

The inquest into Archer's death, held in the morning room at Falmouth House the day following his death, had reached the inevitable verdict that 'the deceased committed suicide whilst in a state of unsound mind.'

Archer's death, more especially the nature of it, shocked every strata of society. When thenews reached London on the Monday evening, omnibuses going down Fleet Street paused obligingly outside the various newspaper offices so that passengers might read the billboards carrying the story. Special editions of the evening newspapers were issued and sold out within minutes. So anxious were commuters to obtain the copies before leaving town that silver coins were being exchanged for the sheets as fast as the newsboys could tug them from their bundles. It was as if Royalty had died.

So many floral tributes flooded into Falmouth House from all over the British Isles and the rest of Europe that three carriages were required to convey them to the graveside; the most touching of all, however, was a simple bunch of violets bearing the inscription 'With baby's fondest love for her father.'

The cortege left Falmouth House at two o'clock. The undertakers issued Algy with black scarf and gloves - though he declined the black-banded hat - and he helped bear the coffin into the glass-panelled hearse before joining those who elected to ollow on foot rather than ride in one of the 30 mourning coaches that contained representatives from every sector of the racing community, from Mat Dawson to Lord Alington; even Baird and Wood paid their respects.

One notable absentee was the Duchess of Montrose, who left for the south of France immediately upon hearing of Archer' suicide - with Seger in attendance. Emily Coleman had shown Algy her letter of condolence.

'No words can tell you how much I have felt for you since I heard the dreadful intelligence yesterday. I feel I cannot help dwelling on the terrible fact that wasting so much for St Mirin must have done him harm, but for months I have not thought him looking well. No doubt he laid down his life for his profession. How we shall miss him.'

That penultimate sentence gnawed at Algy all the way to the cemetery. Did his friend really lay down his life 'for his profession'? His own doubts had increased tenfold in the last 72 hours. Just who did Fred think was 'coming'?

When the cortege reached the cemetery, the crowds massed outside forced the police to control access. Algy helped carry the coffin of his friend to the mortuary chapel where it was met by the same vicar who had presided over Nellie's funeral

A little over an hour later the crowds had melted into the murky twilight and Algy stood silently at the graveside, alone with his thoughts.

'Why, Fred?' he muttered. 'You were the greatest jockey who ever threw a leg across a racehorse. And you go and kill yourself before you've even reached the age of 30. Why, Fred, why?'

Algy vowed he would not rest until he had got to the bottom of it. He turned up the collar of his coat and squelched away, his clothes as leaden as his spirits. Through the gloom he could just make out the silhouette of someone sitting on one of the seats near the gates. As he got closer he could see it was Connie.

'What a ghastly day,' he said, sitting down beside her.

He does not appreciate how ghastly, Connie thought to herself.

'It's coming on to rain again,' she replied, blowing her nose in an effort to buy time.

'Yes, I suppose it is.'

She put a hand on his. 'And you don't want a chill getting into that ear of yours. You may have got away with it once, but you don't want to push your luck.'

'No, of course not.'

'How has it been?'

'Oh, nothing to worry about.'

The flatness of his voice stated his thoughts were elsewhere.

'Connie,' he said, springing to his feet. 'I just can't get Fred's last words out of my head. "Are they coming?" Who was he referring to? Who is "they"? Even if he was absolutely *non compis mentis*, it makes no sense.'

'I suppose...'

'Well,' he said, cutting her off edgily, 'does it make any sense to you?'

'Perhaps he was hallucinating?' she ventured. 'After all, he was delirious with the typhoid fever. He could have been imagining anybody or anything frightening.'

'Bogey men of some kind, you mean?'

'Well, yes, I suppose so.'

'Detectives sent by the Jockey Club to investigate the Jockeys Ring?'

'That sort of thing, yes,' Connie replied, none too convincingly for her brain was preoccupied with thoughts of one bogey man in particular. 'Perhaps he saw Nellie - and the baby boy - coming to take him away. It was the anniversary of her death, wasn't it?'

'Yes, the very day.'

Algy kicked out at a piece of gravel. 'I know what you're driving at, but it just doesn't convince me.'

Connie held her handkerchief to her eyes.

'I'm sorry if this kind of talk upsets you,' he said, sitting down once more and folding an arm around her. 'I know how much you grew to like Fred following that night in the garden at Selhurst.'

Her shoulders began to shake as her breath came in ever larger gulps. Her emotions were churning out of control. She could not keep her guilt hidden much longer. She had to tell someone or she felt she would collapse. The burden, the deceit was killing her. And it had to be Algy.

'It makes more sense,' Algy continued, 'in fact, it only *makes* sense, if he *was compis mentis* and really *was* expecting someone's arrival and, more's the point, was petrified of them! Which means, if I'm correct, it had to be…'

'Me!' she shrieked, prompting a flock of feeding starlings to take flight.

'You?'

'Yes, me!'

Algy looked at her incredulously. 'Have you lost your senses? How could he have been expecting you?'

'No! He wasn't *expecting* me!'

'Then what?' he implored, slapping his gloves against his thigh. 'For God's sake, woman, make sense!'

Connie twiddled with her handkerchief and sat up straight. 'It was me,' she enunciated slowly, 'that brought it about.'

Algy gripped her by the shoulders. 'What on earth are you trying to say? I don't understand!'

'It was Fenner he was expecting!' she sobbed, collapsing into his arms. 'And it's all my fault!'

He held her upright and tried to look her in the eye but she kept looking away. She could feel his anger; she did not want to see it.

'Fenner, I might have guessed!' he snarled. 'But where the hell do you fit in?'

The moment of reckoning she had been dreading was finally here.

'He told me to get you out of the house last Sunday,' she said in a faltering voice, tears flowing down her face and dripping off her chin.

'What?'

'He said he wanted you away from Archer.'

'And you agreed!'

'I just wanted to be with you so desperately. To spend a night together was going to be so perfect - and, Algy, you know it was perfect.'

He glowered at her.

'Or else, I swear, I wouldn't have done it!'

'But for the love of God what were you doing talking to Fenner let alone doing his bidding?'

Connie watched Algy's expression darken as the truth gradually sank in and she grew scared.

'You owe him money, don't you?' he said. 'And you can't repay him?'

Not even a nod of the head was necessary. The tears steaming off her red cheeks gave the answer.

'So, Fenner puts the squeeze on you,' he growled, becoming angrier with every word, 'and demands a favour to wipe the slate clean. Eh?'

She contrived something akin to a nod and for her trouble found herself on the receiving end of a good shaking.

'You stupid bitch! How could you be so stupid?'

'I've had a bad year...'

'But you're worth thousands!'

'I've expenses you don't...'

'I don't what?'

'I give a lot of money away.'

'You give money away! Now I've heard everything!'

'I should say that I donate money.'

'You donate money? To whom?'

'An orphanage.'

Algy let go of her. 'An orphange you said?'

'Yes, that's right.'

'Not the one near Charing Cross...what's it called?'

'St Saviour's.'

'So it was you I saw going in there!' he shouted.

'Yes.'

'This is unbelievable! You and worthy causes!'

'And why not?' she said, suddenly sticking out her chin. 'They have so little and I have so much. I was passing one day when a handful of young ones were being admitted. They looked so lost and vulnerable. One girl was sharing a filthy crust of bread with another. That was it, really. It just broke my heart to watch these poor mites nibbling at something a mouse would refuse to touch.'

'How philanthropic!'

'Sneer if you wish!' Connie retaliated, turning her back on him. 'You and I live a life insulated from reality!'

She peeped over her shoulder, daring to hope her confession might be having some effect. 'So I went straight in and spoke with the custodian about ways of helping.'

'As usual, Connie takes the easy option, pledging money instead of commitment!'

'I do try to call in every now and then!' she said defensively.

'But why the hell did you make such a secret of it?'

'Connie Swynford trying to bribe her way through the Pearly Gates by financing a ragged school?' she said, confidence returning. 'People would have laughed at me and I wouldn't blame them.'

Her revelation had shocked Algy into calming down. 'You must have donated a lot of money to go broke?'

'They always need money. As much as they can get. There are upwards of 500 children in there at any one time. I donated £1000 a month...'

'Jesus!'

'...but I coped all right what with my allowance and my betting.'

'So?'

'Then I lost badly on St Mirin!' she replied lamely, 'and I was left with no alternative but go to Fenner. What else could I do?'

'Go cap in hand to your dear father - like always!'

'I couldn't!'

'Couldn't?' he sneered. 'Why not? He spoils his little girl rotten!'

'Because he's cut me off without a penny, that's why!' she shouted back.

Algy burst out laughing. 'Now I am dreaming! Your father has cut you off! After years of being of paying your bills and doing your bidding, he has finally found the gumption to exercise a little bit of paternal discipline?'

'Yes.'

'Well, that truly is one for my memoirs!' said Algy, throwing his head back. 'I can hardly believe it possible!'

Connie stuck her nose in the air. 'You ought,' she said imperiously.

'Why?'

'Because you're the reason,' she added, glaring at him.

'What?'

For the first time in five minutes the two had each other's undivided attention.

'He hates you, you know that,' she said. 'And he knows that I love you. Then he heard the gossip from Goodwood…'

'Which you started!'

'…and obviously decided he had had enough. We had a horrible row at Denton about it all after I returned from Venice and he said he would cut me off if I didn't cut you out of my life.'

Algy exhaled audibly. 'So you were forced to live off your betting and the only credit available once your father had made his views known?'

'Yes.'

'Fenner must have thought it was his birthday and Christmas rolled into one!'

'Perhaps.'

'There's no "perhaps" about it! It would have taken him all of two seconds to work out that he could use you to get me out of the way so one of his bully-boys could pay Fred a visit.'

'It appears so now. But back then I had no…'

'…idea! Yes, I know! Typical Connie! Always thinking of herself!'

He grimaced at his insensitivity given her recent revelation to the contrary but never had found it easy to forgive the unforgivable. He took a deep breath and tried again.

'I'm sorry, that was unkind and mean-spirited of me,' he said. 'Even so, going to the boxing and getting me up in the ring so that I could be hammered senseless by The Pink was all part of one gigantic subterfuge, wasn't it?'

'I swear, Algy, I knew nothing of the rest!'

'You expect me to believe The Pink turned up by accident?'

'Fenner just told me to get you out of Falmouth House and that if I didn't agree he'd have to get his thugs to take care of you!'

'Charming!'

'I couldn't see you come to any harm!'

'No?' Algy raged. 'Just look at the state of me! I'd call this coming to some harm, wouldn't you?'

'That was not planned,' she wailed. 'At least not by me.'

'Then it must have been that bastard Baird!'

'I swear I don't know! Fenner just told me to keep you occupied for the night.'

'And you most certainly did! I suppose all that was a fake as well - what a girl will do for money, eh!'

Connie lunged at him and thumped his chest with her fists. 'No! Not that! That was real. I admit I'd go to any lengths to get you into bed. You know that. I've never made a secret of that. What happened between us was meant to happen. Money couldn't buy what we had at the Rutland.'

'How sweet of you to say so!' he said, wrapping his arms around her. 'It's truly good to know that I can't be bought that easily even if you can!'

Algy chuckled. He felt he had to relieve the pressure somehow. It was either laugh or cry. Yet there was still something nagging at him.

'How did you ever meet Fenner?' he said sternly, blue-chipped eyes refusing to accept anything but the truth. 'There are plenty of other moneylenders in Mayfair and Belgravia who would have been glad of your custom. Why scum like him?'

Connie squirmed, inside and out.

'Well?' said Algy, his fingers pressing into the soft flesh of Connie's arms.

'Algy, please let me go! You're hurting me!'

'Tell me!'

Algy dropped his hands and Connie broke free, gasping for breath.

'I was introduced to him by...' she panted in the process of rubbing the circulation back into her upper arms.

'By whom?' Algy shouted. 'Introduced by whom?'

Algy's features were frozen in a jigsaw of fury and puzzlement. His mind raced. He ran a hand through his hair and ordered himself to think; think logically.

'Seger!' he intoned. 'It was that bastard Seger wasn't it?'

Connie's solitary response was a snivel which Algy took as confirmation. She peeked at him from the corner of her eye, relieved to be no longer the prime target for his anger.

'And I wager that's how Fred got mixed up with Fenner!'

'Yes, I think so,' Connie mumbled. 'I think he may have been there when Seger introduced me to Fenner...'

'Poor Fred must have been in mental agony,' Algy moaned. 'He set such store in his reputation. It must have got too much for him.'

He halted and shook his head, unconvinced by his own argument. 'Yet surely that's not enough to drive a man to suicide? Not even a man as fragile as Fred.'

Connie had no satisfactory answers. Even had she some, they would not bring Archer back. Her only concern was for the welfare of the man standing in front of her. Mollifying him was her priority now.

'He was morbidly depressed, Algy, we - you - have to accept that,' she said softly, 'And he had tried to kill himself at least once before. Had we not appeared in that did, he may have succeeded down at Selhurst.'

That line of argument was hard for Algy to counter.

'Are you absolutely positive,' he said finally, 'that's everything Fenner told you to do?'

'Yes! He said nothing else to me, I'm positive!'

'Think Connie!' he said, grabbing her elbows and shaking her back and forth.

'But I have!'

'Anything! It might just be vital!'

'There's only one other thing I remember.'

'What's that?'

'I didn't think anything of it at the time,' she continued, drying her eyes, ' but when I was waiting to see Fenner, I overheard him and one of his thugs discussing how they would have to resort to "The Policy."'

The last two words caused Algy to stiffen visibly.

'What is it Algy? What have I said?'

'"The Policy"! That accounts for it.'

'You know what it means?'

'Yes, I know what it means all right.' he said, the veins beginning to stand up in his temples. 'You can't get any lower.'

'Tell me, please!'

'You really want to know?'

'Yes!'

Algy stood in front of her, feet planted firmly in the gravel and hands on hips, the combative look in his eyes leaving her in no doubt that he held her partly responsible for bringing about the horror he was being obliged to explain.

'It's the underworld term for exacting vengeance on someone close to your actual target either because you can't get near him or because he doesn't care what you do to him,' he said in slow measured tones.

Connie began to cry, great weeping tears that ran off her face and matted the rich black fur decorating the collar of her mourning coat.

'To people like Fenner,' Algy continued, glad of the effect his words were having, 'wounding, maiming, or even killing, a wife or child never fails. Make the victim suffer by making his nearest and dearest suffer.'

'Good God...'

'Yes, and in Fred's case only one person comes into that category.'

Connie blew her nose in a conscious attempt to clear her head and regain a modicum of self-respect. She knew who Algy meant.

'Little Nellie,' she sighed.

'They must have threatened to harm her in some way, kidnap her, even ...'

'That incident on The Severals! That was no runaway! It must have been a warning!'

'Yes, a message of intent.'

'Fred must have thought it was him or her...'

'So he did what any father would do.'

Algy stared in the direction of the newly-filled grave covered in wreaths. The truth, and Connie's part in it, made him want to cry out loud, but knowing the truth gave him a strange sense of relief. It set him free. He now knew what he had to do.

'They're not going to get away with this,' he said in a half-whisper. 'Neither of them. I'll not fail in my duty to a friend a second time.'

'What can we do?'

'You,' he sneered, 'can do nothing! You've already done enough damage!'

'But Algy...'

'Go back to daddy where you belong!' he said, walking away.

'I want you!'

Algy turned up the collar of his coat, sending a cascade of rain down the back of his neck, and kept walking.

'Wait! Wait!'

Connie ran after him, her emotions racing faster than her legs. Each step he took seemed to put another mile between them in her eyes. She must make him see reason. Their future, her future, depended on it.

'I can help!' she shouted. 'Listen to me! I know what we can do!'

Algy stopped at the cemetery gates and waited for her to catch up. He was not sure why at the time nor subsequently whenever he thought about the events of that bleak November afternoon. But stop he did.

Connie's face broke into a radiant smile as she puffed to a standstill in front of him. She had no idea what she was going to say but she would think of something.

TWENTY-NINE

'That posh tail's 'ere again to see yer, Mister Fenner, the Swynford woman. Do you want to see 'er?'

Fenner looked up from his newspaper, causing Percy to slide off his lap.

'Cocky, can't a man of your age tell the difference between a lady an' a common brass?' he said despairingly. 'Show the lay-dee in!'

For the second time in a month Connie entered the kind of room in which she should have felt very much at home. Fenner's elegant town house might have passed for any belonging to her upper crust friends had it exuded the attendant conviviality. But it did not.

'Good morning to you, Mister Fenner,' she said, cheerfully disguising a thudding heart. 'And how are you this morning?'

'I am very well, M'Lady, since you ask,' he replied, equally cheerfully. 'My mood 'as been much improved these past few weeks.'

'I'm so pleased to hear that.'

'An' I must thank you, because you 'ave 'ad a lot to do with that improvement!'

Connie let Fenner's sentiment pass without comment.

'So,' she continued, 'May I take it that my debts are cleared?'

'Most definitely, Lady Swynford!'

Connie patted her hair and effected her finest swagger. 'Then I'd like to place another bet.'

'Would you now,' said Fenner, his one good eye expressing genuine surprise.

'Yes, I would.'

'Cash or credit?'

'Why, credit, naturally!'

Fenner sat back in his chair and his features almost, but not quite, creased into a smile as Percy resumed his position. He was forced to admire the lady's effrontery.

'Lady Swynford,' he said in tones suited to a judge pronouncing sentence of death, 'you've just got out o' one scrape by, if I may say so, the skin o' your pretty little teeth an' yet you wish to go through it all over again - is that right?'

'Not quite.'

'An' 'ow's that?'

'Because this time I shall win and you shall be in my debt!'

Fenner almost popped his collar stud.

'Oh, you're goin' to win, are you? I never thought o' that!'

'I refuse to finish this season on the debit side of the ledger,' she explained.

'Some always do!'

'But not I! The season ends on Saturday at Manchester, as you well know. I intend backing the winner of the November Handicap!'

'Don't they all, Lady Swynford! Don't they all!'

'That may be, Mister Fenner. But I shall!'

'But the Manchester November 'Andicap is always a tricky old race to pick the winner. It's not as if 'alf the field'll be non-triers like most 'andicaps is it? This is the last chance to win the price o' some winter corn, ain't it? They'll all be tryin' won't they?'

'They may try as hard as they like,' Connie continued in confident vein, 'but they'll not beat Stourhead!'

Fenner's one bright eye shone brighter. 'Ah, you're goin' with the favourite, are yer?'

'I am. Will you take my bet, Mister Fenner?'

'Now, tell me, Lady Swynford, 'ow much are you wantin' to wager?'

Connie fought hard to subjugate the butterflies fluttering after each other inside her stomach. She filled her lungs and exhaled audibly and forcibly: '£10,000!'

Not a single pore moved on Fenner's face although the startled Percy hissed and spat defiance.

'What a frightful cat!' Connie cried, backing away again.

'Now then, M' Lady,' replied Fenner snootily, ''e speaks very well of you. Don't yer Percy?'

'What price will you lay me?' asked Connie, keeping a cautious eye on Percy.

'Let's see,' said Fenner. 'A credit bet o' £10,000? On Stourhead, you say?'

'Yes, £10,000 on Stourhead to win the Manchester November 'Andicap.'

'That's an awful large bet. You could buy a mansion for that!'

'I told you, I need to balance the books.'

'Well, in that case, since you're so sure, I think 2-1 would be fair, don't you?'

Connie did not consider those fair odds at all, as Fenner knew all too surely. But they would do.

'That's your best offer?'

'Most definitely an', in the circumstances, a most generous one. If it weren't the only daughter of the Earl of Kesteven standin' in front of me, I'd be far less so. But I imagine an' heiress such as yerself is always good for £10,000.'

'Of course.'

'Well, then, Lady Swynford, do we 'ave a bet?'

She delayed as long as she dare. 'Yes. It's a bet!'

Connie turned to leave. Fenner raised a finger.

'Wait a moment,' he said. 'There's one condition. Settlin' will be done on Sat'day immediately after the race.'

'You wish me to bring £10,000 on the off chance I might lose my bet?'

'No, that won't be necessary. I'll be 'appy to take yer mark. I'm sure you're good for it.'

Connie suddenly felt decidedly clammy.

'Whereabouts?' she asked as languidly as she could. 'Manchester, presumably?'

No, my dear,' Fenner replied with a dismissive shake of the head, 'I shall not be travellin'up to Manchester, I can assure you o' that! No, at a place o' my choosin.'

'Here then?'

'No, I 'ad in mind my place o' business. In the Holy Land. You come there. Anyone'll tell you 'ow to get there.'

This was not what she, or Algy, had been expecting at all. She ordered herself to stay calm.

'Come at three,' continued Fenner, 'an' we'll wait for the result to come through an' then we can get matters sorted straight off.'

'A telegram will get through that quickly?'

'Perhaps - but we never take chances!' said Fenner smugly. 'My man on the course will send the result by carrier pigeon as well.'

'Really!'

'An' it's my belief the bird will win that particular race!'

'I hope it doesn't fly anywhere near Denton or it'll never get here. My father shoots anything with wings!'

Fenner's dead-eyed stare suggested he had failed to see the funny side.

'Very well, then,' she said. 'Till three o'clock on Saturday.'

'Sat'day it is,' said Fenner. 'Cocky, show Lady Swynford out.'

Fenner watched her disappear. When the door closed, he ruffled Percy's fur and began to snigger, quite impervious to the cat's angry scratching and biting. He had spilt enough blood and broken enough bones for the entertainment of toffee-nosed folk like Lady Constanza Swynford. How satisfying it now was to have her skewered on a spit for his delectation. The very thought of it made him laugh out loud.

Stourhead was not going to win the Manchester November Handicap. He was positive on that score because Charlie Wood had assured him it had no chance of winning. Charlie was riding the likely second favourite, Silver. And Charlie had things organized.

Fenner permitted himself another chortle. Yes, everything was under control.

******

It was a still trembling Connie who emerged into Gower Street after giving the performance of a lifetime. She had thought of dropping in at Mays Court but decided to reward herself with lunch at Simpson's-in-the-Strand instead.

While Connie indulged herself with the house speciality of roast rib of Scottish beef, Algy was hunched deep inside his overcoat outside the weighing room on Manchester racecourse, lying in wait for Charlie Wood.

Wood spotted him and initiated a number of conversations with various passers-by in order to avoid a confrontation but Algy was more than equal to the ploy and eventually barred his path.

'Charlie, I'd like a word.'

'Brusher, I don't want any trouble from you,' Wood said out of the corner of his mouth. 'I'm as sorry about Archer as the next man...'

'Good! Because I've a proposition that will give you the chance to prove it.'

Wood's body language altered in an instant. He prided himself on detecting a favourable proposition at 50 yards. He sensed this was genuine.

'Let me weigh-in and I'll be straight back.'

Within a minute the two men had a quiet corner to themselves, away prying eyes.

'Let's not waste time, ' Algy said quietly, as he towered above the jockey. 'My friends and I want your absolute assurance that Silver will not win the November Handicap and we are prepared to give you £10,000 in return for that assurance.'

'£10,000?'

'Yes. £10,000. Half now and half after the race.

Algy reached into his pocket. 'This envelope contains 50 £100 notes.'

He stepped closer to Wood and slid the envelope inside the jockey's silks. 'Take it and count them.'

Wood tucked the envelope away and made to speak.

'No questions! Let's keep this discussion on a limited basis, for both our sakes, shall we?'

Wood pursed his lips, keen to speak, but eventually thought better of it and just nodded.

'If you accept, just make a point of pulling up your right boot - but not your left, just the right - when you touch your cap to Lord Lurgan in the paddock before mounting his colt in the next race. I shall be watching. That's all the signal I'll need.'

'All right.'

Algy backed away. 'Then our discussion is over.'

The ensuing 20 minutes seemed to pass like 20 years. Algy took a prime spot on the paddock rails and picked out Lord Lurgan, standing with his colt's trainer, Buck Sherrard. His eyes never left them for a second. Eventually, he spied Wood leading the jockeys out into the paddock.

Wood seemed in no hurry. Finally he reached Lurgan and Sherrard. He tipped his cap. And then bent down and pulled up his right boot.

Algy smiled and began pushing his way through the crowd toward the exit. The rest of the card held no interest for him.

THIRTY

'Edgy,' said Algy, 'You've done a magnificent job!'

The 'job' in question stood before them. Kitted out in a dowdy black suit with matching peaked cap, complete with grubby shirt and blue-spotted belcher tied tightly round her slender neck to give it some masculine substance, Connie looked every inch the street urchin.

'We couldn't have Lady Swynford prancing round the Holy Land dolled-up to the nines in bustles or crinolines!' replied Edgecombe.

'I never wear bustles!' said Connie indignantly. 'But, I must confess, Edgy, you have done a fine job.'

'Thank you, M'Lady. I do hope it will all prove worthwhile.'

'So do I, Edgy!' said Algy, glowering at Connie.

The possibility had crept into Algy's mind that Connie's scheme might fail but he quickly extinguished such an unhealthy thought. Certainly, having to confront Fenner at Rats Castle was an eventuality that he had hoped to avoid but he had mounted a contingency operation.

Everything else, however, had gone like clockwork - bar one exception. He and Connie had spent the previous day informing everyone who had betrayed Archer to back Silver in the Manchester November Handicap. She saw to Deek and Somerset; he attended to Baird and sent a telegram to his father signed 'CW.' They were all assured that Wood and Fenner had everything arranged. But of Seger they could find no sign.

'Are you sure Wood will go through with his end of the bargain?' Connie asked as she rubbed boot-black onto the backs of her hands.

'There's only a rope of sand tying Fenner and Wood together,' replied Algy angrily, 'and Charlie does love a sure thing.'

'Just like you!'

Algy rounded on her. 'Don't be an idiot!' he spat. 'This is utterly different!'

Connie's black-tipped fingers trembled. 'Yes, I'm so...'

'Anything could happen to Silver in the race and he's left with empty pockets,' Algy continued, shaking a clenched fist at her. 'This way he's got five grand in the kitty already.'

'Of course. But won't Fenner suspect?'

'Charlie'll have a story ready for Fenner, you can be sure of that!' said Algy, checking his watch. 'And, anyway, who cares what Fenner does to him!'

'But what about your £5,000?'

'We'll get that back from Fenner, and plenty more besides, when Stourhead wins.'

Connie stopped applying a speck of polish to her cheeks. 'What if it doesn't!'

Algy was starting to wonder whether he had been stupid listening to her scheme in the first place let alone aid and abet her in its execution.

'Look, how many times must I tell you, Alec Taylor has laid him out for this race. Stourhead shows his best form in the autumn. Don't forget, his two wins last year both came in November. So, this year Taylor gives him just three runs in six months. All over distances too short for the horse - a mile and 1 ¼ miles - so the horse hardly beats an egg. Which gets him in here, a race over 1 ¾ miles, with only 7st 2lb. QED!'

Connie gazed at him adoringly. 'Edgy, isn't your master a marvel?'

'Master Algy does make things sound eminently straightforward, M'Lady.'

'The Duchess didn't put her horses with Taylor for no reason!' barked Algy. 'There's no shrewder operator in the game. Stourhead'll win, all right. And that's what was frightening Fenner. That's why he had to take steps to stop him!'

'If you say so, Algy.'

'Now, hurry up!'

Connie followed Algy downstairs and out into Jermyn Street, which welcomed them with driving rain and red-nose temperatures commensurate with late November. They took a hansom as far as St Giles Circus, though it may as well have been a tumbrel: they sat in silence the whole way, Connie playing with her hair and Algy his ear, each mulling over what lay in store. Connie was worried what might happen to Algy if things got rough; Algy was not worried at all - he wanted to get his hands on Fenner.

Connie's motley appearance had the desired effect once they plunged into the Holy Land, no one bothering to give her a second glance as Algy led the way past the woman hawking pigs trotters and then the tannery. He expressly told her to stand tall but to avoid making any eye contact with the local street life. She overcame the problem of walking safely while staring at the ground by pretending to be drunk and hanging on to Algy's arm.

Rats Castle was the same as Algy remembered it from his last visit. The same rough clientele: some half-drunk, one already drunk; two pipe-sucking ruffians playing cribbage; a tail spending her latest tuppenny fee on a gin-toddy.

The main difference from his previous visit was the presence of Mo Fenner, sat in the corner booth like a gorilla in a jungle clearing. Algy's mouth tightened into one thin line and his fists balled by his sides without any asking.

Algy had no difficulty recognizing one of the two men stood either side of Fenner. 'How's your balls, Cocky?' he enquired, aiming a grin at Arnull as he and Connie helped themselves to a seat without waiting to be asked.

Fenner raised a hand as his two bodyguards advanced.

'What an unexpected pleasure to see you, Mister 'Aymer.'

'The pleasure is all yours, I can assure you,' replied Algy. 'Ordinarily, I'd not cross the road to see you.'

Fenner's eyes were two pinpricks of hatred but unlike his henchmen he refused to be baited and restricted himself to dabbing at his watery eye with his handkerchief.

'I'm sure you wouldn't have expected me to come here alone, Mister Fenner?' Connie interjected.

'And how's that mate of yours?' Algy called out to Arnull. 'That was some yell he let out! I'd not heard a noise like that since my sister lost a nail when she was three!'

'Now, then, Mister 'Aymer, that's no way to start proceedins,' Fenner said amicably as the second thug's mouth twisted with fury. 'My son Jack here was all for payin' you a visit after what you did to his pal. If 'e'd 'ad 'his way that pretty face o' yours would be in a right mess be now.'

'Your son, eh?' Algy sneered. 'Yes, I can see the simian likeness now you come to mention it.'

'I told 'him,' continued Fenner, seemingly oblivious to the unflattering reference, 'yer can't go round cuttin'-up the gentry willy-nilly. It's unacceptable. They know people. People who could make life hard for us.'

Jack Fenner stood silently, gums bared, as Algy continued to smile beatifically in his direction.

Fenner concentrated on doing the same toward Connie. 'Ow different you look today, Lady Swynford. What a lady's wardrobe contains these days! Would yer like somethin' to eat or drink while we wait?'

'Thank you very much but I don't think so!'

'Are you sure? A bowl o' somethin' 'ot?'

Connie was adamant. Algy had described the bill of fare at Rats Castle in lurid detail.

'All right, then, we can just settle down an' wait for the result. I trust you've come prepared, M' Lady?'

'Oh, yes! Quite prepared,' cut-in Algy. His temples were thumping to a war-drum. He wanted to throw himself at Fenner and stomp the life out of him bit by agonizing bit.

Fenner glared back. There was nothing he would love better than to launch a pile-driver at Algy's head. But inside the ropes he had carried opponents before dispatching them and he knew how much sweeter it had felt in the end.

'I've got someone waitin' at the St Giles telegraph office for the result to come through,' he explained. 'After listenin' to Lady Swynford t' other day, I thought it unwise to rely on the pigeon-post!'

Connie smiled under protest.

'There might be more Earl Kestevens abroad with their shotguns!' he snorted.

Fenner took out his watch. 'Shouldn't be long now. The race has long finished.'

The false levity was interrupted by the door crashing open and the appearance of Fenner's messenger clutching a telegram. Algy and Connie exchanged furtive glances: each hoped the nervous tension making their skins creep was not as evident as it felt.

Fenner took the telegram and read it. His mouth contorted like a serpent and his fists crashed onto the table, their veins as purple as those lining his nose.

'Do we take it that Stourhead won, Mister Fenner?' Algy asked.

Not only had Silver not won but Stourhead, if Algy had but known, was the horse Fenner least wanted to win. The £20,000 he now owed Swynford was not his only five-figure liabilty.

'Your silence suggests that Charlie has let you down and the answer must be yes,' said Algy. 'He's a lad, is Charlie! Can't be trusted an inch! Wouldn't be surprised if someone had paid him to take it easy in this one and he couldn't be arsed to put you in the picture!'

Fenner's eyes were fast taking refuge behind bags of skin, worsening the secretion from his left. All they could see was Charlie Wood's treacherous face which he was reducing to a bloody morass.

'Sorry to trouble you further, but Lady Swynford would like the money now, as arranged, if you don't mind. Cash will be fine. Then we can be off and out of this shit-hole of yours!'

Fenner's podgy fingers tapped the arms of his chair: he made himself forget Charlie Wood and nodded toward Arnull. Algy watched him go behind the bar and heard the creak of floorboards being lifted. Arnull resurfaced with a small canvas bag.

'Don't let anyone say Mo Fenner welshes on a bet,' said Fenner, snatching the bag from Arnull and tossing it to Algy. 'Here, count it!'

'I'm sure her ladyship is more than capable of counting her winnings!'

Algy handed the bag to Connie while keeping his attention focused firmly on Fenner. He did not believe Fenner would let him leave unharmed. He steeled himself for the first blow. And longed for it.

'It's all here,' confirmed Connie.

'Then we'll detain you no longer, Mister Fenner,' said Algy getting to his feet. 'It was a pleasure doing business with you?'

Algy followed Connie to the stairs and once she was safely half-way up, he turned and walked back to where Fenner was sitting. There was one final thing he had to do if he was to appease his conscience.

'This is only the start, you know?' he snarled in Fenner's face. 'I shall make it my business to see that you get your comeuppance!'

'Yer can't touch me!'

'Can't I? They'll bang you in jug and throw away the key!'

'Fat chance! I'm as safe as the Bank o' England!'

'Bribery? Corruption? Race-fixing?' said Algy, poking Fenner in the chest, starting to enjoy himself. 'That's one thing! Your pals in high places might overlook that, especially if you've greased their pockets!'

Fenner rose slowly to his feet. 'There's some things I know about 'em that's worth more than money!'

He filled his lungs and felt the muscles of his barrel chest warming. He was relishing the prospect of giving this toff a thrashing. He was going to make him cry for his mother yet still leave him crippled.

'But threats of kidnap and then an attempted murder, designed to bring about the death of a much-admired and loved sportsman is another matter!' Algy scoffed. 'No, *Mister* Mo Fenner, no one is going to protect you when you're brought up on those charges!'

Fenner erupted into a full-faced smile which illuminated the purple thread veins that gave the impression of holding his nose together, for he had never felt surer of anything in his entire life.

'Your confidence is ill-founded,' said Algy, returning Fenner's smile. 'Your bosom pal Seger has fled the country! He's left you to face the music! You, and you alone!'

Fenner shifted his feet like he used to in the ring, and tucked his chin into his chest so that his flattened forehead thrust forward like a well-worked anvil awaiting a striking hammer. All trace of a smile had vanished, his skin darkening in line with his humour at each word Algy spoke. It was as if he had donned his fighting face of old.

'Gutless bastard!' he rasped.

'For once we are in total agreement.'

'An' so what if that milksop Archer's in his grave! Best place for the cry baby!'

'So, you admit it, then?' said Algy, thrusting his face into Fenner's, eyes dancing with a go-to-hell glint. 'You admit it was you who was behind all the threats.'

'Yes!' roared Fenner, glad to release some rage. 'Sod him!'

'It was you who tried to have him killed on the ferry to Ireland?' goaded Algy.

'Why not?'

'You who threatened to kidnap his daughter? You who had her attacked on the Newmarket gallops?'

'Yes! Bollocks to 'er an' all!'

Algy was too preoccupied to notice the distinctive sound of cracking knuckles as Fenner methodically stretched and then clenched his right fist by his side. He could feel his ribcage throbbing as he prepared to put his final question.

'And it was you who drove her father to suicide?'

However, now he did notice the change in Fenner's expression. The jaw muscles relaxed and the hard line of his mouth began twitching into a full-blown smile that quickly spread from ear to ear. For the first time since he had descended into Rats Castle, Algy sensed he had lost the initiative and it left him feeling vulnerable and uneasy.

Fenner unclenched his fist and began chortling.

'An' they all told me you were a clever man, Mister 'Aymer,' he said with gathering emphasis, 'an ed-jew-cated man.'

Algy squinted through the fug at Fenner, trying to fathom where this conversation was leading.

'I'd 'ad my fun with Mister Fred Archer,' Fenner said, slyly casting around for sycophantic confirmation from Arnull. 'I made 'im sweat all right! Taught 'im some manners, didn't we Cocky?'

Arnull grinned gormlessly.

'But we settled our differences.'

The veins in Algy's temples felt as if they might burst. 'What?'

'Ee didn't tell you?' Fenner crowed. 'Mister Archer paid me off down in Brighton!'

Algy tried to retaliate but when he opened his mouth to speak no words formed.

'Right 'andsomely, too,' Fenner chirruped, much amused by Algy's obvious discomfort. 'Cheered me up no end, I don't mind tellin' yer. 'E was more use to me alive than dead if truth be told!'

'So, who the hell...'

Fenner folded his arms across his chest and watched impassively as Algy's tormented expression betrayed his shifting thought processes.

'Come along,' Fenner taunted, 'surely a clever man like you can work this out or does old Mo Fenner 'ave to chalk it up on the wall in big letters?'

Algy's right hand raked through his hair and suddenly came to an abrupt halt; a light had finally pierced the fog. 'It was Seger, wasn't it?'

'Bravo, Mister 'Aymer!'

'How could I have been so stupid!' bellowed Algy, smacking his forehead.

'Aint that the truth!' echoed Fenner.

'Seger's behind all this, the Jockeys Ring and everything that goes with it. I should have known! You're just the money and the muscle. You've not the brains for this.'

'Now, no insults if yer please!' said Fenner, fists balling at his sides once more.

'It's Seger who pulled the strings! That explains how you got into the racecourse stables at Goodwood - Seger got you in! And that's why you've been left alone by the Jockey Club. Seger's been guarding your back all along.'

Fenner smiled.

'No doubt in return for a fat commission!'

Fenner released a toothless grin which Algy came within a whisker of removing with a head-butt until its target backed away, palms upraised in mock surrender.

'An', mark this, Mister 'Aymer,' spat Fenner, 'e'd 'ave seen to you in time.'

'I'll treat the intention as a compliment,' Algy spat back, 'but don't think me foolish enough to swallow the wild ramblings of a rancid guttersnipe!'

'I should if I were you. 'E 'ates you as much as 'e 'ated yer mate Archer.'

Algy straightened. 'He hated Fred because he was incorruptible and, yes, he undoubtedly hates me because he lusts after Connie Swynford and he knows she loves me. That's where the similarities end. That's all there is to it. '

'You think so?'

Algy tried to stop himself but failed. 'And because he knew that Fred Archer and I were brothers... half-brothers.'

'Is that a fact!'

'Jealousy, that's the top and bottom of it! He wished he were in my place.'

Fenner stroked his nose and then inhaled deeply. He felt a gush of self-satisfaction warm his senses.

'I wasn't goin' to tell you this, Mister 'Aymer,' he said slowly, forming each word with uncharacteristic precision and unbridled gusto. 'I was goin' to save it for some time in the future. Yer never know when it might come in 'andy.'

Fenner paused to blow his nose, his lips stretching in anticipation of the pleasure he was on the threshold of feeling.

'Lord George 'ated yer for thinkin' you were Archer's brother. Oh, yes. And, 'e 'ated yer more for wantin' to be 'is brother. That's a fact!

'Agreed!'

'E also 'ated yer guts because yer told 'im the very first time yer set eyes on 'im, at that posh school of yours I believe, just 'ow much 'e made yer flesh creep.'

'Correct.'

Fenner closed the gap between them. 'An' that really upset Lord George, that did. All 'e wanted was you to be 'is friend, like a brother as it were. Just like yer wanted Archer to be yer brother.'

'Seger's pathetic longing is of no consequence to me!'

'Well it should be!' hissed Fenner.

Algy felt Fenner's hot rank breath on his cheeks yet more disturbing still was the certainty of purpose his adversary exuded. Algy had not taken a backward step since entering Fenner's lair, but he took one now.

'No, I'll not hear of it!' he shouted, covering his ears with his hands. 'Anything but that!'

Fenner gripped Algy's hands and forced them to his sides.

'I'm sorry, Mister 'Aymer,' he leered into Algy's face, 'but facts is facts...'

Algy screwed his face away.

'...an' the facts is Fred Archer's no brother o' yours. But Lord George is.'

THIRTY-ONE

Algy stood head bowed, fighting to make sense of Fenner's claim.

That Seger might have played him for a fool regarding Archer's parentage was unpalatable enough but the notion of them being half-brothers was sufficiently repugnant to make him feel physically sick. He reached for the nearest bottle and shook his head as its contents seared his throat like neat vinegar.

'Some things is 'ard to swallow, eh Mister 'Aymer?' laughed Fenner.

'Predictable to the end,' Algy coughed back. 'Only cretinous scum could fabricate a story as ridiculous as that and consider it believable!'

Fenner's chest expanded and erupted with a roar that triggered a short right into Algy's stomach. The punch travelled less than six inches but Algy felt as if he had been impaled on an iron railing, his belly-button pinned to his backbone, as he sank to his knees.

Algy grabbed the back of a chair and levered himself to his feet.

'Now I've a surprise for you, Mister Fenner,' he wheezed. 'Gentlemen, I trust you've heard and duly noted every word of Mister Fenner's confession?'

Algy was looking toward the two layabouts who had been immersed in their game of cribbage. Now they rose to their feet and removed their grubby overcoats to reveal the blue uniforms of the Metropolitan Police. One of them waved a notebook in which evidence not cribbage scores had been recorded.

'Fenner, you are not immune to justice, even here,' said the nearby drunk, suddenly sobering-up and getting to his feet.

'Quite so, Bumbo,' said Algy. 'All it requires is to bait a trap that a greedy animal can't resist.'

'And I'm delighted to be here to witness it!' replied his godfather.

'Scotland Yard has been waiting for the right opportunity to put a halt to your operation,' Algy explained gleefully to Fenner. 'They were eternally grateful to receive Lady Swynford's information yesterday afternoon.'

'Damn you to hell!' screamed Fenner, whipping over a short left hook. Algy saw the hairy knuckle heading toward his chin but could do nothing to evade it and was knocked clean off his feet.

Before anyone could lay a hand on him, Fenner had dived through the back door into the rear alley, sending crates and benches flying. Arnull and Jack Fenner immediately hurled themselves at the two policemen in an attempt to cover his flight.

'I've got him,' Algy shouted. 'He can't escape! It's a dead end!'

'Right you are!' Raper shouted back, in the act of wrapping one arm round Arnull's neck, a second round Jack Fenner's and cracking their two heads together as if they were walnuts.

Algy shook the cobwebs out of his own brain and realized he was being stupid even as he stepped into the alley. Fenner would never charge headlong into one of his own booby traps. There had to be a getaway route out here. Algy's eyes travelled from one side of the alley to the other and came to rest on a pile of wood had been torn away from the base of the dead-end, exposing a small iron trapdoor.

What lay at the bottom of the shaft was evident from the stench that gushed forth once Algy lifted the cover and began wriggling into the narrow opening. He held his nose and plummeted three or four feet, squelching up to his ankles in a bog of rotting sewage.

Algy strained his eyes to see for it was also Hades-dark. He used the slimy walls of the sewer to feel his way through the quagmire as quickly as he could given the slippery surface beneath his feet and the attentions of numerous angry rodents. A chink of light suggested he was going in the right direction. The tunnel gradually narrowed, and he realized he would have to crawl on hands and knees in order to get out. He tilted his head back as far from the rising tide of filth as he could manage, held his breath and scuttled toward the light. He emerged into daylight but no fresher air: he was standing in an open cesspit.

He scrambled free and as a hint of lilies-of-the-valley entered his nostrils he felt a wheel of fire scorch around his ribcage: Fenner had struck him a thunderous blow to the midriff.

Algy sank to his knees, grunting and rocking, winded for the second time, sure his stomach wall must be punctured.

'Mister 'Aymer, can yer 'ear me?' growled Fenner. 'I want you to know I'm goin' to beat you to shit an' then drop yer back where yer came from so the rats can pick your bleedin' bones!'

Algy threw his head back and took air into his lungs in short sharp gulps, grateful for each precious second Fenner was wasting by taunting him instead of finishing him off. Hatred, as his father had often told him, heals pain exceedingly fast. Algy coiled himself and then, to the accompaniment of a fearsome shriek, jack-knifed upward, catapulting the top of his head into Fenner's jaw.

Fenner's head rocked backwards feeling as if it were hinged at the neck by white-hot screws.

'Now who's pulp?' Algy yelled, seeing Fenner clutch his jaw, sway and spit out gobs of blood.

'Full o' dirty tricks, eh?' Fenner grunted. 'Who taught a flamin' toff like you to fight dirty, *Mister* 'Aymer?'

'A man who bested you once, *Mister* Fenner! Bendigo himself!'

Fenner's expression twisted with a pain as much mental as physical. 'Might 'ave known it'd be some cheatin' bastard like him!'

He had not been hurt this bad for twenty years and, however reluctantly, he was forced to concede he might be bested again. Outrunning the younger man, he also knew, was an impossibility. He shuffled off down the nearest ginnel and headed for the rooftops.

Fenner knew the precise location of every hand-hold and toe-hold and was soon ascending with the certainty of a fleeing spider. Algy climbed up after him, no less determined though far less nimble, dislodging chunks of masonry as he scrambled upwards, all thoughts of personal safety banished from his mind, motivated by twin thoughts. Archer's death was going to be avenged; Fenner was going to pay.

Grensons were not made for climbing walls dripping with rainwater and Algy had never been one for heights. He feared he would slip and his fear guaranteed he would. His right foot broke off the end of a sodden brick and his body fell with the suddeness of a murderer on the gallows, forcing him to hang on grimly by his fingertips. He fought to establish any kind of toe-hold but the sound of leather scuffing vainly on brick and the sight of chimneys seemingly multiplying as he swung like a timid novice kicking on a trapeze unnerved him further.

Algy knew he had only one chance. Swivelling his hips out to the side, he flung himself back against the wall with every ounce of strength and determination he could muster and prayed the impact would find him a foothold knowing that the rebound would throw him off completely if it did not. He braced himself for the hammer-blows to his knees and cringed as they struck home. But his left boot found a crevice: the tip had jammed into some weak pointing.

Algy hugged the wall and swallowed the rain and sweat flooding down the sides of his nose. His knees throbbed and his shins seemed about to shatter but he managed to feel around for a second secure foothold and begin clawing his way upward until he was in a position to stretch his right hand over the parapet to pull himself up onto the roof.

The hob-nailed boot greeted his exposed hand with bone-breaking force and a pain knifed through his crushed metacarpals that made him scream out loud. Only the hold enjoyed by his left hand on a section of guttering stopped him from lurching backwards and plunging 30 feet.

Fenner turned his attention to Algy's other hand and again raised a boot. Algy bared his teeth to blot out the pain and inched his damaged hand back over the parapet. He groped for Fenner's standing leg and grabbed his ankle. The thought of little Nellie Archer being robbed of her father's love flashed through his consciousness like a lightning bolt and generated sufficient energy for him to twist Fenner's leg from side to side.

Fenner kicked out frantically with his free foot and began to lose his balance. The dilapidated tiles beneath his feet broke loose. First he lost one slippery foothold, then the other. The rooftops began to rotate wildly before his eyes.

Algy heaved one last time, pulling Fenner's ankle back over his shoulder. He heard him curse. Then he caught the briefest glimpse of Fenner's arms flailing like the wings of a shot duck as he went by.

Fenner saw the alley come up to greet him and felt his bowels begin to empty. This sorry realization was the last thought that went through his skull before it struck the ground with the spatter of a dropped egg.

Algy heard the crack and looked down to see Fenner's twisted and broken body lying in an expanding puddle of blood. He loosed a wolfish smile and suddenly felt very dizzy.

EPILOGUE: NOVEMBER 1886

The little girl placed a posy of violets at the foot of the fine marble cross that stood over the bodies of the parents and brother she never got to know.

Algy's eyes and lips refused to stay still. The only way he could keep them in check was by reciting some lines he had composed for *The Sportsman*:

'Fred Archer's dead! The words ring out / O'er verdant plain and valley wide, / And ears distended hear with doubt / The news that he no more will ride. / His last race done, he sleeps in peace, / And what may now his requiem be, / When all his efforts sadly cease? / He rode right well and gallantly!'

Algy stood to attention and licked away the remnants of the teardrop that had cut a lonely trail down the side of his nose and collected on his top lip.

'Fred, you're daughter's safe,' he whispered. 'And so is your reputation. Sleep peacefully, dearest brother.'

Her own task completed, Nellie Rose Archer turned away. She took a couple of wobbly steps and then stopped to wait for Algy - and Connie, who had followed them at a distance. She beamed at the man she called 'Uncle Algy' and clutched his hand as the three of them slowly walked off down the gravel path toward the cemetery gates.

After they had gone ten yards or so, Fred Archer's little girl reached up and entrusted her other hand to Connie.

Lightning Source UK Ltd.
Milton Keynes UK
26 July 2010

157459UK00001B/141/P